HEAVEN IS A PLACE ON EARTH

Graham Storrs

Print edition copyright © 2018, Graham Storrs

ISBN: 978-0-9924988-9-4

Cover design by Graham Storrs. Quadcopter design by Oberwelz Design, Austria (oberwelzdesign.com). Final cover artwork by Patty Jansen (pattyjansen.com). Interior design by Write Into Print (writeintoprint.com).

Published by Canta Libre.

Dedication

Three brilliant and beautiful women are at the heart of everything I do: my mother, Audrey; my wife, Christine; and my daughter, Katherine. I dedicate this book to them.

Acknowledgements

I have been extremely fortunate to have had the help of three fabulous Australian speculative fiction writers in polishing this text and producing the book. I would like to thank fellow writer, Meryl Ferguson, for her invaluable comments on an earlier draft of the book and for comments on the cover design. Another writer, Patty Jansen, who also happens to be an artist, also commented on the cover design and then went on to produce the final version. Finally, Perth-based writer Amanda Bridgeman helped with a final review of the text. Also thanks to my wife, Christine, who read and commented on earlier drafts and who bore with me throughout the process of producing this work from inspiration to publication.

Despite all this help, the text is as you find it, and I have to take full responsibility for that.

Part 1

Chapter 1

Virginia Galton kicked off her sandals and let her head fall back, relaxing into the warm Brisbane sunshine. This is what she needed after the stress of yet another disappointing meeting, just to sit in the Botanic Gardens and let the sun soak through her. Somewhere nearby a water feature tinkled to itself while lorikeets squabbled in the trees. Just knowing that the broad Brisbane River was there if she cared to open her eyes, making its slow, cool progress towards Moreton Bay, was balm to her soul.

And balm was in short supply these days. Her money was running out and customers were getting harder to find. Even the ones she still had were playing silly buggers. The meeting with UnReality was typical. Times were getting harder, they said. They were thinking their worldlets didn't really need such elaborate soundscapes. And, anyway, they could buy stock soundscapes by the hour off the Net. Custom sounds were a luxury and one they had to ask themselves whether they could really afford.

She argued with them about branding and production values, all the while thinking that the two guys running the company were probably ten years younger than her, that they were maybe thinking she was not the bright young talent they were hoping for, that, at the very least, someone younger would be cheaper.

In the end, she had hung on to the Old Vienna contract but with the scope pared back to half of what she'd been hoping for. Now she needed to find another contract to make up for it. Life was getting harder just at a time when it should have been getting easier. She had heard that most people reached their peak earnings in their early forties. Well, the way things were going, she might already have left her peak far behind, and she was only in her early thirties.

She lifted her head and peered out at the river, small boats bobbing at their moorings, a ferry chugging its way slowly upstream. Who held meetings at their offices any more? Who even had real offices? For a company that produced high-end wordlets for the corporate market, UnReality was pretty primitive in its business methods. Offices. And face-to-face meetings. They said it was all about security. Protecting their IP. They said their competition was watching them. Ginny didn't believe a word of it. They were simply paranoid and irritating little jerks and she wished she didn't have to have anything more to do with them.

Be careful what you wish for, darl, she told herself.

On the upside, at least she was out in the sunshine. What had it been? Two weeks? Three? She should probably make the effort to go outside more. She'd read something about it a while ago, about vitamin D and circadian rhythms and how a modern lifestyle was really bad for you. But what could you do about it? It was just scaremongering, anyway. There were laws that made sure food had all the vitamin supplements you needed. Going out was just another time-wasting pain in the neck she could do without. Besides…

Ginny was latched to the Botanical Gardens' augmented

reality, which meant her neural implants took a feed from the sensors all around her, created an artificial reality, and overlaid it onto what her own senses were sending to her brain. On impulse, she switched the level of virtual reality down to a simple informational augmentation, so she could see the gardens as they really were.

The neat lawns and blooming rose beds faded away to rough turf and weeds, the splashing fountain dried up and vanished. The trees were still there, mostly, and the quarrelsome lorikeets. The river still flowed, but the rows of gaily painted yachts vanished, replaced by a handful of half-sunken wrecks. The people walking by, who had been smartly dressed, healthy and cheerful, were almost all gone, having been mere simulations. The two that remained were revealed as drab, pale and overweight. *If being outside is so good for you*, she thought, *how come these guys look like they've just come off life support?* She looked down at her own body and found the sight disturbing. When had she grown so flabby and pale? She wore a simple overall that looked as if she had been gardening in it. *Everybody wears them*, she thought, rejecting the guilt that nipped at her. Why would she wear anything else when it was so easy to augment your own image with anything you felt like wearing? Anybody sane was in full AR or full VR all the time these days. Only a masochist would want to see the world as it really was.

She latched again to the gardens' systems. Reality was even more depressing than usual and it was good to get back to normality. She looked down at herself and was reassured by the long, tanned legs, the flat stomach and firm breasts. She tried to pick out the two sad specimens she'd seen while on minimal aug. One was probably the smart-looking guy in the business suit. The other she wasn't sure about. Maybe the good-looking bloke just beyond that group of teenagers kicking a ball about. Did it bother her that her world – everybody's world – was a complete sham? Not at all. What really stuck in her craw was that the music drifting across from the distant and, she now realised, simulated bandstand, was cheap, out-of-copyright rubbish. No-one wanted to pay for real musicians to write new music any more. It was all recycled old stuff or machine-generated pap.

She stood up and made her way out of the gardens towards the CBD. It was a long walk to the Transit Centre but that would be the only place she'd find a cab. She knew that buses and trains had once run from there too, but mass public transport had gone the way of the dodo. Without the need to commute to work, or travel to the shops, or to travel at all for that matter, it was a miracle there were still taxis available for the few poor souls who needed to shift their bodies around the city. Poor souls like Ginny Galton, with her failing career as a soundscape composer, and her crazy, paranoid customers who made wholly unreasonable demands and, frankly, were virtually ex-customers these days.

The little electric robocab took her out to her unit in Toowong. It had once been a fashionable inner-city suburb in the days when location meant anything. Now it was just another place to live. As she got out, the fare was deducted automatically from her bank account, the size of the bill reminding her that physically moving yourself around the city was for suckers. And the desperate.

Her apartment was larger than she needed, but rents were cheap in the post-boomer world and she liked the luxury of having two whole physical rooms. Maybe she should start thinking about finding something smaller. She looked about herself and, perhaps because she had been outside, she turned down her augmentation to the lowest setting again. The smart white minimalism she loved faded away to reveal the dismal reality. Bare floorboards instead of parquet, grimy walls where there had been posters and artwork, and a beat-up old fabric sofa where the leather-and-chrome one had stood. The only thing that did not change was the Roland electric piano, a real electric piano, an antique her parents had bought her the day she graduated from the Queensland Conservatorium. It was depressing but some self-flagellatory urge made her stay in low aug and take it all in.

Despite her little fleet of cleaning bots, there was dust in every crevice, cobwebs in every corner. The microwave was a mess. When was the last time she had cleaned the place? She walked through to the bedroom. It was large enough for a double bed and a tank, a scratched chest of drawers for her undies and a couple of changes of overall, and that was it. At least the tank looked half-way decent. It occurred to her that, when she was a child, people had had wardrobes and dressing tables, they had put on makeup by painting and dabbing it onto the skin, they had worn jewellery, actually hanging precious metals and stones from their necks and wrists and ears. Things were simpler now. Times had changed.

With a sigh, she switched back to her normal, latched state and the apartment was clean and bright and tasteful again. Promising herself she would dust and scrub the place soon, she sat down on the sofa and turned on the display – not a real display, of course, but a virtual one that filled a whole wall. She scanned the news feeds and checked her messages. She knew she should be calling people and trying to drum up some new work, but she was too low to face rejection just then. She'd do it later. The idea of being bright and positive, trying to sound exciting and interested made her want to shrivel into herself.

The news was boring. The messages were boring. The entertainment feeds were boring. She stood up and walked to the window, a slow kind of desperation welling up inside her. The window showed a panoramic view of the city from a camera feed high on Mount Coot'tha. She had the horrible feeling that she needed to do something but that everything she should do was beyond her.

Hardly thinking about it, she popped up a phone and called Cal.

She hardly new Cal Copplin. Not really. They'd met a few times, well, quite a few times, actually, mostly in the company of mutual friends. They'd had coffee, gone for a walk, talked for the odd hour or so at a party. All in VR, of course. He was older than her but only by about ten years, yet he seemed almost like a father figure. Calm and wise and experienced. And very charming, and kind of cute, now she thought about it. Yes, she realised, Cal was exactly the right person to call. They could meet up. She could tell him all about her crappy day and he'd say soothing, sensible things. He might even make her laugh. He could do that. She listened to the ring tone, waiting for him to pick up, and was surprised at how much she was looking forward to it.

When he finally appeared and said, "Hello, Ginny," she blurted out her own greeting and was half-way to telling him how much she wanted to see him, when she realise it was a recording.

"I'm sorry I can't take your call just now," Cal said in his lovely, English accent. It was funny how she forgot the accent until he spoke and then she loved it all over again. "I'll get back to you as soon as I can, or you can leave me a message."

His face waited there, looking politely expectant. He had an interesting face, not too handsome, not too flawed, and he looked his age, which was unusual. She had the curious feeling that maybe she was looking at his true appearance and not just an avatar. If so, that would make him unique among her friends. Everybody at least prettied themselves up a bit, took a few years off, added a few centimetres to their height, perked up their tits and pulled in their tummies. And who didn't make their eyes bigger, or emphasise their cheekbones? Of course, the twenty-percent rule meant no-one could go too far. Only in role-playing interactives could you change as much as you felt like it. Some took it all too far and looked barely human when you played them, with coloured skin, or steel hair, an extra eye in the forehead, or a beard of living snakes. Fun, no doubt, but you'd have to be pretty weird to want to look like that.

Cal was different. It was as if he liked who he was. He made all the rest – herself included – look just a bit silly and insecure. Some of her friends seemed to resent him for it. They wrinkled their nose when she said she'd invited Cal. They called him "that friend of yours" as if she were the only reason he was tolerated among her acquaintances. It made her defensive on his behalf. Thinking about that, she studied Cal's features. She really would like to see him today.

"Cal, will you stop playing hard to get and pick up? I want you to tell me my life isn't a complete pile of crap. This is not the time for you to go all brooding and mysterious. You have consolational duties to perform. Is that a word? Consolational? Oh well, it is now. Look, call me when you're not doing whatever you're doing that's so damned important you can't speak to me. Bye."

She popped up a zine and began flicking through its

virtual pages. But the news consisted of one politician bagging another, an artificial pop star having to cancel a concert because her software had malfunctioned at the last minute, and some announcement from the Chinese that was going to drive the Aussie dollar lower. She didn't want to hear about any of it. The headlines were like wasps buzzing around her. With a wave of her hand, she shooed the lot of them away. She should work, she supposed. She should work on the Old Vienna project, come up with a track so brilliant that the UnReality jerks would be begging to give her a bigger contract.

She sat at the Roland and doodled her way through some Mozart and Strauss to put herself in a Viennese frame of mind. Then she let her fingers wander free to improvise, searching for an idea that would be a springboard into something wonderful. But nothing would come. How could she compose when she felt like lying on the sofa and crying herself to sleep?

There were places she could go, things she could do, that were guaranteed to distract her. All she had to do was sit down in the tank, unlatch, and travel away into pure virtual worlds were everything was easy and anything was possible. There were sexual fantasies waiting for her there, men with oiled muscles and clever fingers, women with musky scents and smouldering eyes. She knew she only had to go there to feel herself inexorably aroused, for her to be drawn into the wild, passionate tides of her deepest sexual desires until she was fully submerged in them.

She got up and paced across the room, already feeling the urge to yield. But it wasn't what she wanted. She'd done that too often of late and she knew from experience that the relief was only temporary. Afterwards, she would call herself a fool and tell herself she should get a life, get a real lover, anything other than spend her time in the tank doing things she blushed to remember and wouldn't dream of doing in real life.

She called Cal again and got the recorded message. She felt angry at him for letting her down, irrational as she knew that was. "Well, if the mountain won't come to Mohammed," she muttered. She knew where Cal lived. It wasn't very far away, a couple of kilometres at most. She could be there in no time. It was rude to go calling at people's houses, turning up in the flesh, but that's what people deserve if they won't take your calls. The idea of paying for another taxi made her pause at the door. It almost killed the idea.

I'll walk, she told herself. *Crazy, Bohemian, muso bitch. That's me. I'll walk, and I'll bang on his door with my fist like someone in an old vid.* She imagined his face. His real face. She would stand on his doorstep with nothing but basic aug and look at his real face when he opened it, see what his expression was when he saw her there. It was a scary notion, to look into someone's unaugmented face and see what they really felt about you.

By the time she reached Cal's apartment building, she was hot and tired. What was wrong with her today, she wondered. Why this sudden urge to be so primitive? She thanked the heavens for augmented reality. If it hadn't been for the big blue arrows overlaid on the pavement, she'd have been lost in the first few minutes. Yet people hadn't always had map overlays and animated guides to lead them around the city. What did they do before cognitive implants? Memorise that maze of streets? It seemed incredible. *People were made of sterner stuff back then*, she told herself as she stood at Cal's door and got her breath back. Yet Ginny's parents had not had implants – not when they were young. *It's no wonder they're always complaining about how soft we've become.*

There was a display beside the door, offering a menu of units and occupants. Cal's name was there against unit 4. She told it who she was and that she wanted Cal Copplin. Instead of buzzing her in, the display showed Cal's face. Another recorded message.

"Ginny," Cal said. "I was hoping you'd come to find me. If you are alone, please say so now."

"I'm alone," she said, frowning. What on earth was going on?

"Great. Now listen. In a moment, the door will open. Come inside and go to my flat. That door will be open too. I've just sent you an address. When you're inside my flat, call the address and there will be further instructions." Cal didn't look like he was playing about, but Ginny couldn't think what else might be going on.

She checked her messages and there was a fresh one from Cal containing a QNet address.

The door buzzed and clicked open. She went inside, looking about the smart entrance hall as if a boxing glove on a spring might pop out of the wall. Cal's unit was on the ground floor at the front. When she pushed the door, it swung inwards. No tin of paint fell from the ceiling. She went in and closed the door behind her.

Cal's unit was enormous. She passed two bedrooms before she reached a lounge room as big as her entire apartment. Beyond that was a separate kitchen. She hadn't realised Cal was rich. She called out to him but there was no answer. She peered in at the kitchen. It had two microwaves plus one of those fancy new food printers she'd seen advertised. Back in the lounge room, she called again. Then she went to check the bedrooms, deciding Cal must be in his tank. But the first bedroom she found had no tank in it and neither did the second, larger bedroom. Now that was weird. And why would a man who lived on his own need two bedrooms? What possible use could anyone have for a spare bedroom?

She went back to the lounge room and flopped into a sofa, glad to be off her feet. Whatever stupid game Cal was playing, she was beginning to grow irritated with it. And what did he mean, "I was hoping you'd come to find me." In what sense was he lost?

She popped up a phone and dialled the QNet address. There was a short delay and messages flashed by. She caught the word "routing" and then "encrypting" in a stream of numbers and meaningless words. Almost before she had registered this new strangeness, Cal's face appeared on the display.

"Cal! What the hell are you—"

But it was another recording. "Hello, Ginny," her friend said and her stomach clenched just a little. There was something in his expression that she didn't like, a sadness, as if he were about to say something he knew she wouldn't want to hear. "Thank you for putting up with all this nonsense, Gin, but I'm in a bit of trouble and I need you to do something for me. Now, go to the sitting room and you'll see a glass coffee table. Say 'OK' when you've found it."

She didn't need to look far. It was right in front of her. "OK," she said.

"Right, now I want you to switch off your augmentation – just for a moment – then put it back on again. You'll need to switch it right down to zero, Gin. Not even minimal aug. Go completely native, OK? When you come back online, just say 'continue' and I'll explain what you saw."

She looked at the table. It looked smart, but perfectly ordinary. Being glass, she could see right through it. There seemed to be nothing under it. She pushed down the anxiety that was rising in her and told herself not to be such an idiot. It was just some game Cal was playing. A trick of some sort, maybe.

She turned down her augmentation from latched to basic but her systems stopped her going any farther. She had to shoo away warning messages, give her system password and repeat her command before her implants would allow her to switch them off. Even then they didn't quite go away. A message pulsed continually in her peripheral vision to tell her they were waiting for her to restart them. Having finally achieved something like zero augmentation, she looked again at the coffee table. The shock of seeing something lying there on the glass almost made her cry out.

She reached out and touched it, poked it, as if it might bite her. Why hadn't she seen it before? If it had been there on the table all that time, why hadn't she seen it? She knew very little about the technologies that made augmented reality work. Her cognitive implants tapped into her senses, as well as into whatever sensors the local environment provided, and then they computed overlays and adjustments. Depending on how much augmentation you wanted, they would arrange for different degrees of transformation. If you had minimal augmentation, you would get information and images – like hazard warnings and street names – overlaid on top of what you could see. If you were latched to the local environment, you could have the whole scene modified beyond recognition, the way the botanical gardens had been, or her own apartment. Most people went around latched all the time. If you wanted to get away from sensory input altogether, you could unlatch from reality and move into full immersive virtual reality. And for the best VR experience, you needed the tanks.

But, even when you were latched and nothing was the way it really looked, you still expected that everything in the world had some kind of representation in augmented reality. If not, then you might trip over something you couldn't see and break your neck. If Cal had put something on his table, she should have seen it, even when latched to his apartment.

She looked around, trying to find other objects that had been invisible, and had another surprise. Cal's unit looked just the same with augmentation as it did without. The furniture looked the same, the pictures on the wall were real, not virtual, even the floors were just as clean. She stood up and took a few steps into the middle of the room. Through the kitchen door she could see the same appliances, in the hallway, the same umbrella stand. She found her heart was beating faster. It was so creepy it was scaring her. Cal had made the fully augmented view of his home an exact match to its real appearance. What kind of person would do that, and why?

She looked back at the small package on the table. Not an exact match. That one detail was different. Something real, cloaked by the illusions they all shared. She went to it and picked it up. It was small enough to fit in the palm of her hand, light enough to carry in a shirt pocket. The packaging was plain paper – old-fashioned paper, that is, not proper paper, this was inert, unresponsive stuff, made of plant fibres or whatever. She thought about opening it, tearing the paper to reveal what was inside, but she dare not. The invisible package was at the heart of the mystery Cal had created here. Whatever was inside might be even more disturbing that anything she had seen yet.

She switched on her augmentation again and latched to the apartment. The package in her hand disappeared but she could still feel its weight. When she closed her fingers on it she could feel its solidity.

"Continue," she said, almost in a whisper, and Cal's face popped up on the phone display.

"Thanks, Ginny. I hope you found the package – and that it didn't give you too much of a fright. It's not that hard, really, to program your flat to make things disappear. Not as hard as you might think." His light grey eyes looked into hers with an intensity that suggested he was trying to make some kind of point. Half an hour ago, she might have found his unwavering gaze attractive, evidence of his deep and intense nature. Now it looked fanatical and weird. Like everything else that was happening, it made her uneasy. "I want you to do me a favour, Gin," the recording went on. "I wouldn't ask except there is no-one else I trust as much as you." He hesitated. "You know, I thought... I thought we had some kind of connection. I thought, if there had been more time, you and I might... But things have got out of hand and I've got to go, right now." He actually looked over his shoulder, as if there might be someone coming for him. "I know you'll wonder where I am and you'll come looking for me. The flat will recognise you when you come and–" He stopped and shook his head. "What am I saying? Of course, you're already here or you wouldn't be listening to me prattling on like an idiot. Look, the favour is this. Don't open the package. Take it to the address I'm sending you now. Take it by hand. Give it to Gavin. No-one else. Do that and then forget all about it. I'm sorry to be all cloak and dagger, but it's best you don't know what this is all about. The flat will erase all record of you having been here. No-one will ever know unless you tell them. Anyway, I've got to go. I just want to say goodbye and that I regret that we couldn't have… Yeah, well. Cheers."

The recording stopped.

Ginny put the package in her pocket and left the unit. She felt the need to be out and moving. This was all too strange. If she were home, she would unlatch and visit Della. Della was the most level-headed and sensible friend she had. Something about what had just happened seemed dangerous and the unease Ginny felt was slowly turning to fear. She didn't want to get on the wrong side of the law. Her life was difficult enough without that, but it looked like Cal was on the run, and there was that little package, sitting in her pocket like a lead brick.

The sun was high and the day was hot. Sweat beaded on her face as she made her way back through the suburbs. The package was probably drugs, she thought. Or smuggled diamonds or something. She should go to the river and throw it in. But what if this Gavin bloke knew she had it? What if Cal was mixed up with gangsters who would come looking for it? If she told them she'd thrown their drugs in the river, what might they do to her? Maybe they were following her right now.

She stopped walking and looked around. The streets were empty. A few cars and robot delivery trucks went by now and then, and there was a woman out mowing a lawn up ahead. She could see no sign of a tail. Then she remembered the package, invisible on the table until she switched off her aug. Frantically, she shut it all down again. The street really was empty now except for the robot trucks. No cars, no woman mowing. Nobody anywhere. She breathed a sigh of relief, scanning the dilapidated garden fences just in case someone was hiding behind the peeling paint and rotten wood. For a long while she stared at the shabby street before latching again and walking on.

Chapter 2

Ginny was hot and exhausted when she reached her unit. She had not walked so far in years. Just as exhausting were the questions that had hung around her like flies all the way home. She knew she should take the package to the police, but she felt an irrational loyalty to Cal – a man she hardly knew. Not really. Yet he had trusted her. He had landed himself in some kind of trouble and he had turned to her for help. It was like something from a vid, romantic, in an odd kind of way. And the things he'd said, or rather, left unsaid. If he had been at home when she called, if they had finally met face-to-face, maybe something would have happened.

He wasn't really her type. The kind of men she usually ended up with were the little-boy-lost types who needed a mummy to look after them. She could never resist the puppy-dog eyes and the little, helpless shrugs. But Cal was different. He had always been so self-assured and confident. He had never seemed to need anything from her, not even her company, although he'd always been happy to spend time with her.

And now this. A big scary favour, out of the blue. But didn't that mean he must really need her help though?

Someone like Cal wouldn't ask if it wasn't incredibly important, would he?

She was so lost in thought that she didn't see the man standing in the hallway until she had her door open and had taken a step inside.

"Virginia Galton?"

Ginny jumped like a cartoon cat and whirled to face the speaker, stumbling backwards into her apartment. The man shot out a hand and caught her upper arm.

"Steady now. I didn't mean to scare you."

She pulled herself free and took two paces back, her heart thumping. "Well you did. Who are you?"

He was tall and broad shouldered. His face was square cut and clean-shaven. But none of that meant anything, except that his real appearance was within twenty per cent of hot. Of much more interest was the blue and white checked strip that hovered beside him with his police credentials listed below it. For a second she'd thought Cal's dope-dealer friends had found her. Seeing it was the police was a relief, but not a big one.

"I'm Detective Sergeant Richards, Ms Galton. May I come in?"

She actually thought about refusing for a moment but managed to clamp down on her rising panic enough to nod and step back another pace.

"What is it?" she asked. Even the querulous tone of her voice made her sound guilty, she thought. If the cop didn't suspect her of something, he soon would if she didn't get a grip of herself. She waved a hand at the sofa. "Please, sit down. Would you like a drink? I'm going to get some water. It's hot out there."

"Nothing for me, thanks," he said and watched her as she

went to the kitchenette and ran water into a plastic beaker. She took a long swallow, put the beaker down and went back to join him. He sat on the sofa and she took the armchair.

"People are usually at home when I call on them," he said and left it hanging, as if waiting for her to explain herself.

She felt the urge to babble out some reason for why she had been out, but fought it. It was unusual behaviour, it needed an explanation, but a lick of irritation came to her rescue.

"Why are you here, Detective?"

He gave her a charming smile. "I'm sorry, I should have said that straight off. It's Detective Sergeant, but you can call me Dover."

"Dover?"

"As in the white cliffs of. May I call you Virginia?"

"Ginny. Can we hurry this up? I have a lot of work to do. I'm on a deadline."

"You're a composer I see." He must be looking at her file as they spoke, she realised.

"Soundscape artist. Composers write serious music. I write ambient sounds for worldlets." She couldn't help but notice the bitterness in her own voice.

He nodded, as if that made sense of something. "When was the last time you saw your friend Calvin Copplin, Ginny?"

The question took her by surprise and she found herself tongue tied, not wanting to say she'd just been listening to a recording of him, not wanting to tell a lie to the police.

"I haven't spoken to him for a couple of days," she said cautiously. "I called him today but all I got was a recorded message." That was true, and they might check, anyway. "Why do you want to know? Is he all right?"

"Would you say you were close?"

"I don't know. Sort of. We're not dating or anything. Not really. What's happened to Cal?"

"Have you met many of Mr. Copplin's friends? Has he introduced you to anyone?"

She didn't like these questions. She didn't like the way the detective wouldn't answer her own questions. She didn't like being interrogated in her own home. "What's this all about?"

"How did you meet Mr. Copplin, Ginny?"

She shook her head. "No, I'm not answering any more questions until you tell me why you're here."

His gaze held hers for several seconds. He smiled again but he continued to watch her. "Of course, how rude of me. Your friend seems to have disappeared, Ginny."

She tried to sound surprised. "What do you mean 'disappeared'? Has somebody reported him missing?"

"Something like that. Do you have any idea where he is?"

"No I don't." At least that was true. "But this isn't right. I spoke to him a couple of days ago. He's a grown up. Maybe he just went for a holiday or he's visiting friends, or something. You're not telling me something. Why do you think he's missing?"

"Because he is."

"How do you know?"

"Because his tag has stopped responding."

Ginny didn't have to feign surprise or shock this time. "That's impossible," she said. Everybody knew that.

The detective studied her intently, clearly trying to judge her every reaction. It occurred to her that he might be unaugmented, seeing her real face. She hadn't considered it before but it would make sense for the cops to interview suspects with their augmentation turned right down.

"How could he do that?" she asked.

"There are ways."

She blinked at him, adjusting to this new information. The government line was that tags were infallible. That was one of the selling points. Everybody had to be tagged so that the augmented reality sensors could find them and identify them. If you didn't have a tag, you could just disappear. If people were not tagged, they could easily impersonate someone else. It guaranteed that the people you met were who they said they were – even in full VR. It also prevented criminals from walking around undetected. The tags were embedded into people's skulls, distributed right across the cranium, grown from implanted nanotech that was put there at birth. They couldn't be removed, they said, and tampering would have life-threatening side-effects. And people accepted tagging because, without tags, augmented reality – especially virtual reality – would become a playground for scammers and thieves, terrorists and worse.

"I still don't see how I can help you, Detective Sergeant."

"Dover, please. Forgive me for saying, Ginny, but you seem pretty nervous."

She didn't like the man's insinuations, however true they might be. In fact, she didn't like the man at all, with his smooth manner and his stupid name and his suspicions. "I've had a crappy day," she said. "And this is just making it worse. I'm on a deadline and I need to get stuff done." Nevertheless, she couldn't help herself asking, "Why would anybody remove their tag – or whatever Cal's supposed to have done? Surely you can't live without it these days. You can't even buy stuff without an identity check. You couldn't get through a door or take a cab. How could you live?"

The detective shrugged. "I suppose there are other things

you can do that outweigh the inconveniences. You'd be surprised how many people we lose each year." He stood up, ready to go and she stood up with him. "Here's my card," he said, passing her a virtual ID. "In case Mr. Copplin makes contact." He walked the few paces to the door. As he stepped outside, he said, "Of course, he might not have turned his tag off deliberately. Sometimes they malfunction – especially in cases of severe head trauma." Again, he watched her carefully, looking for any reaction. Whatever he saw, he seemed finished. "Thanks for your time," he said, and left.

—oOo—

"Oh my God!" Della seemed more thrilled than shocked as Ginny recounted her day. "He actually said that? Oh my God!"

They were in a bar in New York. Not a real bar in New York, of course. Both Ginny and Della remained in their tanks in their own homes, Ginny in Brisbane and Della in Sydney. But they were unlatched and thus free to visit any bar in the whole of space and time, real or fictional, as long as they could afford the entry fee. Travel was free and instantaneous. So the virtual world was their oyster. It was estimated that there were over three billion worldlets on QNet – of varying scope and quality. There were over two thousand virtual New Yorks alone, covering every conceivable time period and every worldlet designer's personal interpretation of the great metropolis. The "real" New York, built and managed on behalf of the City of New York, was just one among the two thousand.

The Empire Bar was one designer's fantasy of a 1950s cocktail bar set atop the Empire State Building, featuring

22

spectacular views across night-time Manhattan and waitresses with seamed stockings and bright red lipstick. A pianist tinkled out jazz standards and the lighting was suited to quiet liaisons between fat middle-aged men in three-piece suits and their young, blonde companions in tight, satin dresses. Ginny liked to go there when she had lots to talk about and had dragged Della there despite her friend's protests, because tonight was definitely one of those nights.

"And then he told me that Cal had gone off the Net. His tag is no longer working."

"What?"

"I know. This is all so weird, I can't get my head around it."

A waitress appeared and Ginny ordered two more Martinis.

"Steady girl," said Della. "It's all right for you self-employed types, but I've got to go to work in the morning."

"Turn off your drip, then. After a day like today, I need the booze." Most tanks these days would feed an alcohol solution into your veins, at a rate matched to your virtual consumption, so that drinking in bars could deliver the genuine pre-augmentation experience.

Della rolled her eyes and took a pull at her drink. "What the hell? Why should you have all the fun? Tell me more."

"That's it, really. The cop left and I sat and brooded all day until you left work."

"Have you tried calling Cal again?"

"Like every ten minutes!" She sipped her drink and stared out at the tiny lights of cars moving between the skyscrapers. "What do you think, Della? Should I take the package to Detective Sergeant Dickhead and just wash my hands of it all?"

Della looked at her with sympathetic eyes. "You like Cal don't you?"

"What's that got to do with anything?" Ginny said, although she knew perfectly well what Della meant.

"You're worried about him."

"Well, duh. The guy disappears without trace, the police are after him, and before he leaves, he asks me to deliver a mysterious package. Of course I'm worried. The cop said he might be dead."

"And you haven't opened the package?"

"No. I don't want to know what's in it. I don't want to be more involved in this than I have to be."

Della grinned and looked into her friend's eyes. "You're going to deliver it, aren't you? Oh my God, you're going to go and see this crim – what's his name?"

"Gavin."

"Gavin – and give him the drugs, or whatever. You've made up your mind already, haven't you?"

"No. That's why I'm here. So you can talk me into doing the sensible thing."

"Which is what?"

"Well, going to the police, I suppose."

Still grinning, Della picked up her glass and sat back, watching Ginny over the rim. "The philosopher, Jean-Paul Sartre, once had a student come up to him after a lecture and ask–"

"What the hell are you taking about?" Della had studied French Literature at university and was full of anecdotes about people Ginny had never heard of.

Della just grinned more widely. "The student asked the great man for his advice about breaking up with his girlfriend." Ginny sighed heavily and resigned herself to listening to whatever this nonsense was. "Sartre dismissed the lad with an airy wave of his hand saying, 'You already know what to do. Don't bother me with questions to which you already know the answer.' 'But – but –' the boy stammered–"

"Della, for heavens' sake. Does this have a point? I need you to talk sense right now."

"That's just it. Sartre told the student off because the boy must have known already what his teacher thought about the matter and that's why he went to Sartre for advice and not someone else. He didn't really want advice, he just wanted authority for a decision he'd already made."

"And you think that's why I asked you out tonight, so you can tell me what I want to hear?"

"*Précisément* !"

"Well I wish I'd asked Kerry."

"Kerry's too timid. She'd have said go to the police."

"Well, I should."

"Really? And ignore Cal's last request?"

"Cal's not dead."

"But he might be, and if he isn't and there's something illegal in that package, you'd be getting him into even more trouble."

"You're supposed to be the sensible one."

But Della was right on both counts. Ginny had already made up her mind to take the package to Gavin, and she had thought that Della would agree with her, once she heard her reasons. It was irritating to find she was so transparent. She waved the ever-attentive waitress over and asked for two more Martinis. It was an expensive place and the drinks weren't free but now that she knew what she intended to do, getting blitzed seemed like an even more attractive idea than before. She'd regret it in the morning but she didn't want to think about that now.

She downed the drink as soon as it arrived. "Let's go to some seedy old bar somewhere and get pissed," she said. "I want to pick up some young stud and forget about Cal and his bloody package."

Della gulped back her own Martini and raised the glass. "To forgetting!" she shouted, drawing looks from around the room.

—oOo—

When Ginny woke up the next morning, she was still in the tank and still unlatched. The default worldlet was running, which at that time of day was a café on a Greek island, overlooking the Aegean Sea and the rising sun. Her memories of last night were a little blurry but the seedy bar, the pickup, and cyber-sex in some kind of Roman villa, all featured in the mix. She triggered the tank's lid and it lifted off her. Raising her head from the deeply-padded contours of the seat was a mistake. While the padding held it, it had been fine. Now that her neck was doing the job, pain hit her like a plank across the forehead. She let her head settle again.

Too old for that kind of thing, she told herself, and hoped she'd remember next time.

For a long while, she reclined in the tank and let her eyelids fall closed against the bright daylight. She lay there, naked and half buried in the padded interior, and wondered how big a dent she had put in her bank account. It was a time to be economising, not splurging. But, apart from the drinks, and the entry fees to at least three places, she had made several costume changes to suit her changing moods and surroundings, each one having to be hired because, for some reason, nothing she owned was just right for the occasion.

The occasion being getting shit-faced and laid by some complete stranger whose name I can't remember and — Oh God! She recalled that her Romeo didn't even want her number when she offered it to him. Embarrassment and misery flooded her.

And she still had to take that damned package round to some petty gangster called Gavin, only now with a hangover and even more of a need to be working instead of wasting her time.

Her tank was comfortable and warm. A soft and contoured seat that fitted her snugly with separate depressions for each arm and leg, it tilted her back and let her body relax while her mind roved through virtual worlds. A set of drips clipped to a corresponding set of permanently-attached catheters on her upper arm kept her fed and hydrated, delivered alcohol — and other recreational drugs if you were that way inclined — and a cunning bidet-cum-potty arrangement made sure that visits to the bathroom could also be simulated. With enough nutrients in the drips, you could stay in the tank for days. And many people did. With the padded lid in place, you were immobilised and couldn't hurt yourself if you tried. Better than your mother's womb, as the ads for one brand said. Ginny, however, didn't even like to stay in hers for more than a few hours at a stretch.

She climbed out, groaning, switched the tank onto a self-cleaning cycle, and padded across to the shower to let the hot water do what it could to freshen her up. There were two messages waiting for her, one from her mother and the other from the cop, Richards, both asking her to call. Ginny found the idea of talking to either equally unpleasant, but, in the end, even her mother was preferable to the cop.

"Ginny! My baby! Oh, thank heavens you called. I thought

you were just going to ignore me again, even at this awful time."

"Hello, Mum. I'm fine. How are you?"

"Oh, I suppose I deserve it. You sacrifice everything, you give up your life to raise a child, you teach her that your life revolves around making her happy, and what's the result? She cares only for herself. Well, it's my fault I spoiled you so much. And now, in my moment of need, all you can think about are your own feelings. Your Dad said I shouldn't call. He said it would only upset me more."

Ginny gritted her teeth. Even for her mother this was pretty extreme. "Why don't you just tell me what's wrong, Mum?"

"Oh this is a fine state of affairs. A mother having to call her own daughter to break the bad news. If you called me even once a week, you'd know what was going on. We wouldn't be like strangers. I suppose you just don't care. You've got your glamorous career as a composer and you don't care what becomes of your old Mum. You forget who made you practice the piano when you were a little girl, who bought you your first clarinet, who—"

"Mum, I've got to go out in a minute. Was there something particular you wanted to talk about?"

"Something particular? Something particular?" Ginny closed her eyes and tried to stay calm. "I suppose being under sentence of death is something particular. I reckon your mother dying might be worth taking a few moments out of your busy schedule. Or am I wrong? You weren't even answering your phone last night. You were probably out at some fancy party. Sharon's kids are just the same. That boy of hers spends half his life in the tank, spaced out on drugs, while his mother gets the job of filling up his drips so he doesn't just die in there."

"Would that be Sharon's son Jake? The boof-head you wanted me to marry not so many years ago?"

"You'd have made a fine couple. He doesn't care if his mother lives or dies either."

A deep breath. "So you're crook, is that it? You called to tell me how sick you are?"

"Sick? Well that's one way of putting it. Look, I know you don't want to, nobody wants to travel any more, but I think you should probably get on a plane and come down here. I may not have very long."

Despite herself, Ginny felt a touch of anxiety. As much as she knew from a lifetime of experience that her mother was a raving hypochondriac, she supposed that one day there just might be something serious wrong with her. "Mum, what is it? What's the matter?"

There was a silence on the other end of the line, Ginny imagined her mother steeling herself to make some awful revelation. When her mother spoke, there was a tremor in her voice. "Darling, now don't get hysterical. It's all right. Really. I'm coping fine and your Dad's been so wonderful and kind."

Dad's been so wonderful and kind? Now Ginny was really worried. She couldn't remember her mum ever having a good word for her father. "Shit, Mum, what's wrong with you?"

"It's... I... I have breast cancer, darling."

Ginny's temper fizzed up to boiling point in an instant. "Breast cancer? Is that all? They've been able to cure breast cancer for decades! You won't even need to go to hospital. An AIGP will be able to do it all remotely. For God's sake, Mum! Breast cancer?"

Her mother was defensive, perhaps even a little abashed. "People die of breast cancer all the time."

"No they don't. The used to, when you were a little girl, maybe, but not in my lifetime. Jesus, Mum. Did you even talk to a doctor?"

"I got a test. One of those kit things."

"Call a doctor, Mum. Do it right now. Don't waste your money on a human GP, spend a bit and call an AI, they'll tell you all about it and what you have to do."

"I'm sure I've heard of people dying—"

"Well, you're not. You'll be fine. Just call the doctor and they'll sort you out. Look, Mum. I really have to go now. I'm late for something." The silence stretched out a few seconds. "I'll call you soon to find out how you got on, OK? Catch you later."

She hung up before her mother thought of some other crazy problem to keep her on the line.

Standing in the kitchenette, taking deep breaths to calm herself down, she nevertheless sent out a bot to gather the latest on breast cancer, its treatment and prognosis. Just in case. One day her crazy mother wouldn't be crying wolf. One day something terrible would happen. Ginny could easily imagine the tonnage of guilt that would descend on her on that day. The least she could do to avoid just a few kilos of it was to be sure of her facts.

Detective Sergeant Dover Richards picked up on the first ring. "Hi Ginny, thanks for returning my call." He looked fresh and eager, keen to be about his business. "How are you today?"

"Hungover, thanks. Yourself?"

"I don't drink." *What a surprise.* "I forgot to ask you yesterday if you knew any of Mr. Copplin's friends."

"No you didn't?"

"Sorry?"

"You didn't forget to ask. You asked me. I said no I didn't."

"Really?"

"Really."

"I must be going senile," he said, laughing. Ginny waited to find out what the call was really about. "Ah well, sorry to have bothered you. You look like you just got out the shower. Do you always get up this late?"

Ginny checked the time. The morning was half gone already. As before, the cop's tone and his questions irritated her. "Is that a crime now?" she asked, surprised at her own belligerence. The last thing she needed to do right now was antagonise this nosy policeman.

He laughed again. "If it was I could arrest half the city. So you were out on the town last night, then?"

"I'm sorry, Detective Sergeant Richards but–"

"Dover, please."

" – but I'm a bit behind schedule, as you can imagine. I really need to get on."

"Don't you want to know how we're getting on finding your friend?"

The moment seemed to freeze. It hadn't even occurred to Ginny to ask. She realised she had begun to think of Dover Richards as the enemy, not as someone who would help Cal, but who was hunting her friend down to pin something on him. Given the package in her overalls pocket, the evidence that Cal was some kind of crook looked pretty strong even in her own eyes, so her attitude to the policeman seemed a just a little odd.

"I suppose I assumed you'd have told me if there had been any news," she said.

He smiled and nodded. "Of course. And I assume the

same thing about you, Ginny. I'll let you get on with your day, then. Anything good planned?"

"Just the usual." She said goodbye and hung up. Every time she spoke to the man it felt as though he was poking around in her dustbin, or rummaging in her underwear drawer.

She checked the address written on the package. It was too far away to walk but she didn't want to catch a cab and leave a record of her journey. It occurred to her that the police could just track her tag if they wanted to. They could know anything and everything she did. But why would they? Just because she knew someone who had gone missing, what reason was that to follow someone? Besides, weren't there laws? Didn't they need warrants and stuff like that? She told herself she was being paranoid. She derided herself for letting Cal and his stupid package spook her like that. All the same, she vowed that, once she had passed on whatever it was Cal had dumped on her, she was never, ever going to do anything so idiotic again, no matter what.

She went out the back of the building. A shed stood in the yard and she needed something from it. She hadn't been in there since she started renting her unit, five years ago. It was full of old junk and she remembered thinking at the time that some of it was probably worth salvaging and restoring to sell as antiques. Some people liked to have an old piece of real furniture, or some old tool – like Ginny and her electric piano – to display in their home. But she had never got round to it and wouldn't know how to restore an old sewing machine, or whatever, anyway.

The shed had a padlock on it, not a metaphorical padlock that was really an electronic lock that would open at a thought, but a real one, heavy and strong and requiring a key she had lost years ago.

She switched to minimal augmentation and saw the shed as it really was, decrepit and half rotten, the padlock coated in dark efflorescences of rust. The yard itself was a mess, the shrubs and flower beds revealed as tall weeds growing between cracked concrete and heaps of builder's rubble. She said a little prayer of thanks to the landlord who kept the virtual image of her building and its environs clean and attractive. She found a brick in the rubbish and picked it up, surprised by its roughness and weight. Reality was so much more unpleasant than the augmented lives people led. It was easy to see why augmentation had been so quickly and universally adopted once it became available.

Holding one end of the brick in both hands, she brought the other end down hard on the padlock. She had seen something like this in an old vid – or it might have been the butt of a rifle – and hoped it wasn't just poetic license on the director's part. She hit the lock with a jolt that made her drop the brick, and an ear-splitting crack that seemed to shake the whole shed. To her amazement, the padlock was still intact, but the hasp that connected it to the door frame had been knocked right out of the rotten timber and was hanging by one rusty screw. It came away with a light tug and the door swung open.

The gloom inside the shed was criss-crossed by bright beams of sunlight coming through gaps and holes in the walls and roof. There were cobwebs and a layer of grime coated everything. The smell was dry and ancient and took her back to a childhood spent crawling into forbidden places. It had the comforting smell of a place where her mother would never find her. It wasn't a big shed and she immediately found what she came there for.

The old bicycle still had some hints of blue paint on its frame and the chrome on its handlebars hadn't all been bubbled away by the rust beneath it. The brakes were rusted solid and the tyres were flat. The chain was intact but was dry and grey with dust. Despite all the years since she had last touched one, her hands remembered the feel of handlebars, her body leaned just so as she wheeled it out of the shed. She propped it against the shed wall and stepped back to look at it.

Her father had taught her to ride a bike when she was ten. She had been excruciatingly embarrassed at the time. What did she need to ride a bike for? Nobody rode bikes? Bikes were *old*. What if someone saw her on it? But her father had insisted, trying to force her to enjoy it the way he had once enjoyed it. He set her a goal; *ride up the street and back again all on your own and you don't ever have to ride it again.* It had taken her days and days to do it and, as soon as she did, she ran inside and unlatched, rejoining her friends in VR and telling them what a pain in the neck her father was. They all agreed, parents were old-fashioned and weird, always harking back to the olden days.

It had not occurred to her at the time, but now she saw how much she must have hurt her father. She imagined him standing in the drive with the discarded bike at his feet, watching her run back into the house.

She found a little can of oil in the shed, almost rusted through. Yet when she tipped it and squeezed, a thin, greenish liquid trickled from its long plastic spout onto the chain links. She didn't really know what she was doing but she knew the old machine needed oil so she slathered it over every joint and spindle, every link and cog. And it seemed to work. With a little pushing and pulling, squeezing and turning, the callipers closed when she pulled the brake handle and the rear wheel turned when she pressed down on a pedal and lifted up the back. With a little experimentation and by reference to various instruction pages and diagrams on the Net, she learned how to attach the tube from the bicycle pump to the valves on the tyres and pump them up.

Inordinately pleased with herself, she wheeled the bike out the back gate (which refused to open until she had almost demolished it) and onto the road. There was no traffic on this little side-street and almost nothing on the main road except a few robot delivery vans dropping groceries and parcels off at houses along the road. She didn't worry about the robots. She knew they would drive around her or stop if they had to rather than bump into her.

The bike was a little too tall for her and climbing onto it was a nerve-racking experience. As soon as she managed to get her bum on the tattered seat – but before she could begin to pedal – the thing began toppling over. For a while she was stumped by this apparently insoluble problem, trying desperately to remember what she had done as a child to get the machine moving. Again she consulted the Net but this time there were no helpful suggestions. It occurred to her that she had spent so long finding and preparing the bicycle that she would have been half-way there by now if she'd walked. A gross exaggeration of course but her frustration was starting to get the better of her judgement.

In the end, a dim recollection from an ancient movie came to her rescue – a policeman with a foot on one pedal, pushing himself along with the other and then swinging his pushing leg over once the machine was underway. She tried it and almost smashed the bike and broke her neck when she failed to get her leg high enough and came crashing to earth in a heap. For a moment the pain in her grazed palms and the indignity of her position brought tears to her eyes.

What the hell was she doing there, sitting in the middle of the road with a clapped out old boneshaker wrapped around her legs? The whole situation was ridiculous. She had work to do, a living to make. She shouldn't be out in the street wasting her time, a reluctant drug mule for a man she hardly knew and who was probably dead anyway. She stood up and kicked at the bike. Idiotic machine. Why couldn't it just work?

She took a deep breath and picked up the bicycle again. She hated feeling sorry for herself. It reminded her too much of her mother. And that made her angry. Once more she put a foot on the pedal and scooted herself along the road. Determined not to fail again, she swung her leg up and over and found herself sitting high above the whole rattling, wobbling contraption. For a moment, she was so surprised and scared that she forgot to pedal, then had to grope with her feet to find the elusive things as her speed slowed and her wobbling increased. But, having made it so far, she refused to fall over and start again. She located the pedals and pushed hard. The gears clattered and slipped but the chain stayed on and she found herself in a high gear pedalling fast to keep herself moving forward.

She emerged into the main road without even having noticed she had reached it and a delivery truck squealed to a halt beside her. She daren't look at it as all her attention was needed to turn the bike before it hit the kerb at the opposite side of the road. By a miracle, she stayed on the bike and made the turn, her heart racing. It was only as she got the mechanical beast under some kind of control again that she realised she had turned the wrong way. New virtual blue arrows from her nav system painted the road surface but she had to miss the next turn they suggested because she just dare not turn the bicycle. But she was ready for the next one and rattled around the corner with a sense of achievement and a surge of pride.

By the time she had travelled a few more blocks, she had calmed down enough and grown so much in confidence that she was able to remember that she should be using her brakes too. She even considered the possibility of changing gear but didn't manage to pluck up the courage to try that throughout the whole, hair-raising ride.

Chapter 3

When she stopped the bike outside the address written on the package, it toppled sideways and she had to hop and jump to get clear of it as it clattered to the road. She picked it up and wheeled it into the drive. One good thing about her madcap journey was that she had not had a spare moment to think about the mysterious Gavin and how her meeting with the drug dealer, or diamond smuggler, or whatever he was, might go.

Gavin's home was a large, detached house, brick built, on two storeys, a double garage, and a large garden filled with head-high weeds. It was the sight of the weeds that reminded her she was still in minimal augmentation. She latched to the house and street. The lawn became well-tended shrubbery and the house received an instant coat of new paint. She looked back at her bicycle, propped against the gate. The street sensors had picked it up and automatic routines fed her an image with the dirt and rust removed and the chromium restored and gleaming. Spending so much time in minimal aug was giving her a fresh appreciation of the amount of work her implants did to keep the world neat and tidy for her. It was all a grand deception, of course, but a benign one.

Who would settle for reality when you could have augmentation?

She touched the package in her pocket and remembered the shock of discovering it on Cal's table. She turned off all her augmentation again. She didn't know what tricks Gavin's house might play on her senses and she had no reason to suppose he would be a friend. She looked around for a doorbell and didn't see one. With a sigh, she realised that, if there was one it would probably be virtual like everybody else's. So she knocked on the door.

She pulled her hand back as if it had stung her. The door swung inwards. It had been pulled closed but was unfastened. Her heart began to race again, seeing why: the door frame was shattered. Someone had kicked the door in from the outside. She stepped back off the porch frightened of what she'd found but unable to decide to run away. She had to give the package to someone. She had to give it to Gavin. But Gavin was inside the house and someone had kicked in the door. There might be an innocent explanation for that but Ginny didn't believe anything that came to her. The package, Cal gone missing, the police snooping around, only allowed for sinister, scary explanations. Someone had gone in there and done something to Gavin. Killed him, probably.

Still she stood on the drive, wavering. She looked up and down the street. She looked back at the broken door. She took out the package and turned it in her hands. Perhaps if she just went up to the door and threw it inside she could just ride away and forget about it. The police would find it on the floor of the hallway. But that was no good. It would have her DNA on it. She'd heard they could find you from the tiniest traces these days and everyone's genome was on record. They did it at birth when they put in the tag. That's why there was so little crime these days. No-one could get away with anything any more.

Still she dithered. Now was the time to walk away. She didn't owe Cal anything. She would drop the package in a recycler and that would be the end of it. What the hell did Cal think he was doing getting her involved in all this? She was aiding and abetting criminals. She could go to jail. All for some guy she hardly knew and had a bit of a crush on? No, this had all gone too far. She had to get away from there right now and never look back.

She shuffled her feet but still she could not go. What if this Gavin bloke was only injured and not dead? Shouldn't she try to help him? Call an ambulance? Give him first aid? But the idea of going into that house and finding a strange man bleeding out on the floor chilled her to the bone. Could she touch him? Would she even have a clue what to do? The only first aid she knew, she realised, was what she'd seen in cop shows and spy vids. What were the chances of any of that actually being real? She saw herself holding the dying man with blood flowing over her hands as she tried to push his exposed intestines back into a gaping stomach wound. Her throat clenched against her rising nausea. But if she called an ambulance, her tag would reveal her identity. They would know it was her. They would know she had been there and left this man to die.

But they would know it was her anyway. Once the police found the body, they would check the records. The street, the house, would have registered her tag. If she didn't go to them, they would soon be looking for her. The full extent of the trouble she was in washed over her like a giant wave, almost knocking her over, leaving her gasping for breath. Panic was rising in her. She had to get away from that house, she couldn't think while it was standing over her like a giant black cloud.

She turned towards the bicycle and took a step towards it.

"Stay where you are."

She froze. It was a woman's voice, firm and strong. She knew there would be a gun in the woman's hand even before she turned to look.

"Come here. Inside the house."

The woman was short and thin, about Ginny's age. She wore the ubiquitous overalls and had her hair tied in a ponytail. She was standing inside the hallway as if she didn't want to be seen. The gun in her left hand looked the size of an artillery piece. It was pointing straight at Ginny.

"Hurry up. I won't tell you again."

Ginny took a couple of steps towards her, acting without thought, as if having a gun pointed at you robbed you of your will. But a small desperate hope made her say, "You won't shoot me out here in the street."

"Don't kid yourself, darl. Just keep coming and you'll be all right. I won't shoot you at all unless you make me."

Ginny walked towards the stranger. She really didn't want to go into the house, but she could see no option. If she tried to run, it would be easy for the woman to shoot her. There was no-one in the street to see her and raise the alarm and anyone inside their houses looking towards their windows would not be seeing her, they'd be looking out on a tropical beach or the rings of Saturn, anything but a drab suburban street. The woman with the gun stepped back to allow Ginny in and, hating herself for being such a coward, she passed through the doorway into the hall.

It was dark and cool out of the sun, oppressive and claustrophobic. The door slammed shut behind her and

Ginny turned to find the woman leaning with her back against it. "In there," she said, waving the gun towards a doorway.

"You've got me mixed up with someone else," Ginny said, feeling she had to say something, convince the woman she was just an innocent passer-by. She almost believed that was true, despite the package in her pocket. Whatever was going on, it was nothing to do with her.

"Get in there," the woman said. Ginny did as she was told, walking into a sparsely-furnished room with an old sofa and a couple of armchairs. "Now sit. On the sofa." Ginny sat, immediately regretting it. In the low, soft upholstery, she was almost helpless. Doing anything quickly to jump the woman or run was now impossible.

"What are you going to do?" Ginny asked.

"Fucked if I know," the woman said. "Who are you and why did you come here?"

Ginny was confused. How could the woman not now who she was? Basic identity was always available even in the lowest levels of augmentation. With a gasp, she realised she could not see the woman's ID data. She pushed her level of augmentation up but still there was no sign of the woman's identity. When she latched to the house, fully augmented, the woman turned into a person-sized piece of abstract art, standing incongruously in the middle of the floor. In her shock, Ginny almost climbed over back of the sofa, scrambling away from the apparition.

"Stay still," the artwork shouted. It slid across the floor towards her, its shape shifting erratically, reconfiguring itself. Ginny stopped. She was panting and wide-eyed with fright. "Turn your aug down, Ellie. What am I? A pot plant? A hat stand?" She laughed, apparently enjoying Ginny's discomfiture.

The laugh, more than anything, snapped Ginny out of her funk. "You're untagged," she said, understanding, at last. "The house assumes you're some piece of furniture or something and it's making it's best guess of how to represent you." Now she knew what was happening, it was fascinating. Systems everywhere must be doing this all the time. Sensors pick up shapes and usually the computers would know what to do with them, like the weeds in the garden that are rendered as flowers and shrubs. But an untagged person was just a tall thin object to the systems – obviously not a person, because it had no tag. So they tried to find some appropriate household item to match it to, mainly so the people in the house – the tagged people – would see it and not walk into it.

Ginny turned down her augmentation and the statue turned back into a woman. "You can't see my data," Ginny said and felt stupid when the woman sneered at her. Of course, if you were untagged, how could your implants ask the AR systems for information? Questions filled her head. How did an untagged person buy food? How did they buy anything? How did they do anything? But the biggest question by far was, "Who are you?"

"After you, Ellie," the woman said.

She went to one of the armchairs and sat on the arm, resting the hand holding the gun on her knee. To Ginny, the gun still looked enormous and must have been very heavy. Ginny gave her name.

"What are you doing here?" the woman asked, not offering her own name in return.

"I came to see Gavin," Ginny said, not knowing what else to say.

The woman stared at her for a long time. "What business

have you got with Gavin?"

A slight trembling began in Ginny's chest and limbs. She felt weepy and tried not to let it show, suppressing the self-pity that was growing in her. After the shocks and scares she'd been having, and with that gun pointing at her, it was hardly surprising she would have some kind of reaction, but she didn't want this hard-faced woman to see her cry. She kindled the spark of resentment and anger she felt and tried to fan it into defiance. "You killed him, didn't you?" she said.

The woman laughed that sneering laugh again but Ginny thought she could see something else in her expression apart from contempt. Sadness maybe. Pain. "Oh, he's dead all right. In the kitchen if you want to go and see."

Ginny was starting to find her equilibrium again. "Look, whatever all this is about, it's nothing to do with me. I'm nothing to do with all this. Why don't you just let me go and you'll never hear or see me again. I won't say anything about it, ever."

"Shut up. How do you know Gavin?"

Ginny took a breath. The only thing she could think of to do was tell the truth. Maybe then the woman would realise she wasn't any kind of threat and would let her go. "I don't know him. A friend of mine gave me his address." Which wasn't the whole truth, but she was still reluctant to mention the package unless she had to.

"What friend?"

"His name's Cal Copplin."

The woman gave Ginny a fresh appraisal.

"How do you know Cal?"

"Are you a friend of his?" This was the first hope Ginny had felt since she saw the broken door frame. If the woman was a friend of Cal's… But then she remembered the body in the kitchen and her hope shrivelled away.

"How do you know Cal?" the woman asked again.

"I – I just know him. We met. Socially. We've been for coffee a couple of times."

The news seemed to irritate the woman. She stood up and took a couple of paces. "Jesus Christ. So he's chatting up women, going on dates, having a fucking social life. The fucking stupid bastard." She said all this to herself, as if Ginny wasn't there.

"He's disappeared," Ginny said. This woman obviously knew Cal. Her very anger with him suggested they were colleagues, if not friends. Maybe she knew where he'd gone.

The woman rounded on her, eyes hard. "Too bloody right, he's disappeared. Gone without a bloody trace. Left us up to pick up the pieces, too." She took a pace closer. "And he gave you this address did he? Now why would he do that? Why did he send you to see Gavin?"

For all the anger and swearing, Ginny thought she could hear a tone of desperation in the woman's voice. It occurred to her that this tough, menacing woman was worried and maybe a bit frightened. The idea gave her strength. It let some of her own anger loose.

"I've had enough of you waving that gun at me," she said. "Either shoot me or put the damned thing away. I don't know who you are or what you're doing here and I've had enough of being interrogated by you. Now tell me, did you shoot Gavin? You don't get another thing out of me until you start giving me some answers."

The woman returned her glare with a steady gaze, she was clearly not intimidated by Ginny's rebellion and may well have been considering whether to shoot her. Ginny felt her determination wavering. She might die, right here on a dead

45

man's sofa, with a stranger's bullet in her, and no idea why it had happened. She swallowed hard, thinking maybe she should apologise, let the woman ask her questions, do whatever it took to stay alive.

But the woman relaxed, stepped back, and slipped the gun into her overalls pocket. "OK, I believe you. You're just some Ellie patsy with the hots for Cal who let him drag her into this mess."

Ginny didn't like the description but it wasn't too far away from the truth. "All right. That's me. So who are you?"

The woman went back to the armchair and perched on it again. "I'm Gavin's sister, Tonia."

Ginny gave a grunt of surprise. Then the relief hit her. "So you didn't kill him?" The woman, Tonia, didn't answer, but Ginny was sure she was right. "So who did? Someone kicked the door in and came in here and killed your brother. Was it a rival gang or something?"

Tonia frowned. "What the hell are you talking about? I kicked the door in because Gavin went dark. What rival gang? What do you think you know little Ellie?"

Ginny was confused. Did Tonia not know what Gavin was into? "Your brother… He was a drug dealer or something, right? He was working with Cal. Smuggling stuff, maybe. You must know. Why else would someone kill him?"

Tonia shook her head in disbelief. "Did Cal spin you that line? Or are you just some kind of nutjob?" The question seemed to remind her of more important ones. "Just why did Cal send you round here? Have you got a message for my brother?"

"Tell me what this is all about or I'm not saying anything." As soon as she'd said it, Ginny was appalled at herself for saying anything so stupid. This was Gavin's sister, for God's sake. All she had to do was hand her the package and get herself home as fast as she could pedal. She didn't even want to know what was going on. Anything she found out could only make things worse for her.

"Wait, no, don't tell me." She stood up. Tonia stood up too, her hand reaching for the gun. "Look, I don't want to know anything about it. I came here because Cal asked me to deliver a package for him. He said I should give it to Gavin in person. But you're his sister, so you'll do."

She reached into her pocket for the package and Tonia drew her gun, saying, "Steady."

Ginny froze. "I just wanted to—"

"OK, but very, very slowly."

Carefully, Ginny pulled the little parcel from her overalls and held it out for Tonia to take.

"What is it?" Tonia asked. She hadn't put the gun away and she showed no sign of taking the package from Ginny.

"I – I don't know. I assume it's drugs, or diamonds, or something. He's your brother, don't you know?"

"My brother is not a—" She stopped and pursed her lips as if angry with herself. "*Was not* a criminal. He was a good man, a brave man, trying to save dumb shits like you from their own stupidity."

The pain in Tonia's expression was clearer now. "I'm sorry," Ginny said. "I didn't mean to—" She took a breath. No, she would not apologise to the woman pointing a gun at her. "Do you want it or not?"

"Open it," Tonia said.

"What?"

"Open it. Show me what's inside."

"I don't want to know what's inside."

"Just fucking open it!"

"Why do you keep calling me Ellie?" *It's funny the things that seem important when you have a gun pointed your way,* Ginny thought. Tonia wasn't going to answer her, so she began tugging at the paper. It tore easily but her fingers were clumsy and it took her far longer than it should. Inside was a small padded box with three data cubes inside.

She looked at them dumbly then at Tonia. "Data cubes," she said. Not drugs then. Nor diamonds. Just information. "Industrial espionage?" she suggested. "Blackmail?"

Tonia stepped forward and grabbed the cubes, stuffing them into her pocket. The torn paper fluttered to the ground. "You can go now."

But Ginny was watching the woman's expression. "That's not it, is it?"

Tonia walked away from her to stare out of the window. It was as if Ginny didn't exist any more. But Ginny had seen the relief on Tonia's face when the woman saw the cubes. And now it looked as if the she was on the verge of tears. The gun hung like a dead weight at the end of her arm.

Ginny knew that the sensible thing was to walk out the door, out of the house, and go. But she found she could not. She needed to know what this had all been about, what was on those data cubes that meant Cal had to disappear and Gavin had to be killed.

"At least tell me what it is," she said to Tonia's back. "Don't I deserve that?"

Tonia stiffened and Ginny caught her breath. Whatever the hell she thought she was doing, antagonising the woman with the gun was not a good idea. She tried another tack.

"The police have been to see me. About Cal. They wanted to know how I knew him. They asked if I knew any of his friends."

Tonia turned quickly. "What did you tell them? Did you give them this address? Did you mention Gavin?"

The sudden fire in Tonia's eyes set Ginny's heart racing. "No. No, of course not. I didn't tell them anything. I just said I didn't know Cal very well. I said I didn't know his friends. I didn't mention Gavin, or the package, or anything."

"Why not? Why would you hold that back? You thought it was drugs." An idea seemed to strike her and she brought the gun up fast. "You're working with them. You're some fucking tagger's bitch." She stepped towards Ginny and Ginny stepped back.

"I'm not. Honest. I don't even know what a tagger is." She took another step back and fell into the sofa with a yell of alarm. Tonia stepped up to her, the big gun in Ginny's face. Tonia's expression said she was seriously considering whether to play it safe and shoot Ginny now.

"For God's sake! I was just doing a favour for Cal. You've got your data. I'm sorry I stuck my nose in. It's none of my business whatever's going on. Just let me go and you'll never see or hear from me again. I promise."

Tonia said nothing, just glared at Ginny, seemingly still undecided as to whether to shoot her.

"I won't ever talk to the cops, I swear. I don't even like them. That guy Richards gives me the creeps. If I never see him again either I'll be glad."

Tonia's expression changed. "Dover Richards?" Ginny nodded. Was Tonia looking scared now? The woman walked away from the sofa, agitated and frowning hard. "Jesus Christ, girl! Dover Richards isn't a cop. He isn't even a tagger. I reckon he's the bastard who killed my brother. Tell me what he said."

She made Ginny remember word-for-word her two

conversations with the phony cop, while she listened, shaking her head in angry disbelief. When she was sure she'd got as much as she could from Ginny, Tonia made her recite her full name, her QNet address, and her home address. She wrote them down using a pencil in a little notebook with paper pages. "That's so I can find you again if you ever tell the cops anything," she said. "Now get out of here and if Dover Richards calls you again, just keep pretending you're a dumb fuck who knows bugger all. That way he might let you live."

Ginny didn't need telling a second time. She struggled up from the sofa and made for the door, trying not even to look at Tonia.

"It's not Ellie," Tonia called after her. She stopped in the doorway and turned, not daring to upset this strange and volatile woman by ignoring her. "It's the letters, L. E.. Stands for lotos eaters. That's what you are. Now fuck off."

—oOo—

Ginny mounted the bicycle and pedalled away in a hurry. She had to dismount just a couple of streets farther on because she was trembling and crying too much to keep going. She kicked the bike away from her and sat down on the kerb with her head in her hands. She felt sick and angry and relieved and terrified. She might have died. That crazy bitch might have shot her. She had been so scared. She ran over in her mind the stupid things she had done and said, the countless ways she had put herself in danger.

Perhaps worse, she felt so ashamed of herself for being such a coward – a physical coward and a moral one. She had let herself be driven entirely by fear. The woman, Tonia, had bullied her and threatened her, and she had been craven and pathetic in the face of it. But what could she have done? A man was dead in the house. Tonia had a gun. These were vicious criminal types, without compassion or conscience. She couldn't have fought against an armed woman. She couldn't have stood up to her and challenged her. Every time she said anything, it seemed, she had only made things worse.

That pig, Cal, had done this to her. He'd sent her into that house of horrors for whatever miserable criminal purposes he had. He had used her and endangered her, and she hoped he burned in Hell for it. Whatever she had walked into back there, was some criminal conspiracy that had gone horribly wrong. They were killing each other and hiding from each other and it served them all right. She just wished now that she hadn't given that woman her real name and address. But she had been so scared and flustered, she didn't even think of making up something false.

The crying slowly stopped and the shaking gradually died down, so she got back on the bike and rode it home. She saw a builder, working with a flock of robots, fixing up a derelict house on a scruffy lot. He pushed back his hat and stared at her in astonishment as she wobbled past him.

Chapter 4

She tried to immerse herself in her work. She climbed into her tank and went straight to her studio. She loved her office and could always lose herself in there. It was set in a clearing in a forest on the slope of a high mountain. Displays and musical instruments dotted the clearing. The sky was always blue and, where the slope fell steeply away, there was a view across broad valleys and low hills to distant snow-capped mountains. Steps carved into the mountainside led down to a little auditorium on a rocky promontory far below. There people could visit and listen to performances of her work but they could not climb up to the studio where she enjoyed silence and serenity and total privacy. There was no-one in the auditorium that day. Ginny was not a popular composer. Soundscapes were considered the muzak of their day and she was lucky if two or three people a week stopped by to listen to her pieces. But the worldlet of her office came with the auditorium as part of the package and she was always pleased if anyone at all came by to listen.

It was a free worldlet tailored for musical applications and came with the studio, the auditorium, a meeting room for receiving clients, and a little rest room – little more than a comfy chair on a ledge of rock with a small table and a coffee machine. She sometimes considered paying for a custom office. When she made it big and had lots of spare credit maybe. Until then this one suited her just fine.

She made for the studio and pulled up the files for the Old Vienna project. The minute she heard the rattle of carriages and the distant strain of classical strings a wave of utter boredom washed through her. It was almost a physical revulsion. She just couldn't face it. Not today. Maybe not ever.

She went through to her rest-room and poured a coffee, falling into her chair and staring at the perfect sky.

A pair of eagles were hunting over the valley, spiralling up on the thermals and gliding above the hills. It was the same pair of eagles that often appeared just there. The trouble with free worldlets was that they didn't come with a huge repertoire of behaviours programmed in. She had often stared at these two birds, thinking they looked like kites with invisible strings, imagining a little girl down in the valley, running and squealing, tugging the lines to make the birds swoop and soar. Today she felt that she was the kite, only her string was broken. She was being blown about on powerful winds, not gliding gracefully across the sky but tumbling along, out of control and in danger of crashing.

She was tired. Bone weary. Not least from having walked and cycled so much, taking more physical exercise in one day than she had in the previous month. What she really needed to do was sleep, but she was so exhausted she couldn't face the effort of climbing out of the tank and staggering the two paces to her bed. In the end, she forced herself, the prospect of sleeping in the tank again being worse than that of dragging her weary body into bed.

—oOo—

She woke in the middle of the night, groggy and confused, and called for lights. For a second she wondered if the woman with the gun, her cycling along city roads, dodging the robot vans, her hair blowing in the wind, had been a dream. Then she felt the ache in her thighs and knew it had really happened.

She popped up a clock and groaned. Three AM. For a while she lay with her eyes closed and tried to fall back into sleep, but she needed a pee and she was starving. What was worse, the mere recollection of her adventures set her heart racing again and made sleep impossible. It wasn't until she got up that she realised she had slept in her clothes on top of the bed. *This is why you don't have a husband*, she told herself in a parody of her mother's voice. *You live like a hippy. You should get a real job with regular hours.* Instead of amusing herself, the recitation depressed her. She probably would need to get a real job soon, either that or starve.

She grabbed a packet of something from the freezer and put it into the microwave. The little cooker read the tag on the box and set about cooking the contents as instructed. Ginny stared through the window at the slowly rotating packet until the machine pinged and snapped her out of her mindless state. She pulled the box out and took off the packaging. Some kind of Tai soup in a plastic bowl steamed on the counter. With a shrug she grabbed a disposable spoon from the dispenser and sat down to eat.

The entertainment feed was playing some middle-of-the-night political analysis show. The kind that no-one would watch during the day. There was a bill that the pundits had been getting excited about for several weeks now. Something to do with new powers to fight terrorism. She had seen petitions against it in her messages and had deleted them along with all the other junk. A thin-faced woman was arguing that the bill was a terrible threat to civil liberties. A round-faced woman agreed, pointing out that similar bills had been defeated in every OECD country over the past decade or so and, if Australia passed this measure, the country would become little more than a totalitarian regime. A jowly old conservative man seemed to think that the menace of terrorism had to be fought no matter what the cost and, besides, the Government could be trusted not to abuse any new powers the bill would give them. That brought a guffaw from everyone else on the panel.

Ginny switched to another feed, then another, wanting to find something entertaining she could stare at and not think about while she ate her soup. The argument about the bill had disturbed her. Normally she was vaguely liberal in her political views. To be honest, she didn't pay much attention until it was time to vote and, even then, she usually voted Labor or Greens on the ground that they generally seemed more humane than the other lot. But what had happened yesterday made her wonder if people were quite as safe as they believed they were. Criminals with guns, people going untagged, people impersonating police officers, data cubes hidden in plain sight by AR systems that had been illegally tampered with. Maybe the Government did need more powers to monitor what people were doing. Maybe then they could catch some of these people.

People like Cal.

And that was the most disturbing thing of all. She thought

she had been getting to know Cal. She thought she liked him. Yet there he was, mixed up with vicious, clandestine murderers.

She thought again about going to the police but dismissed the idea. She had taken Cal's package and handed it over to that Tonia woman. How did she explain that to the police? Or to a court, if it came to that? She could hardly explain it to herself. *Well, it's like this, Your Honour, I sort of fancied the bloke and he asked me nicely. Can I plead naïve stupidity?*

She watched an African cartoon feed as the soup gradually revived her body and spirit, then she showered and watched a Brazilian soap until the sun came up and she judged it wasn't too rude to call on her friend. Della took the call, scowling and grumbling, but agreed to meet her for breakfast at Cassini's.

"I've only got half an hour," Della said as Ginny entered the restaurant. "I need to be in early this morning. We're doing a big sales presentation. You couldn't have picked a worse morning really."

Ginny grimaced. "Sorry. It's just that I had a very peculiar day yesterday and I'm all on edge about it."

She glanced at the menu and tapped it to order a coffee.

"You're not eating?" Della said. "You dragged me out for breakfast and you're not even eating?"

"Yeah. Sorry. Already eaten."

The restaurant was enormous and full. And it wasn't just simulated ambience. Cassini's was a popular spot. A space station orbiting just above the rings of Saturn guaranteed spectacular views. Today, the moon Enceladus was hanging in the sky so close that Ginny could see the fissures on its frozen surface.

"Who's the presentation to?" she asked, finding herself

56

reluctant to talk about her day, despite having thought of nothing else but getting it off her chest for the past few hours.

"Wouldn't you rather tell me whatever it is you dragged me out here for? I assume you went to give the package to this Gavin bloke. What was the master criminal like then?"

Ginny's reluctance was developing into full-blown paranoia. She really shouldn't say anything else. Della knew too much already thanks to her blurting it all out the night before last. Now Ginny knew about a dead man – one she had not reported to the police – and she had been threatened by an armed woman, and handed over the package to her, with its stolen data or whatever it was. Ginny was up to her neck in something truly awful and the very idea of telling anyone about it – even Della – filled her with horror. In fact, it made the whole thing seem even worse and more dangerous than it had seemed at the time. Even if Dover Richards wasn't a policeman, it wouldn't be long before the real police were involved and then Ginny might wish she hadn't been blabbing to Della about it all.

"Well?" Della asked, giving Ginny a start.

She tried to act nonchalant. "Well nothing really. It was all a big anticlimax. I went round to the address and nobody was there. I just left the package and went home."

"You just left it? A box full of heroin or whatever? Where did you leave it?"

Ginny hadn't expected to be grilled on the subject. "I don't know. On the doorstep. I'm sure he'll find it."

"The doorstep? When was the last time you saw your own doorstep? Well, yesterday, obviously, but normal people aren't always popping out to meet crime bosses. I don't think I've seen my doorstep for days, not since the weekly shopping was delivered. That package is probably still sitting out there. Anybody could find it. Some kids could pick it up and kill themselves. Ginny, what were you thinking of?"

"It'll be all right, really. I'm sure he's got it." *Oh for God's sake.*

"How can you be sure? That stuff might be dangerous, really dangerous. What if it's explosives or something? Or a biological weapon? What if Gavin's a terrorist?" Della put her hand to her mouth. "I hadn't thought of that. What if he is, Ginny? What if there's something really horrible in that package? We should probably go to the police. There might be some kid running around right now with a bioweapon in his pocket. We have to–"

"It was only data cubes." Ginny didn't know what else to do except tell the truth to shut Della up. Her friend stopped with her mouth open and stared, waiting for more. "I took a peek before I left it. I just wanted to be sure it was OK."

"Data cubes?"

"Data cubes."

"Did you look at what was on them?"

"No." She raised a hand to stop Della going off again. "And I don't care what's on them. In fact, I don't want to know. It could be stolen commercial secrets, or even military secrets for all I care. I'm just glad to be rid of it."

Della regarded her with her head cocked. "This isn't like you, Ginny. Don't you worry about what's going on? Don't you care who might get hurt? What if it's kiddie porn and the police could have used those cubes to crack an international paedophile ring or something?"

Ginny pushed back her hair with an exhausted sigh. "I thought I'd just get it off my chest that the package was gone and this whole stupid affair is over and finished. Can you just leave it alone, now? I'm sick to death of it. I haven't done a stroke of work for the past two days and my legs ache from all that cycling, and I'd just like to put it all behind me and get on with my life. So, can we please drop it now?"

"Cycling?"

"It's a long story."

Della looked unhappy. "What are you not telling me, Ginny?"

"Nothing. Can we change the subject now?"

"I still don't like–"

Ginny raised her voice. "I'll go back there and make sure he got the package, OK? I'll go back and face this dangerous criminal and ask him if he got the package. Just so that you don't have to worry, all right? Will that satisfy you?"

Della drew back, looking hurt. "You don't have to be like that. It's your mess. I was just trying to help. Leave your kiddie porn out in the open for anybody to find, or let your dangerous criminal friends sell it. It's all the same to me. I can see you're completely on top of the situation and you don't need my advice." She got up and tossed some notes on the table – metaphorically paying for the coffee. "I've got to be going. Big presentation. Catch you later."

Ginny watched her leave, wanting to call her back and apologise, but wanting her to be gone, too, so that she wouldn't have to go on lying and being evasive.

—oOo—

She climbed out of the tank and kicked it, stomping into the kitchenette to scowl at the inside of her fridge. Nothing there improved her mood, so she flopped onto the sofa and scowled at the wall. She should be working. She *really* should be working. But now Della had filled her head with images of kids blowing their hands off, or dying of heroin overdoses. Ginny had not even considered such gruesome possibilities. Now she couldn't help thinking of what she might have done. She had not wanted to know what was in the package. It was almost certainly something bad, even if it was just data. Half the world was 'just data' these days. Probably much more than half. The thought of what might be on those data cubes, and what Tonia and her cronies might do with it, was one she had been avoiding. And she'd been avoiding it successfully until she'd let Della get under her skin about it.

There were several messages on her queue. One was from the development manager at WorldEnough, a company she had worked for in the past and who were considering a proposal of hers at the moment. She didn't feel like dealing with that right now. If she hadn't won the work, she'd feel even more desperate than before. If she had won it, she'd have another project to feel guilty about not working on. On the other hand, there were only two other messages that were not junk. One from her father and one from Dover Richards.

She knew what her father wanted. Her mother had nagged him into calling her to do something she didn't want to do – apologise, or visit, or whatever. As for Dover Richards, she had it on Tonia's authority that the smarmy creep wasn't a real policeman and was probably the man who murdered Gavin. She definitely wasn't going to take that call.

She got up and paced across the room. What if he came round to see her again? What if he was out in the hallway, right now, waiting for her? He thought she had information about Cal, or the package maybe. What if he decided to stop playing at being a policeman and question her more directly? She stopped pacing and looked at the door. What if he decided she didn't know anything and that he ought to kill her, just so there'd be no loose ends? She kept staring at the door, thinking about him out there, just a few metres away. It struck her just how flimsy a barrier a door was. She always thought of doors as substantial things. They shut out the world. They created a space of safety and privacy inside, an inviolable space, a secure space. But that wasn't true, she realised. A man like Richards probably didn't see doors that way at all. They could be kicked in, the locks shot away, the hinges smashed. Gavin had died after a door he might have once trusted became, not a protective barrier, but a convenient means of entry for his killer.

The urge to take a look outside grew almost irresistible. Yet, even if she had wanted to, she hadn't the courage to open that door, not while a killer might be lurking out there.

The knock came like three rapid gunshots and Ginny cried out in shock and fear, every muscle tensing as if she'd been electrocuted. She stumbled away from the door, wide-eyed with terror. A man's voice shouted something but she couldn't make it out. She looked around. She had to get out. Run. There was a window behind her. She looked at it and outside she saw sunlight filtering through the canopy of a beautiful rain forest clearing. She blinked, momentarily confused. Then she pushed her augmentation down and down until she could see the real street with its scruffy nature strip and the shabby buildings opposite. She was on the first floor. She'd have to climb down somehow.

There was another knock, louder than the first and another shout. Ginny grabbed the window lock, her fingers clumsy and awkward. She couldn't get it open. She broke a nail, sobbing with frustration. *Damn it to Hell!* She had to get out. She'd have to smash the window. She looked about her for something to hit the glass with. There was a chair, over by the door. That would do. But she couldn't go near the door. Not with him outside.

The door burst open with a crash and a man stood there in the hallway, half-concealed behind the wall, holding a black, evil-looking gun, and pointing it straight at her. Her heart seemed to burst inside her chest. Blackness poured in from all sides and she felt herself floating away.

—oOo—

She woke up on her own sofa. The gunman leaned over her. She tried to scrabble back away from him but he grabbed her shoulders and held her down.

"It's all right," he said. "You're safe. I'm with the police. Everything's all right."

He looked so earnest. He seemed worried. He had nice eyes, but they were worried eyes. She tried to look past him, looking for Dover Richards.

"It's Virginia, isn't it?" the man with the worried eyes said. "Virginia Galton?"

She nodded, tight-lipped. Would he kill her now he'd confirmed her identity?

"I don't know who you were expecting, Virginia, but I promise you, I'm a policeman. My name is Mike. I'm sorry about the door but I heard you cry out and then…well, you were whimpering. I thought something was going on in here. I thought someone was hurting you. Look, I'm going to let you go now." He pulled his hands free of her shoulders and stepped back from her. "See? There's nothing to be afraid of."

Ginny looked again around the room. The door was

closed but the catch for the deadlock was hanging loose. There was nobody else with them. "Who are you?" she asked, struggling to sit up. He didn't try to stop her.

With patience, the stranger said again, "My name is Mike. Detective Constable Mike Chu. I'm with the Queensland Police Service. Can't you see my ID?"

Of course she could see it. She just didn't believe it.

"What are you doing here? Why did you break in like that?"

His worried eyes studied her face for a moment, a sure sign he was using minimal aug too. "Would you like me to call up a medic? You don't seem to be quite yourself."

Ginny didn't know what to do. The man seemed so genuine. She looked him over again. Tall, slender, with an Asian cast to his features, and cheekbones she would have died for. His skin was smooth and his eyes large and deep. A hint of a frown ruffled his otherwise flawless forehead. He looked intelligent and concerned.

"I'm fine," she said. "Did Dover Richards send you?"

His head turned slightly in query and for a second or two his eyes unfocused, no doubt as he checked the QNet, or pretended to.

"How do you know Dover Richards?" he asked.

Ginny cursed herself. If this man really was from the police, the last thing she should be doing is giving him the names of criminals and murderers that might connect her to Gavin's death.

"Look, I have no idea who you are or why you're here. You gave me the fright of my life just now and, if you really are a policeman, I have a good mind to call your superiors and lodge a complaint." She shut her mouth and looked away. Why was she behaving like such a complete arsehole?

She needed to get a grip on herself.

Chu looked more puzzled than ever. Then he nodded to himself. "OK. Why don't we just start all over again from the beginning? I seem to have caught you at a bad moment." Ginny didn't say anything, just watched him carefully as he began to act out the scene that might have been. "Ms Galton, I'm Detective Constable Mike Chu from the Missing Persons Division." He flashed up his full credentials. "I wonder if I might ask you a few questions about Mr. Cal Copplin? I believe he is a friend of yours."

Ginny decided to play dumb. "Detective Sergeant Dover Richards already came here and asked me about Cal. There isn't much I can add."

"There's that name again." He gestured towards a chair. "May I?" Ginny didn't want him to sit, or to stay, but she gave a quick nod and he sat down. "According to our records, Dover Richards is one of many aliases used by a person of great interest to us. It sounds like we should be adding 'impersonating a police officer' to the list of reasons we'd like to talk to him."

"You mean he's not a real policeman? He said he was looking into Cal's disappearance."

"And that's interesting too because the department was only notified this morning that Mr. Copplin had gone off the net." A thought seemed to occur to him. "Did you think it was Richards out in the hall just now? Is that why you were so scared?"

Damn the man. He was quick and sharp and her own thoughts were all over the place. It was not a fair contest. Everything she said seemed to make things worse. She realised she had started believing Chu was really a policeman after all. "No. You just caught me at a bad moment. I'm prone to panic attacks. I have been for years." Which was true – or it had been, once. It was five years since Ginny's last attack, but at least there would be medical records for Chu to check and confirm her story. "I've been under some pressure at work. I suppose I was just ready to snap when I heard you outside."

Again, she had the impression he was checking everything she said, even as she said it. And he did look contrite when he said, "I'm very sorry. Is there something I can get you? Some kind of medication? Or should I call someone?"

"No, I'm fine. It goes as quickly as it comes."

He stood up. "You really don't look very well. I should go and come back another time."

She shook her head, feeling guilty that her lie had evoked such concern. "That's all right. Please, sit down. I'll make us a cup of coffee and you can ask me your questions." And, of course, while there was a real policeman in her unit, she would be safe from Dover Richards. "How do you like it?"

She fussed over the coffee and added some biscuits, bringing a tray over from the kitchenette and placing it on the coffee table between them.

"You live here alone?" Chu asked.

"No-one's alone any more," she said, quoting an ad for a popular brand of tank. He smiled and she added, "Never met the right guy. I get wrapped up in my work. I can be pretty antisocial I suppose. Yourself?" Now why did she ask that? What did she care about Chu's private life?

"I have that same problem. Workaholic. What can I say? I love my job."

"You love tracking down missing persons?"

"You'd be surprised where a misper can lead you. I never know what each new day will bring."

"Like finding a crazy woman screaming and – What did you say? Whimpering? – when you knock on her door?"

He smiled. "That kind of thing, yes." Perhaps the turn of conversation had reminded him how curious he was because he said, "Do you mind if I ask those questions now?"

Ginny took a breath and said, "OK."

He went through the same questions the fake cop had asked, only this time round there was less smarm and less creepiness. He said the same things about how Cal had gone offline and that it was not so uncommon.

"Richards said it might mean Cal is dead," Ginny said.

"Sadly, it's the main reason people become untagged. When a person dies, their tag keeps responding but the ambient systems flag the person as immobile after a couple of days. You know, because they're not moving. Eventually, someone goes to check on them to see if they're OK."

"Not you though." It would be inconceivable that Detective Chu could love a job that involved going out to find dead people all the time.

"No, there are medical teams that do that. I get involved when the tag stops responding. That can mean the person's dead too – if the cause of death was a massive trauma to the head – but it can also mean they've managed to untag themselves, or they've gone outside the coverage of QNet."

Ginny blinked in surprise. "Outside of QNet?"

"Australia's a big country. There's an area totalling half the size of Europe that is not fully covered. Plenty of legitimate reasons for going out there. It's the ones who go out without a license that I take an interest in."

"Do you think Cal might have gone out into the bush somewhere?"

"Right now, I have no idea at all. However, if someone

like Dover Richards is looking for him, it might be a smart move."

The questioning moved on to Richards. What had he asked her? What else had he said? Did she have a way of contacting him? Eventually, Chu returned to Cal once more.

"My records show that Mr. Copplin is a freelance IT specialist. Did he ever talk about his work?"

"No. He said it was boring."

"He's a Brit by birth, been in Australia for ten years, took citizenship nine years ago. Did he ever talk about what he did in the UK, or why he came here?"

Ginny cast her mind back, remembering moments, walks, parties. All she had were fragments. They had talked for hours but all she remembered were scenes and feelings, hardly any actual words. "He said something funny about that once. He said – something like – 'Australia is the last free country on Earth.' I thought he was just being romantic, about the outback and all that, the way people are, you know?"

"And he never talked about his work before coming here?"

Ginny shook her head. "I probably didn't even ask him. Why is that important?"

Chu shrugged. "Who knows what's important at this stage?"

But Ginny thought there more to it than he was saying. "So what did he do before he came here?"

"I don't know. That part of his file is missing."

As soon as Chu left, Ginny called the police and asked to speak to someone in Missing Persons. She told them she had had a visit from Mike Chu and could they confirm that he was a real policeman. They were happy to oblige, although the sergeant she spoke to was clearly curious about why she thought he might not be. As soon as she hung up, she realised it didn't prove anything except that there really was a Detective Constable Chu in the Queensland police.

Chapter 5

Ginny had lunch and considered her situation while the TV droned on about the new cyberterrorism bill. It seemed the government was organising a plebiscite on the matter, which was unusual, she couldn't remember ever voting in one before, but it still didn't inspire her to look into the issues and formulate her position on the matter. Anything that gave the police more powers to track down criminals of any sort seemed like a good idea to her at that moment.

With the arrival of Detective Constable Chu, the probability that she would end up in jail for letting herself get mixed up in Cal's affairs, began to loom in her thoughts. She had agreed to visit Chu later to sign her statement – not all of which was true. The fact that Chu confirmed that Dover Richards was a known criminal and Ginny was effectively protecting him by not mentioning Gavin's murder or his sister's suspicions, made her some kind of accomplice. The phrase 'accessory after the fact' came to her.

She switched the TV to a Chinese soap feed and turned off the sound. Beautiful men and women came together in various combinations and locations. Every conversation had an exaggerated emotional temperature, as if everyone in that world lived in a state of unnatural joy or misery, rage or despondency. *Like being a teenager forever,* she thought.

Irritated at herself for staring stupidly at the display when she should be doing things to sort her life out, she picked up the message from the development manager at WorldEnough and set up a call.

Derek Naumann answered, he looked cheerful and fresh, as if he'd been having a good day. "Ginny, thanks for calling back. Do you think you could pop into the office for a meeting?"

"No worries. When would suit you?"

"What are you doing right now?"

That caught her off-guard. She didn't want to go anywhere or meet anyone. But she gave herself a mental kick up the backside and smiled. "Now would be fine. I'll be there in a couple of minutes."

She didn't want to get back in the tank. The thought of being in there if Dover Richards came round scared her witless. She needed to be free to run. No, she'd just lie on the bed – perfectly safe for a short spell in VR – and set up an alarm to pull her out if anyone came to the door. Working through the unit's systems to warn her of anyone standing within a metre or two of her door turned out to be more complicated than it should be and she turned up at WorldEnough's main reception ten minutes late.

"Please go through. Mr Naumann is expecting you," the virtual receptionist said, indicating a door off the lobby. Ginny stepped through it, straight into Naumann's office.

She entered in a flurry of apologies which Naumann flicked aside with easy grace. "My fault for springing it on you," he said. "Take a seat."

Ginny looked around. Once upon a time, offices had been drab little boxes. If you were lucky, your drab little box had a view of something other than the office block next door. Those days were gone. Derek Naumann's office was a huge and ornate salon that might have been modelled on one from the Palace of Versailles at the height of the Bourbon dynasty. Gilded Rococo furniture of the most delicate and elaborate designs drifted in oceans of blue carpet that lapped at wide parquet shores. At least, she guessed, the brochures might say something like that. WorldEnough built virtual worldlets and every office there was an advertisement for the company's products. Ginny sat in one of the white-and-gold chairs and smiled at Naumann, waving a hand at the décor. "This is new."

"Hideous, isn't it?" he said with a grimace. "I keep asking them for something a little less *outré*, but they insist I keep it until the new product line launches. Can I get you a coffee or something?"

No thanks. I need to get back to my unit in case I'm being murdered in my sleep. "I'm fine, thank you. How's business?"

Naumann gave an elaborate shrug and rolled his eyes. In a tone of mock gravity, he said, "Profits are slipping. The shareholders are not receiving the value we promised them. Something must be done."

Ginny had heard this refrain before. What she couldn't see yet was why Naumann had called her in to tell her there was no more work when she didn't even have a contract with them at the moment.

"The powers that be are looking to me to pull their collective butts out of the fire, as usual. They need products that will shake the marketplace, worldlets that will inspire our customers and invigorate their businesses. In short, a miracle is needed."

"I'm not sure…"

"You're not sure if I'm man enough for the task before me?"

Ginny laughed. She'd forgotten how much fun Derek could be. Nevertheless, she wished he would get to the point.

"Ginny, darling, you and I have worked together before. Many times. Let me tell you right now that it was never my idea to stop using you for our soundscapes. The world is run by accountants. Always has been. Cheaper solutions were sought and found."

Cheaper? thought Ginny. If she charged any less, she would be paying them to let her work. Perhaps the thought showed in her expression.

"Oh, I know what you're thinking, and I agree. You get what you pay for. And, trust me," he waved a hand at the room, "there's a good reason why the sound for this little extravaganza is always switched off."

That was another good thing about Derek, he wasn't tone deaf like most people she worked for. "So…you want me to spice up the soundscape for…" She looked around. "…this?"

"Good heavens, no. This is beyond redemption." He winked. "But don't tell the GM I said so. She thinks it's *le dernier cri*. No, this is why I called you in." He moved his hands, working an interface she couldn't see, and pulled a 3D model out of the air onto his desk. "Just artist's sketches so far, as you can see, but it's going to be a whole new line. *Chic*, modern, tasteful and very upmarket."

Ginny peered into the little model, trying to make out the details.

"Why don't you go in and have a look around?" Naumann said.

She could see from his air of anticipation that she was expected to approve. So she got out of her chair and stepped up to the model. There was a door set in one wall that bore the usual entry icon. She touched it and found herself inside a suite of offices. The design seemed to be all space and semi-transparent walls, with small organic touches – a pile of stones here, a vine there. It was a style she had noticed lately in the design feeds she read. The walls reacted subtly as she approached them, changing hue, sometimes giving a fleeting glimpse of ocean and birds. The furniture was minimal, simple chairs, no desks, but when she sat surfaces rose from the floor and drifted down from the ceiling to float around her. They were all mock-ups but one carried a mug of coffee, and others were alive with information displays. When she rose, they slid smoothly out of her way and merged into the room. She walked around a little and admired the other rooms, all variations on the theme, then made her way back to the door and stepped through into Naumann's Louis XV museum. By contrast it seemed cluttered and excessively elaborate.

"Well?" Derek asked. "Isn't it just wonderful?"

She smiled at his enthusiasm for what, to her, seemed like just another fancy office. "It certainly makes the old product range look a little…conservative."

"So tactful, darling." He looked pleased to have his current office insulted.

"Bit of a departure for WorldEnough, isn't it? You'll be head-to-head with the top-end office suppliers."

"I know, delicious, isn't it. We'll be coming in at about half their wholesale cost. We shall mop the floor with them. This is just a taster, we have a whole range planned, with luxury features at the pricey end and a cut-down budget version for the plebs. You should meet the designer. Young Korean bloke, barely out of nappies. What about the soundscape?"

Ginny had been dreading the question but tried not to let it show. She hated this part. They always expected her to be instantly inspired, to have brilliant ideas, and then pitch them in thirty seconds. Fortunately, Derek's enthusiasm wouldn't let him keep quiet, giving her a few more precious seconds to think.

"We've been thinking Japanese. What's that theatre they have? Kuboki? Something like that. With maybe tinkling water, breezes rattling paper partitions. You know the kind of thing. And hard-surface reflections for internal sounds like footsteps and putting objects down. What do you think? Is that the way we should go?"

"It's…not bad," she said. What she meant was, *It's a terrible cliché and anyone with any sense would hate it on principle.* "But maybe we can come up with something a bit more exciting. Something as modern as the design itself." There was something about the organic touches and the sudden swirls of life from the wall images that teased her with the possibility of auditory analogues. A rising excitement seemed to lift her. This could actually be an interesting project. She could see herself really enjoying it.

"Derek?" She looked away from the model into Naumann's eyes. "Are you really giving this one to me?"

He tilted his head in reproach. "I wish I could, Ginny, but then I'd have the auditors all over me. Processes must be followed. I'm asking three companies to come up with ideas and quotes. You're one of them and I expect yours to be the most interesting submission by far. Please say you'll put in a bid."

She forced a smile. It would mean lots of work, all unpaid, and she still had the Old Vienna project to finish. But what an opportunity.

"You know I'm a one-man-band, don't you?" she said. "I fit my marketing efforts in between earning my living. When do you need this by? My life's kinda complicated just now."

"When can you do it?"

"Give me a month."

"Two weeks it is, then. Here…" He used his invisible interface again. "I've just sent you the request for proposals. The model's in there."

She looked wistfully at the bright little rooms on Naumann's desk. It was exactly the kind of work she wanted, big, interesting, with plenty of scope to be creative and have fun. A few days ago, she'd have been over the Moon to get this opportunity. Now all she could think of was how impossible it would be to do a good proposal while dodging murderers, and the police, and trying to finish a completely soul-sucking project for the guys at UnReality. Yet she had to try. *Murderers come and go*, she told herself, *but the fridge is always there, demanding to be restocked.*

"Thanks for this Derek. I will do my best," she said. They shook hands and she left with a slowly knotting stomach.

—oOo—

A restless, fretful night left Ginny in no doubt that she couldn't stay in her unit a minute longer. Dover Richards could find her there. If he wanted to kill her, she was a sitting duck. It didn't help her peace of mind that the lock on the front door was smashed. She'd called the landlord's agent but they had been evasive about when they could send someone round to fix it.

She considered calling Della to see if she could sleep on her couch, but Della was another person she didn't want to see at the moment. Even if she didn't bend Ginny's ear about confessing to the police, she would ask endless questions to which Ginny might have to spin endless lies. No, she had only two choices, check into a hotel, or go to Sydney to stay with her parents. A hotel would be expensive – too expensive if she stayed there more than a couple of weeks – but at least it would probably have a tank in the room and she could get on with her work. Staying with her parents would be the usual torment, but it would only cost here the airfare – whatever that might be – and she could stay away as long as she needed to. She checked her bank balance and decided it had to be her parents.

The plane banked as it climbed, pushing through the rain, leaving Brisbane Airport to be swallowed by the suddenly wet Spring weather. The plane was a small, unmarked, windowless tube, painted a dull grey. Inside, its fifteen passengers filled fewer than half the available seats. The steward, Andy, who occasionally patrolled the aisle, cast his eyes over Ginny's fellow passengers. To Ginny, most of them appeared to be in drugged sleep. Their heads lolled and their mouths hung open, their bodies slumped in their seats. She had never seen so many people unlatched at the same time, lost in virtual worlds, working or playing, oblivious to their environment. One woman had told Ginny she intended to stay that way until they reached Sydney. The steward regarded those ones with a happy smile. They would be no trouble at all, Ginny supposed.

A handful of passengers were latched, though, staring about them with expressions of wonder or interest, as they took in the "view" or the in-flight entertainment, smiling at Andy as he went by. The young man smiled back, offered them drinks, meals, keeping them comfortable. That was his job: helping them through the ordeal.

Ginny had often wondered why people flew at all. Why, in this day and age, would anyone need to, let alone want to? Even unlatched, it was a gruelling experience with no proper bed or tank to lie in. And if you went augmented or native, it was hell. Yet, every week, she now knew, another couple of dozen would make the trip. She had not been able to imagine what on Earth would make it necessary to move your body so far. Well, now she knew. Although it seemed unlikely the others were all hiding from murderers.

Ginny watched the steward as he happily patrolled the uncarpeted aisle of the windowless plane, checking that no one had slid out of their seat and that all the latched ones were fed and watered.

"Hi there," Ginny said as he went past. "Do you think I could get some water?"

"Of course, Ms Galton," he said. No doubt her name, seat, flight details, were all there. Including her network status, it seemed. "If you'd like to latch to the plane you'll have a much better flight," he said. "And if you want to unlatch, we have full QNet connectivity throughout the journey. No need to suffer the grim reality."

Ginny smiled at the disconcerted steward. People told her she had a good smile, big and generous. It seemed to put the young man more at ease. "It's all right. I like to give it a break now and then. If you'd just bring me that water."

The truth was that Ginny had been running on minimal aug ever since she met Naumann yesterday. She daren't latch to anything in case a pot plant or a post box turned out to be an untagged assassin. It sounded like crazy paranoia just to think it but Ginny was taking no chances.

She waited until Andy was gone, then re-opened the virtual folder on her lap. She flicked through the pages of the research she was doing. Her recent brush with Brisbane's underworld had left her feeling stupid and ignorant – not to mention vulnerable. There was clearly a whole world out there she didn't know or understand and this endless trip was her chance to fill in a few gaps in her education.

And she was learning some very surprising things.

Like that being untagged was neither as impossible nor as uncommon as everyone seemed to believe. The authorities even had a name for it, "turning ghost". Maybe her friend Cal was dead or maybe he'd turned ghost. Dead didn't matter to the police. Turning ghost would normally be no big deal either. Thousands turned ghost for one reason or another each year, it seemed. Whether it was deliberate or just an accident, the tag teams tracked most of them down in the end and brought them back online. "Tag teams" or just "taggers" was what criminal types called the police missing persons officers. The division the nice Detective Chu worked for. She heard Tonia's voice saying, *You're some fucking tagger's bitch.* The hatred in her tone still made Ginny shiver.

When she chased down the term "lotos eaters" – obviously a term of contempt on Tonia's lips – she found it came from Homer's *Odyssey* – one of those books Ginny had always meant to get around to reading one day. According to what she found, a bunch of guys landed on a North African island and started eating drugged lotus fruits. Which made them stop caring about their quest to get home and just want to hang about getting stoned. Not very helpful, Ginny thought, until she found a footnote that mentioned that "in popular culture the term is used by members of the infamous September 10 terrorist group to refer to anyone who uses AR or VR technologies."

So she chased down that reference and found September 10 was bunch of nutjobs who spent their free time sabotaging communication lines. September 10 was growing in stature as a terrorist movement after some audacious and effective attacks. It was named after the day in 2049 when the US government made electronic tagging compulsory for every man, woman, child and domestic animal in the country.

Naturally, by 2049, most people in the States were tagged anyway. If you weren't tagged, how would the stores know when you came in to be served? How would your message services know where to find you? How would people who were latched know not to walk into you or drive right over you? If your tag didn't keep the network informed about where you were and what you were doing, you might as well not exist.

And that, of course, was the reason for the law. It could be very useful for certain people not to exist. People who didn't want to be found or people who were doing things they shouldn't be doing. Such people became known as ghosts – and governments, Ginny discovered, are scared of ghosts. In the twenty years since the US passed its law, similar laws had been passed in the European Union and then in most other states around the world.

But it wasn't just criminals and misfits who dodged the taggers. There were also many people who objected to tagging as a matter of principle or of religious conviction. Some of these people organised themselves into terrorist groups and some of these groups formed uneasy but horribly effective alliances to disrupt and destroy the societies they hated so much.

So there were tag teams to track down the untagged and it was a serious and deadly business. The amazing thing to Ginny was that it was all so low-key. She had never seen anything about taggers on the news, and she'd certainly never heard of the September 10 terrorist group. It made her nervous to think of all this going on below her radar. Maybe she should pay more attention, scan a wider set of feeds.

She closed her displays and stretched her legs, wondering how much faith she could put in all those conspiracy theory feeds she'd been dipping into. Looking around she found the sight of her lolling, staring fellow passengers disturbed her. It was creepy, she realised, seeing it all in a way she never had done before. The unlatched were deep in full immersion virtual reality, free of the constraints of the real world, their sagging bodies kept artificially relaxed so that they didn't hurt themselves as their minds roved through simulated worlds. In unlatched VR they could be where they chose to be, their bodies altered by up to twenty per cent from their natural form. And that could make a lot of difference if done well. Latched or unlatched, when you moved out of minimal augmented reality and let the machines take over your sensorium, you gave up all hope of ever seeing anyone as they really were. The vast majority of people thought this was a good thing – a damned good thing. The next best thing, in fact, to Heaven itself.

The world had been waiting for this since the first thought flickered across the first brain. Now they embraced it in their billions. Inevitably, a lot of people grasped too tightly and wouldn't let go, even if it killed them. Artificial realities were not Heaven but they could easily become the road to Hell.

Was that what had made Cal kill his tag? Had he suddenly

decided to become a conscientious objector, to ghost out for the sake of his sanity? Or did he want to save the world? Maybe September 10 had got to him, convinced him, blackmailed him, seduced him. She shook her head, unable to accept that Cal – who had seemed so level-headed and nice – could have been recruited by terrorists. Killed by them, maybe. She wouldn't put that past the unstable Tonia or the slimy Dover Richards.

—oOo—

Sydney was a quiet place, empty and decaying like most cities. *Haunted by ghosts,* Ginny thought. *Of every kind.* She picked up a cab at the little airport. The huge old roads were empty, unlit. No one used them except the robot freighters endlessly moving food and manufactured goods out of the robot farms and factories to the robot warehouses and then to the houses.

The cab was small and plain. The giants of the past – Ford, Honda, General Motors – had long since sold up and gone into the telecoms business. Now cars were made by tiny specialist manufacturers and maybe they'd be out of business too in a few years time. Global warming, pollution, the Oil Wars were all just fading nightmares. They'd been overtaken by events.

Ginny travelled augmented, feeling safer with a thousand kilometres between herself and Brisbane. She watched maps unfold across the unlit freeway, watched ads pop up around her as passing systems sensed her tag. She had decided to surprise her parents – mostly to avoid them saying no. But the only flight had been late in the evening and she thought it would be better to turn up on their doorstep in the morning than in the night. So she had booked a hotel. On top of the staggering cost of the flight, the room had seemed relatively cheap.

When she was close to the hotel, she latched into its augmented reality. The road ahead lit up. Welcome signs appeared. All the wrong turnings turned dim and the right way was a bright and spangled one. The effects were cheap and tacky, but that was to be expected, the hotel business was in terminal decline too. People did their business unlatched these days, meeting in common virtual realities. Whole worlds of artificial business venues existed. Who would travel hours to meet in some dump of a conference centre, when they could hold their meeting in Ancient Greece or a crater on Mars? Who would commute to a downtown highrise when they could stay put and work on the Mont Blanc glaciers or the Oslo Fjord?

It was the same story for holidays. The hotel was a dying concept. For the few people who still travelled, you took whatever you could get.

Ginny, still latched, left the cab and walked into the hotel lobby. She looked around at the deep plush carpets and the Italian marble pillars and her nerve broke. She went native and found herself in the dimly lit and run down reality she had expected. Where the smiling receptionist had stood behind an impressive marble desk, a roboteller was bolted to a beat up wooden counter. Ginny checked around her. She was alone.

"Good evening, Ms Galton," the teller said. "We're so glad to see you here at the Sydney Hilton."

"Just tell me what room I'm in."

The machine told her and she went straight there. She locked the door then wedged it shut with a chair. She checked the window. Good. There was no balcony and the walls were sheer and would be hard to climb.

Look at me, she thought. *Acting like a spy on a mission. Maybe I should sweep the room for bugs and hide my documents in the lavatory cistern.* But it wasn't really amusing at all. Being anxious all the time was no fun and she looked back wistfully to the time when all she had to worry about was money.

That had been just two days ago.

She lay on the bed and dealt with the day's messages. Della had sent a sweet apology for being in such a huff that morning and Ginny replied saying it was all her fault, really. She didn't mention she had left town and was lying low, beginning to understand that what she was going through was not the kind of thing to burden your friends with. The urge to talk to someone about it was strong, though, and she had recorded a long ramble about meeting Detective Chu and how he was a tagger and pretty cute with it, before deleted the whole thing and started again, avoiding anything to do with her troubles. She mentioned the job opportunity that Derek Naumann had sprung on her and used it to explain why she would be out of circulation for a couple of weeks at least.

You're disturbingly good at this lying business, she told herself after the message was sent. *Let's see if you can come up with something convincing for your mother tomorrow to explain your first physical visit in ten years.* She fell asleep, fully clothed, with a mash-up of the past two days churning through her mind, explaining to Chu why she had Gavin's body in her kitchen, Dover Richards politely sneering at her ideas for the WorldEnough project, Della and her mother nagging her to join the September 10 group because Tonia needed her bicycle. On and on, round and round, more bizarre all the time but also more stressful. She woke up at one point, undressed, and showered. It was three AM. She watched a Nigerian documentary about the space program which dissolved into further, tortured dreams. At six AM, she woke up exhausted and sat on the edge of her bed for half an hour, watching the sun rise over a mountain lake through the virtual window of her windowless hotel room.

Chapter 6

"Hi."

Her father stared at her as if she was an obscure optical illusion he was trying to fathom.

"Virginia?"

She waited for him to get over his surprise and step back out of the doorway so she could enter.

"You brought a bag," he said, eyeing the big canvas shopping bag that had her meagre wardrobe in it.

"You'd be surprised how hard it is to find anywhere that sells luggage in Brisbane. Is Mum about?"

"Here," he said, taking the bag off her and walking ahead down the short corridor. "Come on through." Raising his voice, he called, "Cheryl, it's Virginia come to see us." He stopped and turned to Ginny, then put his free arm round her in a hug. "Well this is a surprise. What on earth brought this on? She's not that bad, you know."

"I don't know what got into me, Dad. I rode a bike the other day and I remembered how you taught me all those years ago."

"A real bike? I didn't know they made them any more."

"Maybe they don't. I found this one in a—"

"Darling! You came!"

Cheryl Galton pushed her husband aside in her rush to throw her arms around Ginny. Not in the least offended, Ginny's father relinquished his hug and stood back, smiling on, as his wife enfolded their daughter.

"Oh darling, I spoke too soon. It was quite treatable. Nothing at all to worry about. And look at you, flying all that way to be with me. I feel so ashamed but I'm so glad you're here. The worry has been so awful. I try talking to Bob about it but–" The mention of her husband's name reminded her of his presence. "Bob, be a dear and put the kettle on, would you. Your poor daughter has just travelled all that way and you're just standing there looking useless."

With an "Oh, yes. Right," Bob set down the bag and wandered off to the kitchen.

Cheryl sighed and shook her head, letting Ginny see how patiently she put up with her father's stupidity. "Come and sit down, darling and I'll tell you all about what the doctors said."

And that's it, thought Ginny. *No explanation necessary.* She should have known her mother was so self-obsessed that everything was automatically about her. Anyone could have turned up at the doorstep and Cheryl Galton would immediately assume they were there because of her. No question that your only daughter might turn up after a ten year absence because she has problems of her own. No need to make enquiries as to her health or well-being, just sweep her up into the vortex that is Cheryl Galton and carry on as usual. It made Ginny's muscles tense, a visceral memory of the reasons she had fled to Brisbane all those years ago. And yet it was an easy and comfortable role to play, as a bit player in the great drama of her mother's life, a part she knew by heart and understood to the core. Later, Ginny knew, her part would change from heroine to villain as her mother began to feel the potential burden of coping with a house guest at such a time of trial and tribulation, but that too would be familiar and easy to deal with.

There was no guest room. Ginny would sleep on the sofa. Making the few domestic arrangements that were required to accommodate this unexpected visitor and fetching a doona and a couple of pillows stressed her mother so much she retired early, leaving Ginny to chat to her father over a cup of cocoa he made in her honour.

"I can't remember the last time I drank cocoa," she said, cradling the cup between her hands. "Not for real, anyway."

"How's the music business?" he asked.

"Humming along." It was an old joke between them. "It's been a bit of a struggle lately but something big might be on the cards. I need to do a proposal. I was hoping I'd get a bit of P and Q here to work on that."

Her father pulled a face. "Good luck with that. I think your mum will probably want to spend a bit of time with you." Code for, everybody under this roof is part of Cheryl's audience.

She smiled to let him know she understood the situation. "I'm looking forward to spending time with you," she said. "Both of you. I spend too much time in the tank anyway." He raised his eyebrows in agreement. It was what everybody said these days.

"You're free to borrow mine while you're here. I'm only working mornings now. It's just a temporary thing, they say, until the business picks up, but, you know…"

"Shit, Dad, Are you looking for another job?"

"Who'd have me at my age?"

He was right. In the post-boomer age, anyone over fifty was lucky to have a job at all and her father must be sixty by now. "Would you be all right, if…"

"Don't worry about us. We've got our superannuation. That'll see us through 'till we reach pension age. If worst comes to worst, I'll sell the Ferrari." She didn't even bother to look up whatever a Ferrari might be. He stood up, clearly uncomfortable talking about his troubles, and said goodnight. "You just hurry up and write that smash hit musical so we can all retire in luxury."

"Yeah, no worries. I'll start on that as soon as I've finished the score for the next Bollywood blockbuster."

She sat alone after he'd gone, feeling anxious and low. No wonder her mother was acting up. She'd find a million things to complain about, a million non-existent problems to whinge about, but she would never mention what was really worrying her. *At least*, Ginny told herself, *I'll be here to deflect some of it from Dad*. The prospect of which made her feel even worse. Still, she was here now and she'd have to tough it out, fret about her dad, put up with her mum, finish Old Vienna, and come up with a kick-ass proposal for WorldEnough.

Think of it as saving your worthless neck from the bad guys, she thought. But it wasn't much consolation. Hardly any at all, really.

Part 2

Chapter 7

"Can't it wait, Rafe? I'm up to my bloody eyeballs here."

Rafe Morgan had been christened Ralph Morgan, there having been a brief fad forty years ago to name babies after the megastar animated hero, Ralph (pronounced "Rafe") Williams. As soon as he could, he changed his name officially to Rafe, just so he could stop explaining how to pronounce it to everyone he met.

"I just need you to approve some expenses," Rafe said. "I'm planning a trip."

"You'll be lucky, mate. Why the hell did they have to have a plebiscite anyway? The polls have been showing the bill's a bloody shoo-in for weeks. The last one had it at eighty-two per cent approval. Eighty-two! Nothing's been that popular since they assassinated that televangelist guy back in sixty-five. What was his name now?"

Rafe let his editor rant for a while. Becky was a good editor and a good friend, but she did like to have her little rants.

"I reckon they just want a cast iron bloody mandate to give the voting public the shafting they right royally deserve. Since when do you ask me to approve expenses? It must be one helluva trip. If it's a sex scandal involving mining robots in the Kimberley, I'll sign, otherwise piss off."

"You have such refined taste. No wonder our readers love us. I need to go to Brisbane for a few days."

"What? Physically go? Like on a plane?"

"It's the only way my source will meet me."

"Can't your source come to Canberra? I need all hands on deck for this bloody anti-terrorism bill."

"You don't need me. I'll only write pieces about how the Cabinet is stuffed with right-wing fascists and that the bill is designed to crush all opposition and turn the Liberal Party into an Aussie Politburo."

"You'll write whatever well-balanced, carefully reasoned dingo's droppings I tell you to. What's the story?"

"In Brisbane? I don't want to say yet. It might all come to nothing. It's related to the bill and, given the kind of organisation my source claims to belong to, I'm pretty sure you don't want to know anyway."

Becky considered him in silence for a minute. Then she said, "You're sure you're OK, Rafe? You haven't been back long. Maybe you should, you know, ease back into it."

Rafe looked her in the eye and said, "Becky, I'm fine. What else can I do but work? And what other kind of work could I do but this?"

"I could put you back on the political desk – just until you get back in the swing of it."

He grimaced. "I don't think so. I'd go mad in a week." He tried another tack. If Becky didn't let him do this, he really did worry whether he could stand it. "Look, you know me. I'm only happy when I'm out there in the jungle with my elephant gun, tracking down the big stories. It's what I live for."

Again, he got the meaningful stare from Becky. Maybe this

time she saw the pleading underneath the bravado. "OK. It's approved. But keep in touch. And don't do anything too stupid. And remember we can't afford legal fees, so if you end up in deep shit, no-one's going to pull you out."

Rafe grinned and winked at her. "I'll see you in a few days."

He stepped through her office door into his own office. Becky favoured clutter, heaps of paper, and the clack of typewriters, as if she were running a newsroom in the 1950s instead of a modern socio-political newsfeed. Rafe's office was spacious and tidy, impersonal and silent. It was so bereft of any personal touch, he might have rented the space for the afternoon. He popped up a phone, made a couple of calls to finalise his arrangements, and left. This time the door took him back to his tiny studio apartment. The lid of the tank opened and he jumped out, grabbed the bag that was already packed and sitting by the bed, and set off for the airport.

—oOo—

Rafe enjoyed flying. He liked the cosy informality of the airports, with their low, scruffy buildings with the little electroprop aircraft rolling up to the terminus in the bright sun. He liked chatting to the other passengers as they hung about under the fans, sipping beers. People who travelled these days were always such an interesting bunch. Of course, the flight itself was about as dull as it could be, but, like everyone else, he either slept or unlatched and got some work done. He was always sorry when the captain ambled in off the tarmac and announced that the flight was ready. If he was lucky, there'd be a quick exchange of virtual cards with whoever he'd been talking to while everyone grabbed their bags and shuffled out to the waiting plane. And who knew where a new contact might lead?

Today was a good day. He met a guy from one of the big mining companies making his way up to inspect mines in the Bowen basin. The guy looked like a 1950s film star, square-jawed and broad shouldered. It struck Rafe how perfect the guy would look in Becky's office, perched on the edge of her desk, maybe, with a cigarette and an American accent.

It was always good to know people from the major industries. You never knew when you might need an insider's perspective, or an invitation to visit corporate HQ. Rafe collected such people like others collected old ebooks, or pre-3D movies. This guy was a bit too chatty and a bit too keen for company, so once Rafe had the man's card, he made sure he wasn't sitting with him for the whole flight. Which was just as well because Rafe slept most of the way, catching up on an endless chain of broken nights.

—oOo—

Brisbane was hot. Even in mid-Autumn, it was thirty degrees in the shade. Rafe sweated as he waited on the verandah of the little terminal building for the cab to arrive. He already missed the civilised coolness of Canberra. Whatever anyone might say about he nation's capital, you couldn't deny that it had seasons and its people knew how to cope with them. Up here, in the sultry, sub-tropical humidity, the dwindling population seemed to take a twisted pride in surviving whatever nature threw at them, as if having air conditioning was the mark of a weakling. It was no wonder people were migrating south in droves. These days you rarely needed to live close to your job, so why not live somewhere comfortable? People lived where they liked and let the robots cope with the long hot summers. Only machines and lizards moved in the northern interior these days and most of the towns up there had become ghost towns.

The cab – which, he thanked God, was air conditioned – took him, at the leisurely pace of all robotic vehicles, on a long, meandering tour through the Brisbane suburbs. It was a big, sprawling city and he'd had enough of it by the time he reached Portland Apartments, a three storey, nondescript block of units in dazzling white. He stood in the shade of the entrance porch avoiding the sun and looked around. He liked to get a bit of atmosphere when he interviewed people, some feel for where and how they lived, a few seconds of recorded visuals, a few comments to remind him. Today, he said, "Boring, stifling, anonymous suburb." Then he rang the bell.

A woman's voice said, "Come in. Up the stairs. Unit 6."

There was something hard about the voice. The door clicked open and Rafe felt his stomach knot. He hesitated, remembering. He had never hesitated before. The old Rafe would have pushed his way in and bounded up the stairs, keen to get on. But the old Rafe had been invulnerable, untouchable. The old Rafe had been a fool.

Steeling himself, he opened the door and stepped inside. The hallway looked harmless, clean and modern, with no deep shadows. He swallowed and walked to the stairs, grasping the metal handrail and pulling himself forward. He'd come a bloody long way for his nerve to fail him at the last minute, he thought, his feet mounting the steps as if they had no significance. If he just kept going, putting one foot in front of the other, he'd get through it and out of there. And, if he did, the next one would be easier. If he didn't, if he scurried back to Canberra now, he might as well climb into his tank and stay there forever.

The first floor corridor was much like the one below. He took a breath and walked slowly along it until he stood facing a plain brown door with a brass number "6" screwed onto it. He waited for his heart to slow down. *It's just an interview,* he told himself. *Just someone with information they want to get off their chest. You go in, you make small talk, you ask your questions, you leave. You've done it a thousand times before.* So why did it feel like the first time? Why did it feel like putting his head in a lion's mouth?

Of course, he knew exactly why.

The door flew open and a woman stood there, scowling at him. He stepped back in alarm, almost ran.

"What the hell are you doing out there?" she asked, sounding as cross as she looked. She stepped towards him and he stepped back again as she peered past him, then over her shoulder, checking the corridor was empty. "You're Morgan, right? From the Sentinel?" He nodded, trying not to behave any more stupidly than he already had done. She studied him briefly. "You OK?"

He snapped out of his funk. "Yes, yes, I'm fine. It's... It's the heat or something. I just needed to take a moment You're Tonia Birchow?" He held out a hand, realised how damp his palm was, wiped it on his chest and held it out again. The woman looked at it with distaste, then at him, showing no inclination to touch him. He withdrew his hand, feeling ridiculous.

"Come in," she said and walked away into the apartment.

He dropped his bag inside the door and closed it after him. Then followed her.

She was a small woman, thin and intense. Her hair was tied in a ponytail which made her look a little younger than she probably was. About thirty, Rafe guessed, although her dark eyes and furrowed brow suggested someone older. She stood facing him in the lounge room, appraising him.

"Where are you staying?" she asked.

"A hotel in the CBD," he said. He found he didn't want to say which one.

"You're not auged," she said. It was clearly a challenge to explain himself.

He shrugged. "I usually conduct my interviews on minimal aug. I like to see what people really look like. When you're latched it's too easy to…" He cast about for the word.

"To be deceived," she said. He nodded.

"How are you going to vote?" she asked.

"Vote?" If this was the woman's idea of small talk, she could probably use a few lessons. He hadn't even been invited to sit down yet. "In the plebiscite? I dunno. Against, I suppose."

"Why's that?"

"Look, Ms Birchow, maybe we could get started?" Her look told him to shut up and answer the question. Irritated, he said, "Because the government's got enough damned power as it is without giving them the right to do whatever the hell they like just on the suspicion of criminal activity."

"You're in a minority. It's in the bag. Isn't that what all the polls say?" He considered trying again to get the conversation back on track, but the woman seemed obsessively interested in what she was saying. "You're a journo. You've probably written loads of pieces about what a dead cert the new bill is. Is that right?"

"Not me, but–"

"Well, you're all wrong. The bill won't pass. You'll see." She glared at Rafe, as if daring him to contradict her. Then she nodded and went over to a cupboard where she pulled a folder of papers out from under some other junk and brought it back to Rafe. "Here," she said. "Take it."

He took it. "What's this?" He opened the flap and looked inside. There were pages and pages of paper documents. Paper documents. He looked up at her.

"That's everything you need," she said. "When you've read it, you should probably burn it."

"Paper?" he said.

"You'll find its safer than electronics. Less chance of it leaking out onto QNet."

"But what is it?"

"Read it and you'll see. OK. That's it. Time to go."

"Go?"

"Yeah. Out the door. On your way."

Rafe blinked at her in confusion. "But what about the interview?"

"What interview?"

"The one I just flew twelve hundred kilometres for. You said you had information about the terrorism bill. You said there were secrets you needed to pass on. My contact in Canberra said I should listen to you. He said you were the real deal, whatever that meant. Now you won't even talk to me?"

"Everything you need is in that folder."

"What if I have questions?"

"You won't."

"Oh yes I will. Can I come back here tomorrow?"

She thought about it. "Sure. No worries. Come back tomorrow. All right?"

He didn't like what was happening. He held out the folder. "You could have sent this by courier."

Her expression had so far been closed. Now it was turning to anger. "Read that lot tonight and come back here tomorrow with your questions."

He was still reluctant to leave. He still didn't trust this odd turn of events. His hesitation seemed to infuriate her.

"Why the fuck are you still here? I told you to get out. Did I pick the wrong journo? What kind of moron are you? You've got the story of a lifetime there in your hands. Just go and fucking read it."

Her hand went to her pocket and he saw the fabric move as she grasped something long and hard – a gun, maybe, or a knife. His heart thumped in is chest. Thumped again. He couldn't speak. His throat was so tight he could barely breath. A gun. Or a knife. It was happening again. Just like Melbourne. He stepped back. His vision twitched, a wave of light-headedness washed through his mind. Memories flashed, assailing him like attacking birds. Memories of fear. Memories of pain.

He fought against the rising panic. This wasn't Melbourne. This woman wasn't Sam Hopwood.

"OK," he gasped. "I'm going. It's all right. I'm going now." He realised the woman was watching him, squinting at him as if he'd grown an extra head. He backed to the door, not daring to look away. He stumbled but his back hit the wall saving him from a fall.

"What the fuck is wrong with you?" Tonia said. She took a step towards him and panic overwhelmed him. He saw the door handle beside him, grabbed it, and tore the door open. He remembered leaping down the stairs with Tonia shouting "Hey!" behind him.

Then he was outside, panting and lost, with a pain in his left ankle and no idea how he'd got there or how far he'd run.

The folder was still in his hand, trembling because his hand trembled. He squeezed his eyes shut as if he could squeeze out the fear and humiliation, but with his eyes closed, he saw Sam Hopwood again, a smile on his face, and a knife in his hand.

—oOo—

Rafe tipped his head back and let the warmth of the bathwater seep into his bones. He straightened a leg and the water chinked and made ripples that lapped on his chest. His hotel room felt anonymous and safe. Even so, he had balanced a beer bottle on the door handle so that he would have some warning if anyone tried to sneak in. He'd seen the trick in a Chinese spy interactive when he was just a boy and had been so impressed, it had stuck in his memory.

There's too much stuck in my memory, he thought. *That's the problem.*

He thought again about calling Dr. Godleigh and again dismissed it. If Becky thought he couldn't cope with the job, she'd put him back on sick leave. Or fire him. And he needed to work. He needed something to occupy his thoughts besides the memories of that time in Melbourne. Anyway, he knew what Godleigh would say, "Time and patience, Rafe. That's what will heal you. Give yourself the space you need in your life and let your mind heal itself." She'd go nuts if she knew he was back at work and on the trail of a criminal conspiracy to fix a vote in parliament. She'd tell him what a complete idiot he was being. Well, maybe she wouldn't say it. But that's what she'd think. And it was true, of course, but what could he do when something like that just dropped into his lap?

Run a mile, you dickhead. That's what you could do.

He squirmed in the bath, the noise of it echoing around the tiled room. Maybe he should take that job on the political desk, writing fluff pieces quoting the opposition's sound bite of the day, getting excited about which politician was rorting their expenses that week, which family values minister was screwing his interns, or which political adviser was writing her memoires. Maybe he couldn't do this any more. Maybe he never did have the stomach for it.

He was forty years old and he should be near the top of his profession. He was no failure. He'd done well, but he had not done really well. He hadn't done anything they'd give him an award for. The Sam Hopwood story had been it. That was the one that would have made his name. It had the lot, sex, big business, drugs, illegal brain mods, but most of all it had Sam Hopwood, the dashing, charismatic psychopath who had drawn so many people into his net and systematically corrupted and debased them. Rafe had picked it up when no-one else was even sniffing around it. He'd dug deeply in the mire that surrounded the man until he'd pieced together the whole story. And then he found Angel, Sam Hopwood's ex-wife, and persuaded her to talk. He had been so close to nailing it.

But then Hopwood had found him.

The torture had lasted three days. Mostly Hopwood had used knives, all kinds of knives, in all kinds of places. Sam Hopwood had wanted Rafe to give him the names of all his sources, so he could hunt them down too and make sure none of them could ever testify against him. And Rafe had resisted. He'd kept quiet. He'd endured the unendurable for a whole three days before the pain had become so intense, the exhaustion so numbing, he could no longer remember why he was there or what he was protecting. He'd told Hopwood everything, even making up things to tell him so that he would stop the pain and let him sleep. And Hopwood had smiled and smiled and said what a good boy he was being and that he could die now. And if there had been any joy left inside Rafe, he would have welcomed the release. As it was, he simply waited for it to happen, not caring either way.

When the policeman lifted Rafe's head and said, "Holy crap, he's still alive," Rafe could tell by the horror in the young man's eyes that the torture had been just the beginning, his suffering had only just begun.

He got out of the bath and towelled himself down, trying not to look at the scars.

"You're a bloody hero, mate," one of the cops had told him, sitting beside his hospital bed after yet another operation. Rafe's three days in Hell had given the police the chance to find Angel and, through her, Sam Hopwood. It saved Rafe. Several people owed their lives to Rafe, the cop said. But all Rafe could think was that someone else was writing his story. In the weeks of his hospitalisation and the months of his recovery, the feeds had fed. They'd been like crows on the roadkill of Rafe's big exposé. There was nothing left for him. He was interviewed and lauded, but it was no longer his story. He had become its subject, not its author.

He moved quickly to the bedroom, putting on the pyjamas he had laid out. He always slept in pyjamas now so that he could not see what Hopwood had done to his body. Even so, the awareness of his graven flesh rarely left him. He snatched up the folder Tonia had given him, tossed pillows against the bed head, and sat down to read, determined not to think about those three days.

The documents inside were printouts from newsfeeds,

business communications, excerpts from parliamentary white papers, personal messages from and to people he'd never heard of, hand-written notes in various hands, most of them unsigned and undated, photographs, extracts from software design documents, and other, less identifiable diagrams and descriptions. There seemed to be no order to it all and no sense.

Looking at the jumble of apparently unconnected and no-doubt illegally obtained information, it occurred to Rafe that Tonia Birchow might simply be a lunatic. He'd met many such in his time. Once you had your by-line on a high-traffic newsfeed, you were targeted by every conspiracy nut, UFO believer, and wannabe Deep Throat on the planet. Finding the reliable sources who were really onto something among all the crazies was a key skill in his line of work. Maybe this time his instincts had let him down.

The very idea that he might be losing his touch knotted up his stomach. He screwed up his eyes and fought down the fear. Self-doubt had been his constant companion since his encounter with Sam Hopwood. Sometimes it overwhelmed and crushed him. For a man who had been confident to the point of arrogance all his life, this fear of his own incompetence was perhaps the deepest scar that Hopwood had inflicted.

He snarled with anger at himself and spread the contents of the folder across the bed. If there was something here, he would find it. If he didn't find it, it would be because he had let his eagerness to get back into the saddle lead him astray. He'd just go back to Canberra and start again, pick up a new thread, unravel some other story. A false start was no big deal.

He began sorting the documents into piles by type. After

two minutes, he stopped and put them all together again. Then he started laying them out again, this time putting them in chronological order. The oldest documents were news stories from the USA that were more than twelve years old. They were all about the introduction of anti-terrorism legislation much like the bill Australia was about to vote on. They had a familiar tone. The legislation seemed like overkill, it involved terrible infringements of civil liberties and personal privacy, it gave the Government extensive powers to monitor people and to interfere with their network activities, all in the name of security. As with the current legislation, there was widespread support across the country. Then the vote came and the bill was unexpectedly thrown out.

There was a similar clutch of news reports from the UK. The government there had tried to put up a similar bill ten years ago and that too had been voted out. Since then, there had been votes in China, Russia, the other European countries, all over the place, in fact, and each time the same kind of legislation had been proposed and rejected by the people. It was a story Rafe already knew well. Even so, the Australian government was determined it would be the first to succeed, and it looked as if they had the numbers on their side. He could understand why Tonia had said the bill would be voted down. It seemed that, wherever it was put to the vote, people who were all for it beforehand, changed their minds when it came to the crunch. People seemed unable to bring themselves to give that much power to their governments.

Beneath the row of newsfeed reports, he laid out the other documents, the messages, the notes, the diagrams and so on. All the documents with no dates, mostly the hand written ones, went into a separate pile. A definite pattern emerged.

Most of the computer design documents clustered around the UK vote. So did most of the commercial correspondence. Then there was a gap before a slow build-up of correspondence and other news reports, unrelated to the legislation, began to pile up around the present day.

He looked again at the names in the current correspondence and that from ten years ago. Only one name occurred in both places, Cal Copplin.

He spent another hour laying the sheets out in different orders, by people they mentioned, by locations they related to, by subject, by sender, by recipient, trying to find other patterns. Then he lay back against the pillows and worked his way through the notes. Most of them were short and cryptic. People, places, perhaps projects were referred to by code names. Several mentioned September 10, or S10, which got his attention. September 10 was the government's favourite whipping boy at the moment, any act of terrorism against the national communications network was blamed on them. In fact, it was the organisation most frequently trotted out to justify the current cyberterrorism proposals.

He turned another page and read, "Approached by CC (S10 UK?) Provided docs attached. Poss. recruit this cell. Need more background. Pls advise. TB."

He put it down on the bed and stared at the ceiling. What the hell had he stumbled into? Was the woman he'd met today running a terrorist cell? Was all this some kind of confession? Evidence against her own people? If so, why go to a reporter and not to the police? The more he thought about it, the more agitated he grew. If this material was all from September 10, he was sitting on a goldmine. Or a ticking bomb. He had never heard of September 10 killing anybody but then he hardly knew anything about them at all.

Political scandals were his thing, not terrorist organisations. He was definitely out of his depth and the thing he should do, right now, not even waiting for the morning, was to go to the police and dump the whole lot, get on the first flight to Canberra and keep his head down.

The next document was a letter, in a different hand from the previous one. It had no date or address. Rafe read it.

Tonia,

I did as you asked but I've got to say I'm shaking all over still. I wish I had your nerve but I don't. It looks like you got Dad's genes and I got Mum's. I don't know if I'm cut out for this, Ton. I mean, I believe in The Cause and everything but I just don't have what it takes to do what you do.

I got that little gizmo you sent that looks like a gold crucifix on a chain. The guy who brought it said I should wear it all the time – even in the shower – to establish a credible pattern or some such. Then, when I get the tag removed, the device takes over as me and I can leave it at home when I go out to do secret squirrel stuff. He made it all sound so mundane – and I suppose it must be for you and him and the others. For me, it's just another scary reminder of my scary new life.

Anyway, I'm booked in with your doctor friend to have the tag removed next Friday. I hope she knows what she's doing. But I suppose she must since she did you and didn't manage to fry your brains – not so you'd notice. Look, I wish we could meet up and talk. I'm going nuts thinking about all this on my own. I can't remember the last time I got a good night's sleep. We can't all be fearless warriors, like you. Some of us need our hands holding while we save the world from injustice.

Don't worry, I won't do anything stupid. Just drop by one day, alright?

Love,

Gav.

Chapter 8

Rafe woke up on the bed with crumpled documents all around him. Through the window of the hotel room, he could see the sun already high above the bay and its long, low islands. The view itself meant nothing, the room probably didn't even have a window, but auged illusions tended to stay in sync with local time. He glanced at the bedside clock – another aug illusion – and was astonished to see it was nearly eight AM.

Cursing, he jumped up, showered, crammed the documents back into their folder, stuffed the folder in his bag, and hurried out. He called a cab and was back at Tonia's unit within an hour. This time, no-one answered the doorbell and no-one came when he pounded on the door. He went out to find something to eat and failed. When he returned, there was still no answer. He sat in the hallway and waited for four hours before he gave up and left.

He found a stall selling food from a printer at the airport, so he printed off a meat pie and a custard slice and ate them as he pondered his next move. He could go back and wait for Tonia Birchow to reappear, or he could go home and forget about it. Going home was by far the more attractive option. Yet he lingered through two cups of coffee that only a man with no other option could drink, and went out to the taxi rank, unable to give up on the story until he had at least spoken to Tonia again. The documents she had given him were teasers. He couldn't make them add up to a coherent picture. They told him Tonia was a terrorist, probably the leader of a September 10 cell, and that she was concerned about the upcoming vote on the anti-terror bill, connecting it obscurely to other, similar pieces of legislation all over the world. There were links to other people, her brother, Gav – Gavin? – and the Brit, Cal Copplin. But what did any of it mean?

He wished he knew more about September 10, but he daren't look up anything on QNet for fear of setting off alarms in government basements where, no doubt, computers watched night and day for any mention of terrorist organisations. If he were in Canberra, he could ask Jan, she tracked all this stuff for the Sentinel. She'd have all the background. Dare he call her and ask? Not unless she'd agree to a quantum-encrypted call and if he asked for that, she'd know something funny was going on.

He took a cab back to Tonia's unit and spent another three hours sitting outside her door. By then, he was convinced the fearless warrior woman wasn't coming back. He was also wishing he had printed off a couple of extra pies. He leafed through the documents as he waited, hoping for fresh inspiration but the only thing he found was a page from a small notebook with the name and street address of a woman called Virginia Galton. The page carried no hint of who she might be or what her connection was to September 10. Perhaps she was the doctor Tonia's brother had visited to get his tag deactivated. Perhaps she was Tonia's dentist. The only thing that made Virginia Galton stand out was the fact that hers was the only address in the folder, and she lived right there in Brisbane.

"Bugger it," he said, climbing to his feet. His back ached and his legs were stiff. He'd missed the only flight to Canberra for the day – perhaps for several days – and he needed to find a hotel and somewhere to eat. He wrote a virtual note and fixed it to Tonia's door. He might have used paper since he was carrying so much of it around with him, but he had no pen or pencil and had no idea where he might get one. If Tonia had any kind of aug, she'd get the note. If not, well it was probably better if he never met her again. The note said, "Call me. Rafe." It seemed safest not to say anything else.

He went back to the same hotel and they put him in the same room. He spent the evening reading through the contents of Tonia's folder again, this time setting up a whiteboard in his office so that he could draw timelines and lists of names and the places and organisations they were associated with. He wrote it all in code, Tonia was Warrior, Cal Copplin was Recruit, and so on. He didn't use the hotel's tank, but stayed on the bed, slipping in and out of his office and the hotel room, not daring to take images of the documents into VR with him, but memorising the content, in case those computers in the government's basement were snooping around.

It was seven PM when he started. When he checked the time again it was past midnight. The virtual whiteboard in his office had multiplied. Luckily virtual spaces could expand as required. Each board was full of notes and figures, every detail hard won from the jumble of documents Tonia had given him.

He was certain now that Tonia ran a September 10 cell,

that she had recruited her reluctant brother and probably Cal Copplin. There were other members too but It was Cal Copplin that was central to what they were planning. Rafe went to stand in front of board number five. At the top of the board, he'd written "Master Plan" and underneath were several islands of information associated with references to action that he'd seen in the documents. He still had no clue as to what Tonia had in mind, but he could see it was going to happen soon – before the vote on the anti-terror bill.

On the board labelled "Membership", in large capital letters, was the word "Pocahontas" with a large question mark after it. It was his code name for Virginia Galton. Tomorrow he would visit her and see if he could get some answers.

Reluctantly, he left his office and sat up on the bed. As before, it was littered with paper. This time he tidied it away and slept under the covers. But his sleep was broken and shallow. The material in the documents went round and round incoherently, but no new insights came. He kept coming back to the Galton woman. Would she be another hard-faced terrorist with a concealed weapon and eyes that watched you like a cat watched mice? Was she the doctor who had hacked Tonia's brother's tag? He hoped it was the latter. He could deal with a doctor. He didn't know whether he could face another cold hard criminal. If Galton was like that, he'd just turn around and walk away. If he spotted even a hint of a weapon, he'd get out of there, go home, and hand the whole thing to Becky to reassign as she saw fit. As for him and his career, well maybe that was all over anyway. He'd panicked when he met Tonia. He'd run like a rabbit. He'd lost his bottle. He should look for some other line of work. Something that kept him safely out of the way of crazies and crims and terrorists.

Maybe.

Tomorrow would be the decider. Tomorrow, if he could face Virginia Galton and do his job without cracking up, maybe he could stick with it.

He fell into a fretful doze, a drugged misery of memories and fear, the old dreams of Sam Hopwood and his knives, the dreams that had plagued him asleep and awake ever since he'd regained consciousness in that Melbourne hospital all those months ago.

—oOo—

"Virginia Galton?"

The woman let out a cry and jumped back, trying to shove the door closed. He rushed forward and put his foot in the jamb to prevent her.

"I'll call the police!" she shouted.

"You're breaking my foot," he shouted back.

"Get away. Leave me alone."

"I just want to talk. I'm a reporter with the Sentinel. Rafe Morgan. Maybe you've heard of me? I'm chasing down a story about the new cyberterrorism bill. Your name came up. I'd just like to ask you a few questions."

"My name? I've got nothing to do with terrorists."

Despite the pain in his foot, Rafe noticed she had answered a question he hadn't asked. "I don't think you're a terrorist, Ms Galton. Can we just talk, please?"

"I don't believe you. Go away. I'm calling the police now."

"What don't you believe?"

"I don't believe you're a journalist."

"Look me up. My picture's in the Sentinel brochures." He

was pretty sure he could push the door back and get in, but that would just scare the woman even more. "Please open the door, Ms Galton. I'm Rafe Morgan, a journalist. I've been out here ringing your bell all morning. If I'd been a burglar, or whatever you think I am, wouldn't I have broken in before now?"

"You waited for me to come out and ambushed me."

"I was waiting for you to come home. I thought you were out."

"Why would I be out?"

Rafe took a deep breath and tried a new tack. "I got your name from Tonia Birchow."

There was a gasp from the other side of the door and then silence. Rafe cursed himself. It seemed the lovely Tonia had the same chilling effect on all her acquaintances. *Ah well, in for a penny…*

"You know Tonia Birchow then. And her brother, Gav?"

"Gavin," said the woman behind the door. There was a hollowness in her tone, a hint of despair. "Who are you? What do you want?"

This was getting silly. "Look, Ms Galton. I'm a reporter. I'm going to take my foot out of your door now and let you close it. Please just check my credentials and confirm what I say. I'll wait out here while you do that." He pulled at his foot but couldn't get it out. The damned woman was pushing on the door with all her strength. "You'll have to ease off on the door a bit so I can get my foot out." There was no response from the other side, just the unrelenting pressure on his foot. After a while, he put his shoulder against the door and shoved hard enough to push both door and woman a few inches into the apartment. He yanked his foot back as fast as he could, almost losing a toe as the door slammed shut with a force that shook the wall.

He limped across to the other side of the hall and sat down to check his foot for broken bones. Whatever kind of reception he had expected, this was not it. The woman was scared out of her wits. The good news was that she obviously knew something. The bad news was that she wasn't being exactly cooperative.

Seconds ticked by, turning slowly into minutes. He got up again, wondering whether to try ringing the bell, but it was hardly as if the woman would have forgotten he was there. No, patience was the only way. Even so, what the hell was she doing that was taking so long?

The door opened a crack and a woman's face peered out at him. He stepped towards her and she slammed the door again.

"Ms Galton?" he called through the door. "Just check my credentials. Please."

"I did."

"Then may I come in, please?"

"Credentials can be faked."

"Oh, for God's sake!"

She opened the door again, a bit wider this time. It was his first good look at her – a woman in her early thirties, slimmish, longish dark hair, probably not bad looking if you took away the suspicious frown and the bruises under her eyes left by too many sleepless nights. He knew those bruises. He saw them in the mirror every day. In his own case he knew full well why that was, but what was keeping Virginia Galton awake at night?

"I phoned your editor," she said.

"Becky? Then you know I'm who I say I am."

"She said to get your useless arse back to Canberra and

stop pestering women while you're on her expense account."

"Well that sounds like Becky all right. Can I come in now?"

She held the door wider but didn't move to let him enter. "Why didn't you call, or visit me at my office?"

"I'm sorry but I want to use QNet as little as possible. It's the story I'm working on. I was worried that if we met in VR or even if we talked on the phone, people might be able to listen in. I don't want that. Not yet. I need to find out who's who before I trust anybody – even the Government."

He saw her mouth twitch. "You're even more paranoid than I am," she said.

"You don't know the half of it."

He stood there waiting while she stood there weighing him up. He had time to notice the hand that was holding the door. It was a beautiful hand, long, with delicate tapering fingers. An artist's hand. At last, she stepped back and he went in. Crisis over, he looked around the apartment and realised there were other pressing needs. "Do you mind if I use your bathroom, only I've been hanging around in your hallway for hours." She looked taken aback but waved him towards a closed door beside what he could see was the bedroom. "And I couldn't beg a cup of coffee off you, could I? I'm dying of thirst."

—oOo—

"So?" she said, putting Rafe's coffee down in front of him. "What do you know about Tonia and her brother?"

Rafe shook his head. "I want to know who you are first. Then I'll answer your questions."

She sat down in a chair opposite him. He could see she

was keeping her distance. "You've got a bloody nerve," she said, but seemed to accept his condition.

"What do you do for a living, Virginia?"

She gave him a baleful stare. "If we're on first name terms now, Rafe, you'd better call me Ginny. Only my mother calls me Virginia and I've just had three glorious weeks of it."

"Right. Ginny, then. What business are you in?"

"Why don't you read my bio?"

"I would normally, believe me, but I can't do that without a QNet query. And that might bring me attention I don't want. For that matter, it might raise a few flags against your name and maybe you don't want that either." He was fishing for a reaction but he didn't get one. "So we need to do this the old fashioned way, through conversation."

"We don't need to do this at all."

"No, we don't, but from your reaction when you met me, I reckon you're in some kind of trouble and you'd like to hear what I know maybe more than the other way round. Is your job some kind of secret."

She scowled. "I design soundscapes for worldlets."

"Soundscapes? So you're not a doctor or some kind of medical professional?"

"Are you really a journalist? You don't seem very good at this interviewing thing."

Rafe took a deep breath. She was right. He was making a complete balls up of it. Time to start again. "Sorry. Look, here's the thing. Someone got in touch with me and said they had information about the upcoming cyberterrorism bill. I agreed to meet them here, in Brisbane. They wanted a real, physical meeting. As it turned out, that was so they could hand me some documents. Paper documents, that is. Those documents suggest a connection between my informant and a terrorist group called September 10. They also contained several other names. One of them was yours."

Ginny's reaction was to stand up and pace away from her chair and then back to it. "I'm nothing to do with terrorists. I don't know anything about it. I did one stupid favour for a friend, that's all. Just one stupid favour."

"Which friend was that? Tonia Birchow?"

"Tonia? That psycho?"

"So you do know Tonia then? I met her myself yesterday. Charming woman."

"Is she your informant? Is she the one in this terrorist group?"

"How do you know Tonia, Ginny?"

Whatever progress he thought he'd made in gaining Ginny's trust, seemed to have been undone. The woman said, "The problem is, I don't know you, Rafe. For all I know, you're working for the police, or ASIO, or maybe you're with the terrorists. Being a journo might just be a cover. Spooks have cover. Cops have cover. So do criminals. This interview is over. I want you to leave now."

Rafe didn't move. He'd fought too hard to get a seat to give it up, and he hadn't drunk his coffee yet. "Ginny, I can see you're scared, and, considering what you're mixed up in, I don't blame you a bit. This is scary stuff. To be honest, I'm scared shitless myself. The thing is, we've both got monkeys on our backs now and the only way to shift the little buggers is to share what we know and help each other out." Even as he said it, he realised it was true. This woman was no terrorist. She had stumbled into something dangerous and didn't know what to do about it. It had made her so paranoid she didn't think she could trust anybody. He was willing to bet she hadn't even told her best friend. What's more, he was in the same position. He needed a friend and confidante as much as she did.

"You just spent three weeks at your parents' place," he went on, letting his intuition guide his words. "That was to lie low wasn't it? You were hoping it would all blow over if you gave it a bit of time, right? But it didn't. No sooner do you get home than there's a stranger accosting you on your doorstep, wanting to rake it all over again. Who else has been on at you, Ginny? Tonia and her friends? The cops?"

She turned away from him, shoulders hunched. "You need someone you can talk to, Ginny. To be honest, I could use someone myself. Even the little bit I already know about this is driving me nuts." She didn't respond. "Tell me about this favour you did. Someone you knew – a friend maybe – dropped you in it, didn't they? Was it Tonia? Or Gav?" Still no response. He took a wild leap. "Was it Cal Copplin?"

She spun round to face him, eyes wide, and said, "How do you know Cal?"

He blinked in surprise. "I don't. He's just another name in the sheaf of papers my informant gave me. But he's an important name. He's of great interest to September 10. They seem to have been tracking him for years. I think they might have recruited him."

"No," she said, shaking her head. "Cal's not a terrorist." But there was doubt in her eyes. She knew something that maybe suggested her friend really was one of the bad guys.

"But he asked you to do a favour for him, isn't that right? And the favour led you to Tonia. And then..." And then what? He was out of guesses for now, but fortunately Ginny started talking.

"And then a killer turned up. A man named Dover Richards. He surprised me out in the hallway, just like you did. He wanted to know all about Cal. And later a cop turned up from Missing Persons. Another man in the hallway. He wanted to find Cal too."

Rafe's mind was racing. "So there's a tagger after him. Cal ditched his tag, right? Went off the grid? They can do that. They've got a doctor who helps them. I thought you might be the doctor."

"Me?"

"It's all I could think of to explain why Tonia had your name in her papers. But you're not a doctor. You're not anyone – if you'll forgive me saying."

"Feel free."

"So it's something else. It's Copplin. He's the important one. How come you're friends with a terrorist?"

Ginny threw up her arms. "I'm not. Cal's just, like, a normal bloke. I met him. We had a couple of dates. We talked. He seemed nice. He's not a terrorist any more than I am."

"Maybe you're more of a terrorist than you think you are. What was the favour he asked you to do?"

Ginny scowled at him and walked away, towards the kitchenette. Rafe realised he was hungry. He wished he could find a good restaurant and get lunch but a virtual restaurant was useless. Without a tank, there would be no point eating.

"Have you got any food in the house?" he asked. "I mean, real food?" Ginny scowled at him in response. "Well, do you know somewhere that sells food? I mean a real fast food place or something?"

She turned to the fridge and seemed about to open the door when she stopped. "Are you really travelling on an expense account." He nodded. "OK, then, you can take me to lunch. There's a place in Toowong that serves real food.

Very pricey. For the jaded rich who want to try something different. They've got a chef and everything. It's only a fifteen minute walk from here. I've always wanted to go and now's the time. Come on."

Rafe didn't much like the sound of it – Becky would kill him when she saw the bill – but if that's what it took to get the story, she'd understand. Or, at least, she'd forgive him one day.

—oOo—

"I heard about you," Ginny said, studying him. "You were on the feeds."

Rafe nodded and scanned the menu in vain for anything that cost under a week's wages.

"They tortured you or something, nearly killed you. You're famous."

"What about you?" he asked, wanting to change the subject. "Written anything I'd know?"

"I write soundscapes not pop songs. Ever been to the National Museum? You're from Canberra didn't you say? I worked on the Dali exhibition there last year."

"Yeah, I saw that. You did that, huh?" He tried to look impressed, but he hadn't really noticed the soundscape. In fact, he'd never really considered that someone actually wrote the ambient sounds he took for granted wherever he went.

"Not my best work," she said. "Very conservative bunch at the National Museum."

He glanced at her, not sure if that was meant to be a joke. He grinned anyway, just in case.

A robot rolled up to them and took their order. Ginny seemed to be intent on bankrupting his employer while Rafe tried to mitigate the damage by ordering the cheapest dishes he could find. If his guest noticed, she did not comment, but chattered away about her various clients and some big proposal she'd just put in to a wordlet design company he'd never heard of. A lot seemed to be hanging on it, so he tried to sound interested and make intelligent comments, all the while trying to get the conversation back to Tonia Birchow and her gang of saboteurs.

"So, tell me how your meeting with Tonia went," he said at last, cutting across an ecstatic monologue on the subject of how much better real food tasted than sim food, or printer food, or the processed rubbish they deliver from the supermarket warehouses.

Ginny closed her mouth and looked at him across a spoonful of desert that had been making abortive sorties towards her mouth for quite some time. There was a flicker of defeat across her features and Rafe realised she had been deliberately waffling on about anything and everything to keep him off the subject. She put down her spoon and regarded it for a moment.

"She pulled a gun on me," she said. "The woman is certifiable." Rafe swallowed hard. Perhaps he hadn't been so paranoid yesterday when he'd fled Tonia's apartment. Maybe she had been armed after all.

"Why would she pull a gun on you?"

"Because I went to her brother's house, to deliver this package Cal gave me."

"Her brother's house? You mean Gavin?"

"I mean, the late Gavin. As in, he was dead in the kitchen, according to Tonia."

"Had she killed him?"

"I don't think so. But who knows? I thought she was

going to kill me. She said I was working for the taggers. I didn't even know what a tagger was. In the end she let me go."

Rafe pressed her for the details and, by the time he'd finished his coffee, he had the whole story. "And you have no idea what was on those data cubes?"

She shook her head. "I should have opened the package. My friend, Della, says all kinds of people might be in danger because of me."

Rafe could only agree, but he said, "You thought you were helping a friend."

"But they blow things up," she said. "They could disrupt services or even kill someone."

"September 10 you mean?"

"Yes, I looked them up after I met Tonia."

"I wish you hadn't done that."

"Why? The police already know I'm involved. Besides, it hardly looks suspicious if I try to find out what September 10 is. I mean, if I was one of them, I'd already know, right?"

"Do the police know you met Tonia?"

"I don't think so?"

"Or about the package Cal asked you to deliver?"

"No."

"So your sudden interest in this particular terror group might just seem a bit surprising to anyone who's monitoring your Net usage." She frowned at him, as if trying to work out how serious he was. "Never mind," he said. "Tell me what you found out."

A movement near the door caught his eye and he looked up to see a man talking to a robot waiter. The waiter led the newcomer over to one of the many unoccupied tables. "Now there's a coincidence," he said.

"What?"

"I know that bloke. I met him just–"

The realisation hit Rafe like a jolt of electricity. Fear ran through his body like a fire. He stood quickly but as quietly as he could. He needed to act while the man was distracted with taking his seat and dealing with the waiter. He grabbed Ginny by the arm and pulled her to her feet, saying, "We've got to get out of here. Come on, quickly. Don't make a sound."

She rose, looking around to see what had spooked him, but he hustled her towards the door. A waiter rolled after them and he waved the stupid machine away. The last thing he wanted was any attention being drawn to them. He tried not to look at the man, but he couldn't help stealing a glance as they reached the door. They were OK for a few more seconds. The man was looking at the menu. He hadn't checked yet that Rafe and Ginny were still at their table.

The bill flashed up in his aug as they stepped outside and he flicked it away. They needed somewhere to hide and fast. The restaurant was in a row of what once must have been shops and eateries on a broad street that curved away around a corner to his right. Opposite was a massive building without windows that might once have been a shopping mall but was now clearly a distribution warehouse. Robot trucks of all sizes were driving into and emerging from a wide black tunnel that led to the interior. He considered hiding in there but dismissed it at once. There would be security. The robots would challenge him, perhaps even arrest him. No, his best bet was to escape down the road.

Ginny was starting to resist his tugging and asking what the hell was wrong. "Someone followed us to the restaurant," he said. "Someone's been following me for days."

"Who?"

Then he saw what they needed. "Come on." He grabbed her tighter and dragged her with him across the road. Vehicles stopped and waited politely for them to cross. He led her to the entrance where the delivery trucks were emerging. "That one," he said, pointing to a flat-bed truck loaded with large crates. The crates were fastened down with webbing.

They reached the truck just as it slowed to a halt before turning onto the main road. "Climb on," he said. Ginny resisted and he pushed her forward. "Climb on. It's easy." It was, too. The electric truck's bed was low and the webbing made for easy hand-holds. At the speed it moved as it edged around the corner, a child could do it. "Get on the truck, Ginny. He'll notice we're gone any moment now and come out to find us."

She hesitated a moment longer but, perhaps responding to the desperation he must have been showing, she grabbed the webbing and pulled herself onto the bed of the truck. He was up beside her in an instant. They were on the opposite side of the crates from the restaurant. "Keep low," he said, unnecessarily. Ginny was already crouching out of sight. The truck began to pick up speed, whining up through its gears to reach its maximum twenty-five kilometres an hour. Rafe risked a quick look through the webbing at the back of the load and saw the man come rushing out of the restaurant, scanning the street left and right but not spotting his quarry.

"Oh my God," Ginny said in a low, frightened voice. Rafe turned to find her ducking down again, having also taken a peek at the man from the restaurant.

"What is it? Do you know him?" She nodded but didn't speak. "Well? Who is it?"

She swallowed and licked her lips, as if her mouth was dry.

"It's Dover Richards," she said.

—oOo—

They stayed with the truck for a long, long way, before climbing off at a junction and continuing on foot to a small, ramshackle park. A robot mower was just finishing when they arrived and they sat on a bench that had seen better days. The air was full of the smell of cut grass.

"So Richards followed you from Canberra to Brisbane?" she asked.

"Yes. I met him in the airport lounge. He said he was a mining engineer. I've still got his card."

"Couldn't it have been a coincidence?"

"What, that some guy picks up my trail in Canberra and is still on it two days later in Brisbane – at a real food restaurant of all the unlikely places – and he just happens to be the same guy that our terrorist friend said killed her brother?"

"Yeah, all right. So no coincidence then." She stared into the distance, pouting. "So what does he want? Why is he following you? How could he possibly know you're involved with September 10 and Tonia and all that?"

She was right. Dover Richards had been onto him before Rafe himself even knew what he'd become mixed up in. "He must have been monitoring Tonia's calls. It's the only possibility. But who is he? If he's not a cop and he's not with the September 10 crowd, it must mean there's another group out there, one we have no clue about."

"Except we know they kill people, and follow people."

Rafe wasn't even sure about the killing part. They only had Tonia's word for it. "Maybe they only kill terrorists."

A small grin creased Ginny's cheek. "You're just trying to

cheer me up."

Surprised, he grinned back. "That's me, always thinking of others."

He studied the woman beside him while she studied the shrubbery at the far end of the park. He liked her. More to the point, he trusted her. Just a pleasant, not unattractive woman, making her way in life, not completely alone, doing something not uninteresting, not uncreative. Not unlike himself. In another life, if they'd met in some other way, they might have become friends, lovers even.

The ludicrous idea of a jaded hack like him starting up a new relationship almost made him snort in derision. There was a time, fifteen, twenty years ago, when it was all he wanted. He'd found Zoe and they'd set up a virtual home together. She lived in South Africa and he was in Sydney at that time but they lived together in virtual space for nearly five years. She was endlessly fascinating, intelligent and witty. The cybersex was beautiful. She had been a one-woman intellectual fireworks display. And she had him dazzled. But while she had grown brighter with each passing year, Rafe had grown duller, more cynical, less able to shake off the mundane. He blamed it on the crushing tawdriness of his work. She said he had simply failed to rise above the limits of his imagination. When she left him, it felt like watching the angels leave the Earth.

"I can't go home tonight," Ginny said, interrupting his maudlin mood. "He knows where I live."

He snapped back to the park, the hot Brisbane sunshine, the smell of mown grass. "There's a hotel I've been using," he said. "It's not bad."

She shook her head. "I can't afford hotels. I just blew a bundle on going down to see my folks."

Not really my problem, he thought. "What about friends? There must be someone you could stay with."

She pursed her lips. "Probably the only one I could ask, I don't want to get involved. Who'd thank you for maybe bringing an armed killer to their door?"

He nodded. He shouldn't go back to the same hotel either. Richards would know he'd been there. It would be the first place he'd check. But how many hotels were there in Brisbane? Two? Three? It wouldn't take long to find him wherever he went.

Again they drifted off into silence until Ginny said, "I've got it. I know where I can go tonight. You could stay there too if you're worried about going back to your hotel."

"Where?"

"Follow me. It's not far." She jumped up and held out a hand. He took it and let her lead him.

Chapter 9

The entrance to Cal Copplin's apartment building seemed unremarkable, latched or not. Rafe peered up and down the street before turning to the woman beside him. "Looks clear to me," he said.

"I sort of expected there'd be police tape across the door or something," Ginny said. "Or one of those 'Crime scene. Do not enter.' signs."

"It's not actually a crime scene," Rafe said. At least, he hoped it wasn't. Just the empty apartment of someone who'd gone missing. "And how are we going to get in?" he asked, again.

Ginny sighed. "I think the door will just open for me."

They crossed the street and Ginny pushed a button only she could see. They had agreed beforehand that Rafe would remain on minimal aug while she latched to the building. After a moment, she said, "Ginny Galton," and the door clicked open. So far, so good. They were inside the building at least.

Ginny led him to Copplin's apartment and to Rafe's surprise, the door unlocked itself as they approached. Ginny flashed him an excited smile and walked straight in. With a last look up and down the hallway, he followed her inside, closing the door behind him.

The apartment was cleaner and tidier than almost any he had ever seen, as if Copplin hadn't relied on the rough-and-ready services of the dombots but had actually done the cleaning himself. He'd heard about people who were like that, but he'd never met one. "You know, the police might be monitoring this unit in case Copplin returns."

Ginny shook her head. "I don't think Cal would let that happen."

"Pardon?"

"There was something about the way the unit responded to me last time I was here. I got the impression Cal has these systems under his thumb. It's sort of how I knew the unit would let me back in."

"It must be nice to have faith." He went to the kitchen and looked in the fridge. It was full of food. "Thank Christ for that," he said. The prospect of having nothing to eat until tomorrow had been nagging at him. He hadn't walked so much in years and he was already hungry. The fridge was stocked with enough food for them to stay several days if they needed to. He grabbed the kettle and took it to the sink. "Why don't you ask the unit where your friend is if it's so smart?"

"I'm not sure I want to know."

"Coffee?" Ginny nodded and he set about hunting through the kitchen cupboards for mugs and ingredients. "Can you cook?" he asked, realising that Copplin had pans and utensils of the sort he'd only ever seen in VR.

"I can microwave."

"Yeah, me too."

"I could ask the unit if there are any more messages from Cal."

"Can't hurt?"

"You're joking, right?"

Rafe gave a sheepish grin. "Yeah, stupid thing to say. But you should try it, anyway."

"Right." Ginny went silent for a moment as she communed with the apartment. Her eyes widened. "Oh God, there's a message."

He put down the spoon he was holding and went to join her. "Hold on. Let me latch so I can hear it."

Ginny nodded and waited for him to give her the OK. "You know, it's bloody weird that this place looks the same with and without aug," She nodded again, a quick, nervous bob of the chin, and popped up the message.

Cal Copplin's face appeared. He looked relaxed and untroubled by the mayhem his disappearance had sparked. He seemed to be sitting in the apartment, so Rafe guessed the recording had been made before he ducked out of his life.

"Hello again, Ginny," the recorded voice of Cal Copplin said. "If you're watching this, it's because you came back to my unit. And the only reason I can think of for why you might do that is because you're in trouble and you've come back looking for answers. I'm sorry. There was always a chance the little errand you did for me would go wrong, but this is my attempt to help you sort things out."

"Pause it a sec," Rafe said and Copplin's image froze in the act of drawing its next breath. "Is that your friend? Does he seem to be normal? Does he always talk in that pompous, convoluted way?"

Ginny gave him a frown. "Do you always put other people's friends down before you even get to know them? Yes, it sounds like Cal. Maybe he does sound a bit up himself. I always made allowances because he's a Brit."

And a control freak too, Rafe thought. The whole recorded messages from beyond the grave thing seemed just a bit over the top. *Still, it takes all kinds...* He nodded at the message display. "OK."

Ginny scowled at him but he pretended not to notice. After a moment, she continued the playback.

"I hope you're all right," Copplin said. "Gavin's a nice guy – that's why I sent you to him – but some of his associates can be a bit overwhelming. Maybe Gavin told you what this is all about. If so, I hope you'll have the sense to keep quiet about it. If not – trust me – it's better if you don't know anything – or anyone, especially if the police ask you. In this matter – as in so much else – the police are not necessarily going to act in your best interests.

"Obviously, I have no idea what kind of trouble you're in. Maybe you're just nosy and looking for clues. Maybe you're on the run and your life is in danger. Whatever you need from my flat, just take it. I won't be coming back. If you pull the dishwasher out from under the counter, you'll find some useful items taped to the back of it. That's about all I can do for you, I'm afraid. Oh, I should say this, though: nothing is what it seems. If you have to trust anybody, the only person I know who won't lie to you is Gavin's sister, Tonia." Rafe and Ginny exchanged glances. "She might shoot you, but she won't lie.

"You might also want to consider leaving the country. Ask Tonia if you want to know which countries are safe, I've lost track myself. The thing is... Well, I'm doing what I can, but my success is not guaranteed. Things might easily fail to go as planned. Goodbye again, Ginny. Take care of yourself."

"That's it?" Ginny cried, addressing the sad-eyed image in the air before her. "A load of vague rubbish? How's that supposed to help me? You fucking bastard! You knew you'd dropped me right in it, didn't you?" She turned to Rafe. "That's why we just happened to meet by chance. That's why he came on all flattering and flirtatious. That's why–" She stopped herself on the cusp of a sob. "He just used me. He just set me up and strung me along, just in case he needed a favour one day. That's all it was ever about."

Rafe had to agree it seemed very likely. The guy in the recording might have said he was sorry but he certainly didn't look it. There was no remorse in Copplin's manner. He was just a control freak tidying up some loose ends, well aware he'd probably wrecked this woman's life and doling out his bullshit advice as a sop to his own conscience. It seemed incredible that Ginny hadn't spotted it sooner. Even so, he said, "I'm sure there was more to it than that." It was all he could bring himself to say.

Ginny went to slump down into the sofa, probably to consider why her taste in men was so shockingly poor, while Rafe went to the kitchen and wrestled with the dishwasher until he had it clear of its housing. On the metal plate at the back of the machine were taped a small silver cylinder, a small black box, a folded wad of paper documents, a semi-automatic handgun, and two spare clips of ammo. "Christ," he said, looking at the gun.

He heard Ginny's footsteps as she came up to see what he'd found. "I'm going back to Canberra," he said. "On the next available flight."

—oOo—

They hardly spoke that evening. Ginny watched news feeds and immersed herself in entertainment worldlets, but Rafe didn't want news and he was in no mood to be entertained. The sight of the gun had deeply unsettled him. Ginny had taken everything off the back of the dishwasher and laid it all out on the kitchen counter. Rafe didn't even feel tempted to look at the documents. He just wanted nothing to do with them. Now the gun was a constant presence in his mind. It seemed to be calling to him from the kitchen, saying, "What are you doing here, you fool? Get out now. Go to the police. This story will get you killed. Or worse."

Unfortunately, he shared Cal Copplin's view of the police. Even under existing anti-terror laws, Rafe could be held for weeks without access to lawyers on the mere suspicion that he knew more than he was telling. And that's if they bothered to follow their own procedures. Worse than that, with a co-operative judge to keep extending his interrogation, he could be held indefinitely. Being a journalist wasn't likely to help him much, especially since he had been loudly critical of police corruption and police incompetence in the past.

Of course, it would all come right in the end. He really believed that. His story would be believed, his innocence would be obvious, and they'd let him go. But Rafe didn't think he could face an interrogation, however short, however gentle. He'd had enough interrogation to last him a lifetime. A single moment handcuffed to a table while someone threatened him and bullied him would be like a month in Hell. The very thought of it set his heart thudding and his stomach knotting. He'd go mad. He'd rather be dead.

He couldn't go to the police. Not with all these unanswered questions. Guilt by association was a police investigation technique he knew only too well.

And that left getting on the next flight to Canberra with his tail between his legs and telling Becky his lead was a dead end. Lying. Letting September 10 do whatever they were planning. Keeping his head down, saving his own skin at the expense of whoever else might get hurt. But it was the best he could do. Anyone who knew – really knew – what he'd gone through at Sam Hopwood's hands would understand. No-one would think he was a coward. He'd come back too soon. The scars were – literally – too fresh. He saw that now. He just needed to take it easy for a while. Ease back into it slowly.

And there was always Ginny. She could go to the cops. She could do the right thing. It wasn't all on his shoulders. He looked across at the woman lying on the sofa, completely unlatched, deep in some VR fantasy world, seemingly unconscious. That was because the strange Mr. Copplin didn't have a tank. Who in the world didn't have a tank? That, right there, was a sure-fire sign that the guy was a crazy terrorist. The government wouldn't need its new anti-terror legislation if they just rounded up and locked away all the creeps and misfits who didn't use a tank. How do you work, how do you have any kind of social life without a tank?

And yet Copplin had managed it. At least enough to seduce this poor naïve woman and drag her into his insane conspiracy. Rafe felt sorry for Ginny. How could he not? But not sorry enough to hang around and let her drag him into more trouble. Staying in Copplin's unit had seemed like a neat solution to his problems for a while there, but now there was that gun, yelling at him from the kitchen, and yet another wadge of incriminating documents that he daren't even look at in case they contained more names he shouldn't know, more facts he shouldn't be aware of.

Ginny's eyes popped open and she caught him staring at her. A small frown crossed her face and he fought the urge to explain himself, as if she'd openly accused him of leering at her while she was unlatched.

"Got to have a pee," she said, sitting up. "I'm hungry too. I can see why they invented tanks." She got up and went to the bathroom. When she came out, she went to the kitchen and poked around in the fridge. "There's a few microwave meals in the freezer, do you want one?" He told her no. He was hungry still, but he couldn't face eating. Five minutes later she was back on the sofa, forking something that smelt like Thai food into her mouth. The smell made his stomach heave.

"You still going back to Canberra?" she asked.

He nodded.

"Then what?" He must have looked as puzzled as he felt. "Then what?" she repeated. "You write your story and move on? Is that how this works?"

"Not quite. I won't be writing the story."

She nodded as if she understood. "And what about Richards?"

"What about him?"

"He followed you here. Maybe he'll follow you home. He just has to hang around at the airport when the Canberra flights leave, or, better still, wait at Canberra airport for you to fly in."

Rafe didn't like this. "Why should he? He was only tailing me so he could get to Tonia?" At least, that's what he'd assumed.

"So why was he still following you after you went to Tonia's place yesterday?"

"Did you think of this while you were playing ScareWorld III?" It was a stupid dig, but he was irritated, not least, he now realised, because Ginny was clearly more calm than he was.

"I was at a J. C. Bach concert, actually. Listening to classical music helps me relax."

Rafe clenched his teeth. *Why did he follow me?* "Maybe he found Tonia. Maybe I did lead him to her. Maybe he killed her or spooked her and that's why she wasn't around this morning. Maybe he wanted to know if I had any other September 10 contacts in town."

"Maybe. Or maybe he thinks you're one of them. Maybe he's from a rival gang, or Tonia's lot managed to upset the September 10 hierarchy somehow."

Rafe got up and strode across the room. You could go mad wondering what the hell was really going on here. The apartment felt small and claustrophobic. He wanted to unlatch and find somewhere with room to breathe, to shake this feeling of the walls closing in on him. He even thought about going outside. But Richards could be out there, waiting for him.

He went into the kitchen and snatched up the silver cylinder. It looked like a single, seamless piece of metal. He tried pulling it and twisting it. Ginny was watching him from the door. "You should be careful with that," she said. "What if it's a grenade or something?" He froze, then put the object back on the counter. Damn it, the woman was right. It could be anything, a tube of nerve gas, or a phial of some hideous doomsday virus.

"The only way past this is through it," he said.

"What?"

He tried to unclench his jaw. "We're in this up to our eyeballs and we're stumbling around like bloody sheep. We need to know more. For a start, we need to know who the players are and what they're after. It's only by getting in deeper that we'll ever be safe again." He looked at the little black box and decided not to touch it. Then he looked at the wad of paper. His eyes wouldn't look at the gun. They kept flinching away from it.

"All right," he said. "How about this? We camp out here for a couple of days while we put this all together, work out as much as we can. If we need more, we'll go out into QNet and get what we need. We shouldn't be pussy-footing around. We're already in more danger than either of us can cope with. We can't make it much worse, but maybe we can make it better."

"You mean we should go to the police?"

"No!" He took a breath. "No, I don't think the police would be a good idea right now. They'd probably burst in here and arrest us both for aiding known terrorists, or whatever."

"But there's that detective, Chu, the tagger. He seemed OK. Maybe if we–"

"No. Remember what Cal said. We can't even trust the police." He really needed to convince her of that. "We need to do this without them. You know what they're like when they hear the word 'terrorist'. We'll be locked away for weeks with no civil rights and no hope of clearing up this mess." Ginny looked unhappy but didn't argue. Relieved, he tried to give her something in return. "It'll be all right. We'll do this together. We're safe here for now. We've got some time to get to the bottom of it. Maybe the stuff Cal left us will fill in the blanks. Look, I want to show you something." He passed her the address of his office. "Unlatch and meet me there, OK?"

She nodded and went to lie down on the sofa again. Rafe

went to the bedroom and lay on the bed. In a moment, he was in his office, with Ginny at the door. He let her in and stood back to reveal all the whiteboards summarising the information he had from Tonia.

Her eyes were wide as she took it all in. "This was all in that folder from Tonia?"

"We should read the stuff Cal gave you and see if we can do the same with it, add it into this lot. Then we might see what it's all about." He explained the name swaps for her so she could make sense of it.

She stood in front of the timeline that showed the progress of anti-terror laws around the world and matched it to the involvement of the various players. He could see her look from the first occurrence of Cal Copplin's codename – Recruit – in the UK ten years ago to the more recent ones in Australia. He sat down in the big, leather swivel chair from which he did most of his work and gave her time to soak it all up. She moved on to another board and then another, eventually returning to the timeline.

"Tonia says the bill won't pass in Australia," he said.

She didn't turn away from the board. "I'd vote for it."

"So would eighty percent of the country, according to the polls." He glanced at the calendar on his wall. "In fact, we'll know in a couple of days. The plebiscite is on Saturday."

"Then what? If people say yes, then what happens?"

"Then it goes to the parliament. The bill is tabled in the lower house for Monday. If it passes, it will go up to the Senate, but that's just a formality given the government has a majority in both houses. It'll be law before you know it."

She turned to look at him and it struck him that she was subtly more attractive in VR, a better match for her beautiful hands, slightly taller, slimmer, longer legged. He was subtly better looking too, of course, and for the first time felt a little ashamed of himself, a little embarrassed for Ginny. Such a small, everyday deception, and one he wouldn't have noticed except they'd spent most of their time together so far on minimal aug.

"I don't really know what the bill's about," she said. "I mean, I'm always hearing people going on about being for it or against it, but I don't remember ever hearing any details, just that it's supposed to help government agencies fight terrorists."

"Yeah, well, that's what it's supposed to be about, and it's probably a good thing, really, only there's a few clauses in there that have the civil rights people up in arms – and with good cause."

"Like what?"

Reluctantly, he asked his office librarian for a copy of the bill. He didn't want to spend his time educating someone who couldn't be bothered to check on what her government was asking her to vote on. In his view, people should take the trouble to keep themselves across that stuff. It infuriated him that, when it came to elections, his vote only counted as much as some moron's who watched the news once in a blue moon and didn't even know what the issues were, let alone where they stood on them. But that was democracy for you. Half the country thought whatever the tabloid feeds told them to think.

He tossed her the document. "It's clause 23.b.iii," he said as she picked it up. "Nicely buried where few would bother to look. I forget the wording but it's something to the effect that 'in the national interest' and in matters of 'national security', the government has the right to monitor and filter any information on QNet to prevent the spread of sensitive information, or to modify such information so as to disguise the truth from or to mislead those who might choose to act against the State."

Ginny shrugged. "Sounds OK to me. What's so bad about that?"

He made an effort not to sound as irritated as he felt. "It's the vagueness. The whole thing is wide open to abuse. A filter on the whole QNet? With the government able to change information to suit whatever it thinks is in the national interest? Doesn't that make you the least bit anxious? You do realise that everything goes through QNet these days, newsfeeds, financial transactions, all our aug and VR? Even the parliament itself meets in VR nowadays."

"I think you're overreacting a bit, aren't you? The bill is about stopping terrorists. If the police feel they need more powers to manipulate the information these people are getting, I'm perfectly happy to help them out."

"If I may say so, that's a very naïve position. If you give the government new powers, sooner or later they'll start using them. Maybe not the present government – although I wouldn't put anything past that lot – but maybe the next one, or the next. What if, down the track, a right-wing religious party got in power and they thought it wasn't in the national interest to let atheists become teachers? How would we ever find out if the filter changed every atheist's job application to show they had criminal records for child molestation when the interviewer saw it, but then changed it back again when the applicant looked at it?"

Ginny put the bill down on a table. "Now you're just being silly. And paranoid. Is this why September 10 is against the bill? Or is it just because they're terrorists and they're protecting their own interests?"

Rafe gave up trying. He knew this was a no-win argument, having had it so many times before. Besides, he needed to get Ginny focused on the material on the whiteboards and how they could turn it into something more substantial. "I don't know," he said. "But they've been tracking similar legislation all over the world. It's extremely important to them. Do you know where the name, September 10, comes from?" Perhaps sensing another lecture on its way, Ginny shook her head and looked away. "September 10 was the date of the vote in the US House of Representatives on their own equivalent of that." He tapped the bill on the table.

Ginny frowned. "That's not what I read. Anyway, if they're a US organisation, what are they doing here?"

"Good question. Let's find out." He jumped up and blanked out all the whiteboards. "Time we got an expert opinion." He made a call to the Sentinel office and was routed to Jan, the feed's terrorism specialist. "I've been avoiding making this call," he told Ginny, "but it's time to start shaking things up. Jan? How's it going? That's the way. Look, can you pop into my office for a sec.? I need to pick your brains about something I'm working on. Yes, I'm sorry it's so late, but this will really only take a minute."

A woman appeared at the door, young and pretty, and Rafe let her in. "Jan this is Ginny. Jan is our terrorism expert, aren't you mate?"

Jan looked a bit bewildered. "I wouldn't say expert, exactly." She turned a self-deprecating smile on Ginny. "I've got the Africa desk, so that kind of thing tends to land in my inbox."

"Jan, look, I'm chasing down one of my sordid scandals and someone involved might just possibly have some vague connection to S10. Can you give us a bit of background, like where they come from and why they're operating here in Oz?"

Still looking bemused, Jan said, "Well, they started in the States. Named themselves after the date of some anti-terror legislation—"

"See? I told you she knew her stuff."

Taken aback by the interruption, Jan seemed to lose her train of thought for a moment, then recovered. "They were US only for a couple of years, then the UK voted on a similar bill and they turned up there, blowing up comms towers and hacking worldlets, nothing very serious. They've never hurt anyone directly, but there have been a few indirect casualties – people who couldn't call an ambulance because the local Net was down, that kind of thing. Anyway, suddenly they were all over Europe and then everywhere – a full-blown international terror organisation. No-one's quite sure what their agenda is. I've never seen a coherent manifesto or anything. There was something a few years ago about governments lying and people being duped. The usual rambling kind of stuff. They just seem to be anti-QNet or something. They started operations here a couple of years ago and their activity has definitely ramped up ahead of the big cyberterrorism bill vote. You've probably seen their slogans geotagged all over the place. 'The truth will set you free.' 'Kill us rather than deceive us.' 'Better dead than led.' That kind of thing." She gave a sort of giggle and stopped. She looked at Rafe, waiting for questions.

"Do you have any names?" he asked.

"Not off the top of my head. I'll give you access to the file if you like. There were a lot of arrests in the States and a big trial but that was donkeys' years ago. Is that it?"

Rafe looked at Ginny who shook her head. "Yep, that's it.

Thanks, Jan. See? Didn't take long."

Jan smiled, apologised for not being much help and left, promising to see to that file access as soon as she got back.

"That was your expert?" Ginny asked when they were alone again.

"Well, she knew more than we did. Maybe there'll be something in the file."

Ginny nodded without enthusiasm and sat down, deep in thought.

Rafe brought his whiteboards back to life. In the face of Ginny's obvious disappointment he grew defensive. "I know it's not much yet, but we've got Copplin's stuff and now there's Jan's file. Let's put that together and see where we are then, all right?"

Ginny sighed. "I don't have much option, do I? I can't hide out at Cal's for the rest of my life. And I'd rather be dragged out and shot by the terrorists than spend another three weeks at my parents' house. You're right. The only way past this is through it. What do we do next?"

Chapter 10

Sheets of paper were scattered all over Cal's floor and furniture. After a solid hour of reading, Rafe and Ginny began collating the information they had gleaned. They quickly slipped into a method of working which involved Rafe staying in his office, updating the whiteboards, while Ginny spent most of her time in the real world, shuffling documents into different clusters and popping in to give Rafe an update every few minutes.

Cal's documents were something like Tonia's but all in one hand. They were his own notes, diagrams, message printouts, and feed dumps. One document was a list of places Cal had discovered around the city that had weak or limited QNet coverage. One was a list of online suppliers that were "friendly to the cause" – the cause being S10, Rafe assumed. The suppliers seemed mostly to be electronics and computing shops, although notes beside some of them made it clear they supplied all kinds of other things – including weapons and explosives. There was no doubt that Cal was an active and willing member of Tonia's cell.

When this finally dawned on Ginny, she went and sat in the bedroom on her own for a while, but it wasn't long before she was back. Rafe found it hard to make out his reluctant partner. She was bright enough, and quick, but she had that stultifying naiveté that afflicted almost everyone apart from his fellow journalists and the people they mostly dealt with – politicians, crooked business people, the police, media-hungry celebrities, and out-and-out criminals. Rafe couldn't remember the last time he'd spent so much time in the company of anyone who wasn't either on the make or chasing after people on the make. It wasn't as refreshing or renewing as he might have expected. In fact, it was a bit creepy. It was as if this woman had a part of her brain missing – the part that was always looking for an angle, always trying to outsmart you and use you. It made him feel uncomfortable around her.

As with Tonia's stash, a lot of Cal's documents related to computer systems design. Rafe knew nothing about the subject but knew a man who did. Unfortunately the man lived in Canberra and there was no way to show him the pages without scanning them into his office worldlet – something Rafe was still reluctant to do. He made a mental note to ask Ginny if she knew a computer whiz closer to home. Yet the diagrams and notes were highly suggestive. References to various "security layers", "secure worldlet interface architectures", and "the Parliament worldlet message protocols" made him yearn for more information. The Parliament worldlet in particular could be pure gold. It might be the most secure worldlet in the country, the place in which the Government met. Was there a September 10 plot to disrupt it? He knew hackers tried to bring down the Parliament worldlet all the time. It was a prime target – like the Kremlin and the Capitol worldlets – but to the best of his knowledge, it had never succumbed. Had S10 finally found a way? Hackers in Argentina had brought down their country's parliament once, and kept it down for a week, seriously disrupting the government and leading to a state of emergency being declared. But that was twenty years ago. Surely nothing like that could happen these days?

Still, Rafe set up a new whiteboard he labelled, "Potential Targets" and wrote, "The Parliament worldlet". By the small hours of the morning, the whiteboard still had only one potential target on it. Rafe was standing in his office frowning at it when Ginny came in.

"I'm going to crash," she said. "I've been running on strong coffee for the past couple of hours and it's not helping any more, just making me feel sick."

Here in his office, she looked fresh and immaculately well groomed, of course. But, even a few hours ago when he'd last gone for a pee and seen her crawling about on the floor, shuffling papers into new configurations, she had looked like the living dead. "Yeah. Right. You get your head down. I'll just finish up here and I'll join you." She raised an eyebrow. "Well, not literally, obviously. I meant… Well, you know what I meant."

She nodded towards the whiteboards. "How are we doing?"

It was a hard question to answer. Rafe looked around the room. There were about twenty whiteboards now, some covered in dense scrawl in multiple colours, some almost empty. Did it all amount to a coherent story? He sighed and took the plunge.

"This is what I think. Twelve years ago, the US put up this really crap piece of anti-terror legislation. Ironically, it seems to have brought a new terrorist organisation into being just to fight it."

"September 10."

"Correct. S10 then took on a life of its own, continuing to oppose something or other, even after it had won its case and the legislation had failed. When the UK tried to get up essentially the same thing, it gave S10 a whole new lease on life. It went international and never looked back." He paused. Even Jan had known all that. What had he and Ginny learnt that was new?

"The story gets interesting when Cal Copplin appears. He's a top-notch systems architect from the UK. He's employed by the Brits to design the systems necessary to support the legislation. From what I've seen, he was the head honcho, technical lead for the whole project. I can't make much sense of what his designs mean but they're impressively complicated and it looks like they worked. There are test results and other documents to suggest that they built it and had it ready to roll out. Unfortunately, the bill was defeated and the systems were never deployed. Score two for S10.

"Perhaps Cal was pissed off about that because, just a few months later, he turns up in Australia, applies for citizenship and settles here. The interesting thing is, though, that he took a job as a field technician for a computer company."

"Why is that interesting?"

"Because the guy was a major high-flyer. He would have been over-qualified to be Technical Director of any company in Australia. Instead, he becomes a lowly field engineer. I'm thinking that your friend was either very pissed off indeed, or he was deliberately keeping a low profile." Rafe moved over to the timeline board. "About four years ago, Cal is recruited into S10. That's at the same time the first green papers on the cyberterrorism bill start appearing in Australia. Then, a few weeks away from the vote, he disappears altogether."

Ginny shook her head. "So they're planning something,

probably involving Cal and his specialist knowledge of this kind of security system, and it's all going to happen any day now. Honestly, we don't seem to have got very far. I don't feel the slightest bit safer. Do you?"

Rafe had to admit she was right. "I don't think we can give up though," he said. The energy seemed to drain out of him as if someone had opened a tap in his ankle. "There's lots of other things we can explore."

Tomorrow. He couldn't do any more tonight.

—oOo—

The pain in Rafe's back almost made him cry out as he struggled to sit up after a night spent fighting with the sofa. The blankets he'd found in a cupboard were lying on the floor, having failed miserably to stay on top of him as he tossed and turned. He rubbed his sandpaper jaw and padded blearily to the bathroom to see what Copplin had by way of shaving implements. But the bathroom door was locked and he could hear the shower running.

He felt old and achy and made himself a coffee while pondering the fact that there was a naked, not unattractive woman just a few metres away and he just wished she'd hurry up and get out of the bathroom so he could stand under a hot shower and wash the kinks out of his spine. *Old age*, he told himself, but he knew that wasn't true. His mind veered towards his mutilated, scarred genitalia, and he wrenched it away, angry and scared. Of all the things he didn't need to dwell on right now, his future life of certain celibacy was close to the top of the list. *We can fix you up,* the young doctor in charge of his reconstruction had told him, just a few weeks ago. They'd grow new parts for him, new skin, new muscle

147

tissue. He'd be as good as new. Induced pluripotent cell therapy, the doc had said. No worries.

But Rafe had told them to leave him alone. He'd had enough of being cut up and mutilated. He just wanted to forget about the whole thing. And deep inside him, where his inner voice was muffled and incoherent, some dark part of his psyche wanted to keep the scars, wanted to own them.

"If you don't put it in the cup, it just doesn't work." He jumped and the coffee cube he'd been holding fell from his hand onto the worktop. Ginny stood there in one of Cal's robes, her hair wrapped in a towel, grinning at him. "Earth to Rafe," she said. "Are you always catatonic in the mornings?"

He tried to force a smile but failed. "Do you want one?"

"Oh yeah." She bustled in and moved him aside. "Why don't you let me make it. You look like you're in withdrawal or something. Shit! You're not, are you?"

"No, but thanks for asking. Of all the ways I'm totally fucked up, that is not one of them. I'll be back in a mo." He went to the bathroom and by the time he came out, feeling only marginally better, the drink was steaming on the coffee table, Ginny was dressed, and she was frying bacon and eggs.

The smell made him realise how hungry he was – and the sight of real food frying in a pan gave the morning a strangely exotic feel.

"This Copplin guy must be some kind of throwback. I haven't seen eggs and bacon since I was a kid. I didn't know you could still get them."

"I hope you don't mind everything a bit burnt. I've only ever seen this done in interactives. I've never tried it myself. It's surprisingly tricky."

"It's supposed to be really bad for you," Rafe said, as the plate of scorched eggs and bacon was handed to him. There were fringe types who swore that only genuine food, from plants and animals, was safe and healthy, but Rafe had seen documentaries on modern food production and it seemed clear to him that the more control you had over what went into your food, the more certain you could be that there was nothing dangerous in there. Even so, the smells and flavours that filled his head as he put the first forkful into his mouth made him wonder if health and safety were the only concerns you should have about the food you ate.

"So what's our plan for today?" Ginny asked.

He looked up at her to see whether she was joking but she seemed genuinely to trust that he would know what to do. It was a little bit scary.

"We're going to visit a computer specialist," he said.

"OK."

"Only I don't know any. Not in Brisbane, anyway. What about you?"

"What? Do I know any computer specialists?"

"Yeah. You must know somebody. Someone who could look at Cal's documents and tell us what they mean."

"You know I'm a musician, right?"

"Yes, but you must know somebody. What about those companies you do soundscapes for? They build worldlets, don't they?"

Ginny looked uncomfortable, a forkful of bacon half-way to her mouth. "Well, yes, but…"

"So they must have computer guys. Good ones. Can't you call one of them and ask around?"

"Well I could, I suppose, but…"

"But what?"

"Well, they're my customers. I don't want to scare them off by turning up with a pile of terrorist documents and some wild story about disappearing people and murderers on the loose."

Rafe put his fork down and gave her a look. "Seriously? You're worried about losing some work when we're trying to save our necks – and prevent a terror attack on the parliament?"

Ginny pressed the heel of her hand into her forehead as she grappled with her dilemma. Rafe already knew she was hard up and her business wasn't doing well, but she still seemed to be having more trouble making the decision than he thought she should. When she finally looked up she said, "All right. All right. There is a company I know that's big enough to have some good techs." She pushed her breakfast away from her, obviously no longer interested. "Give me a few minutes to set it up." She lay down on the sofa and zoned out. Rafe finished his breakfast, along with Ginny's bacon, and took the plates to the kitchen. He had barely begun to fathom the mysteries of the dishwasher – everything he ate came on disposable plates, or was fed into his body through his tank's drips – when Ginny sat up and scowled at him.

"Everything set up?" he asked. Her scowl intensified. "What? Are we good to go?"

"Yes," she snapped and set about putting the paper documents into a neat enough heap to stuff back into the folder.

Rafe thought about demanding what the hell was wrong with her, but left it alone. He picked up the silver tube and the black box from the worktop and studied them. Maybe the computer guy could say what they were. Ginny pushed past him, grabbed up the gun and the spare clips and thrust them into her pockets.

"You weren't going to take it, were you?" she said. "I've seen the way you keep looking at it sideways, like it's going to jump up and shoot you. It scares the shit out of you. Well, maybe you haven't had one pushed in your face lately. The next time we meet Tonia, or Richards, or whoever's lurking out there waiting to kill us, I'm not going to be completely bloody helpless."

Her lips were hard and thin, her eyes glinted at him as if the whole damned business was his fault. He felt an answering anger surge inside him but he kept himself from snapping back. "Is it far?"

"What?"

"Is it far to your customer's premises? Is that where we're going?"

She looked at him as if he was stupid. "We're going to see their Deputy Engineer. We'd be off to see the Chief Engineer, only he lives in Ballarat and I don't fancy travelling two thousand kilometres. Luckily the Deputy is just the kind of nerd we need and she lives in Stanthorpe. That's just two hundred and fifty K away. We can be there in four hours. I ordered a taxi."

Rafe shook his head, despairing at his own idiocy. Of course there was no reason why this company Ginny knew would have any physical premises anywhere, let alone in Brisbane, or that any of its employees would be anywhere except in their tanks at home during working hours, or that any of them would happen to live in the same State. They were lucky to find someone so close. He just hadn't made the adjustment yet to this fugitive life of doing everything in physical reality. It was like living in the twentieth century or something, except worse, because at least then they had trains and buses and private cars. Once you were outside the civilised world of unlatched VR and tanks, you might as well be living in the outback without a personal flyer. A smile slowly spread across his face. Now why didn't he think of that sooner?

—oOo—

They took the cab to the Transit Centre and rode the lift to the roof. There they found a row of quadcopters waiting for customers. Rafe tried to ignore the hire rates appearing in his aug as he led Ginny over to a two-seater and flipped open the canopy. Becky was going to kill him – figuratively, he hoped – but that was tomorrow's problem. He might be out of a job, but at least he'd be alive. With any luck.

"Can you fly one of these?" Ginny asked, hesitating.

"They fly themselves. Get in. I've always wanted to try one."

The virtual display popped up as he sat down. It had maps and indicators of various kinds, and a big red button labelled 'Start Engines'. Beneath the label was the small print about how starting up the machine was deemed acceptance of the terms and conditions and charges. He hit the button and saw a large sum of money disappear from his company expense account.

Ginny was in her seat and scrabbling for her safety harness. "For God's sake don't let it take off before I'm strapped in."

The canopy dropped into place, cutting out much of the rising whine of the four rotors. He told the machine where they were going and a gratifying 'destination accepted' sign came up. "Here we go," he said, raising his voice as the engine and rotor noise grew louder. He felt the whole machine thrumming with power. The four rotors, each on a gantry extending from the corners of the cockpit, lifted from the ground into their flight configuration and the machine began to tremble as if it was as excited as Rafe and as keen to be airborne. And then, as smoothly as the lift they just been in, the quadcopter surged into the air. Ginny clutched the arms of her seat with her eyes screwed shut, but Rafe felt the exhilaration of soaring into the air above the rooftops of Brisbane.

The little flyer kept going up until Rafe could see the ocean out to the west and the hills to the east. The altimeter read two thousand metres dead when the fans tipped and they began to creep forward, heading south, rapidly picking up speed. There wasn't another aircraft in the whole sky and, looking up, Rafe lost all sense of motion, all sense of direction. He floated in the depths of the blue sky like a disembodied spirit. The whine and tremble of the quadcopter only serving to shake him loose of the planet below.

"Now I know why they don't put windows in airplanes," Ginny said, breaking the spell. She still hung onto the seat arms despite the smoothness of the ride, but at least now she was looking around.

"Isn't it great?" Rafe asked, partly to tease her and partly because it was how he felt. He glanced at the instruments. Their groundspeed was already close to a hundred and fifty kilometres an hour and they were racing over the outer suburbs of the sprawling city below. "We'll be there in no time."

Ginny said nothing, just stared out at the ground below as if she expected it to rush up and slap her. Rafe amused himself by poking around at the quadcopter's controls, to see what he might be able to make it do. After a while Ginny lay back in her seat and closed her eyes again.

"No good deed goes unpunished, I suppose," she said.

"Meaning what?"

"Meaning if I hadn't done that little favour for a friend, I wouldn't be dangling in mid-air waiting for a rotor to fail."

Rafe wasn't buying it. "You knew what you were doing was probably illegal. And he wasn't just a friend. You fancied him and you willingly got yourself into this. So don't sit there trying to convince me what a martyr you are."

For a moment, she glared at him, then looked away. "Shit, I'm turning into my mother."

"Women have a habit of doing that."

"Yeah? Well not me. I always thought I'd turn into my dad. My mum's a complete drama queen. Everything's about her. Everyone around her gets sucked into her ongoing production of the Great Cheryl Galton Show. The fact is, she needs constant attention. If there wasn't someone there to feed her need she'd just vanish in a puff of smoke. That's why she glommed onto my dad. He's the exact opposite. If he wasn't attending to the Queen twenty-four seven, he wouldn't know what to do with himself. He wouldn't know who he was any more."

Rafe was only mildly interested, still exploring the flyer's user manual. "But you identified with your dad?"

"When I was little. I thought he was the sane and sensible one. I used to feel sorry for him that my mum made his life such a misery. I used to try to help him out. We had, like, a little conspiracy going. The oppressed majority. It wasn't until I'd dated a handful of needy, grasping, life-sucking blokes that I realised being like my dad wasn't what I wanted."

She fell silent for a moment, gazing out at the fields and towns sliding past below them. Rafe applied himself to the instruction book but Ginny started speaking again. "I thought I'd finally broken the cycle with Cal. I thought I might have found a grown up relationship at last, one that didn't involve neurotic grasping or giving. Turns out the bastard was playing me all along." She gave a bitter laugh. "Same game, really. He took, I gave."

Rafe, hearing the misery in her voice, realised he'd have to comfort her or distract her. He chose the latter. "See that range of mountains ahead?" You could hardly miss the line of forest-clad hills marching across the horizon from north to south, rising precipitately from the gently rolling farmland over which they were passing. He looked across at her. "I think we–"

The sight of the wet streaks down her face brought him to a dead stop. She turned her face away.

"I'm sorry," he said, although he wasn't sure why. He didn't know this woman and he had no idea why she was sitting there, silently weeping. Why had the sight stabbed him with a pang of guilt? "I didn't know you and Cal were, you know, serious."

She shook her head, still looking away. "It's not that. It wasn't serious. Not really. It's… It's just me. My life. Everything is so screwed."

"You've been upset ever since you set up this meeting." At least he'd noticed that.

She sighed. "I worked myself ragged while I was at my parent's place, putting in a bid for some work for a company called WorldEnough."

"Isn't that the company this guy were going to see works for?"

"Yep. I asked the development manager if we could talk to his guy and he said he was going to give me the contract. It had been through the review panel and I was streets ahead of the competition, he said. So he didn't want me talking to his tech guys before the winner was announced because, if any of the other bidders got wind of it, they'd be able to say I had unfair access during the evaluation period. He wanted me to wait until after the announcement in a few weeks' time." Rafe could already see where this was going but he let her finish. "I said I couldn't wait. I had to talk to someone now. Today. He said fine, but it was one or the other. If I talked to the tech, I'd have to withdraw from the bidding process. He wouldn't budge, even though he was urging me to just wait a while. So I insisted and I recorded my official withdrawal right there in his office."

"Jeez, this is the job you were telling me about that would save you from going broke, isn't it? Don't you know any other companies?"

"WorldEnough is the biggest and the best. They're the only ones I'd trust." She flopped back in her seat and closed her eyes. "God, I'm stupid!"

Rafe took her hand and leaned closer. "No you're not. It was a big sacrifice, but there was nothing else you could do. If we don't sort this out, we're dead. I'm almost certainly going to lose my job too over this, as soon as my editor sees the expenses claim. But we have to see this through, Ginny. There's nothing else we can do."

He thought maybe he'd helped her get it in perspective. Yes, her professional life had taken a bad knock, but that was better than being dead or a fugitive. She looked at him, wide eyes brimming with tears and then her face crumpled. She grabbed at him, clumsily pulling him into a hug, and wailed into his shoulder, "And my Dad's losing his job. And he's sixty."

Chapter 11

Stanthorpe was a sprawling town of the sort that might once have been called a regional centre, in a time when regions mattered. Just eighty years ago it had been a sleepy town of two thousand souls making a marginal living from tourism and the surrounding fruit farms and vineyards. When the climate-driven mass migrations had begun, a few decades later, the town had become a favourite spot for Asian refugees to settle. There had been a brief but glorious boom time for the fast-expanding settlement that had stopped when the Immigration Control Act had slammed the country's doors. By then, Australia's population had doubled and Stanthorpe's population levelled off at around forty thousand.

The quadcopter found itself a landing spot on top of what had once been a multi-storey car park – now converted to housing units. Rafe and Ginny left their flyer ticking and cooling in the weak Autumn sunshine and took the stairs down to the ground. They were latched to the town's systems, following directions on foot to the home of Kelly Anh, Ginny's contact.

It was cold, ten degrees cooler than Brisbane, and neither of them was dressed for it. Partly to distract himself from the weather, Rafe did his best to keep up some kind of conversation, but Ginny had fallen into silence not long after her mid-air outburst. At the risk of starting the tears again, he said, "Look, I'm sorry about your father. What does your mother do? Can they live off one salary?"

Ginny snorted. "Mum's an artist." She struck a pose as she said it that implied melodrama, intensity and self-obsession. "She had an exhibition once, before I was born. Since then the 'establishment' has worked hard to ensure that she never sold another piece. That's her story anyway. Sometimes it's just that Australians are so narrow minded and can't appreciate her work." She rolled her eyes. "She has the kind of talent that can only thrive on a global stage, you see. We're all too parochial for her."

"Is her stuff any good?"

"I don't know. She smashed half of it and locked the rest up in the garage in a big tantrum when I was little. Her 'breakdown', Dad calls it but, trust me, I was there; it was just a big tanty. Even as a kid I could see she had me well outclassed in that area. She hasn't made a thing since, but she sneaks down to the garage now and then to brood." Ginny herself brooded in silence for a moment. "Of course, even at the time of her famous exhibition, the days of people making art out of real stuff were long gone. She just never seemed to see that no-one wanted it any more. They wanted things to decorate their virtual worlds and brighten up their aug. Have you ever seen a piece of physical art?"

"Just mouldy old statues in parks and such – if you turn off your aug you can still find them."

"Even the Mona Lisa isn't real any more." From her tone, Rafe guessed Ginny was disputing with her crazy mother rather than with him. "They stuck it in a vault sixty years ago. I've heard they don't even remember where they put it. Last time I was in the Louvre, I went to see it. You can pick it up, examine it, magnify it, get tons of commentary and analysis. Hell, you can lick the bugger if you like. What's the point of physical art when you've got access like that from the comfort of your own tank?"

"This is it."

"What?"

"We're here. Kelly Ahn's place."

Rafe turned down his aug to minimum and looked around. They were in a street that looked as run down and decayed as any other. The delivery truck traffic was light. There were single storey houses lining the road in both directions but the building they had stopped outside was a huge, blocky, brick-built edifice with an imposing arched doorway. An old church, he guessed, built at the turn of the century by one of those well-heeled protestant splinter religions that had flourished back then. A flock of huge black birds wheeled overhead, featureless silhouettes against the blue sky. Short-necked and long-tailed they flapped their giant wings lazily, keening like flying reptiles from a distant epoch. He looked back at the street without bothering to query what the birds were. There was no-one in sight so he stepped up to the door and pressed the buzzer.

It took a long time but a woman eventually appeared. Kelly Ahn was dishevelled and flustered. Her overall needed cleaning and her black hair could have been a nest for the giant birds outside. Ginny stepped up and introduced herself.

"Yeah, yeah, yeah," the engineer said, waving aside Ginny's half-finished explanation. "Derek said you'd be coming. I didn't expect you'd turn up in your meat. Come in, come in."

Ahn's manner was brusque and she spoke fast in

159

Mandarin Chinese. It took Rafe's implants a moment to cut in with the translation but his software soon caught up, suppressing her real voice and substituting a very good imitation. She led them through an entry hall into the main body of her home – a vast space of bare brick walls, arched windows and, at one end, a ten-metre tall crucifix behind a stone altar. Looking up, he realised there was a clear ceiling not far above him, suspended on fine wires from the vaulted roof high above.

Ahn must have seen him looking. "Gotta have a ceiling in a place like this or you'd freeze to death in the winter," she said.

"Are you religious?" he asked, wondering why anyone would want to live in a place like that at any time of the year.

"Sure! I worship the Holy Dollar." She laughed as if she'd made a great joke. "Come on. We'll go to my lounge room and talk." She led them past an area full of comms racks and servers, and then another full of benches piled with electronics junk. They passed a carpeted section in which two small children were being tended by nannybots. The kids stopped screeching briefly and stared warily at the strangers as they moved past.

"OK, what's this all about?" Ahn asked as they reached another carpeted area with chairs and sofas. She waved them at the seating and called to a dombot to fetch them coffees and cakes. The little machine scurried off and Ahn took a seat. From Rafe's perspective, she was sitting right below the giant crucifix, the ancient symbol looming above her like a warning.

Ginny started thanking the woman for her help and her hospitality but Rafe didn't want to waste time. He spoke across his companion. "We've got some documents we'd like you to look at."

Ahn studied him for a moment, probably reading his credentials, then turned to Ginny. "Derek never said anything about a reporter."

"Rafe's a friend of mine," Ginny said. "He's helping me out. These documents are from another friend. One who's gone missing. We think they may have something to do with the design of the Parliament worldlet."

Again, the engineer said nothing. Finally, she nodded. "OK, upload them and I'll take a look."

"We can't do that," said Rafe and took the sheaf of papers out of his bag. "That's why we had to come in person."

"First meat, now tree pulp," said Ahn. She got up and walked over to Rafe, took the documents, and sat down again, flicking through them. "Is any of this legal?"

Ginny opened her mouth to speak but again, Rafe cut her off. "We don't know. We'd like your opinion on the software designs. We need to know what they're for."

Ahn looked at him and then back at the documents. "Come back in an hour."

Ginny leaned forward, ready to stand up. "No," said Rafe. "We can't let those documents out of our sight. You can't copy them or scan them to QNet. It wouldn't be safe to do that."

Ahn stood up and handed the sheaf back to Rafe. "I think it's time you left."

Rafe made no move to take the documents back. "Kelly, you already know too much. There are people who would kill you if they found out you'd seen those pages. And don't think of calling the police. You don't want to be a suspect in a terrorist investigation. What would your kids do while you were being held without trial for three months?"

The engineer looked at Ginny. "Does Derek know why you're here? Does he have any clue what you're into?"

Ginny shook her head, looking ashamed. She glanced back at the two children, perhaps realising for the first time that she had put the whole family in danger. "I'm sorry. There was no-one else we could turn to. We're not criminals. We're not terrorists. We just got into this by accident. If you could just look at the papers and tell us what they mean, we might be able to find a way out of this without getting killed, or arrested. Please help us."

Without a word, Ahn walked over to a table, slapped the sheaf of documents down and leaned over it, lips pursed. "OK," she said. "OK. I'll take a look. A quick look. Then you two get out of here and fuck off back to wherever you came from. Deal?"

"Deal," said Rafe. "Just one more thing, though." He got up and joined her at the table. He took the metal cylinder and the black box out of his pockets and put them carefully down beside the documents. "We need to know what these two gizmos do as well."

Chapter 12

They walked back to the flyer together, hunched up against the cold, Stanthorpe wind. The sky had clouded over while they were with Kelly Ahn and rain was threatening. Rafe did not like the idea of walking around wet in that icy wind.

"I should go back and thank her again," Ginny said.

"For what? Anyway, you thanked her enough."

"What's she going to say to Derek, do you think?"

"Look, if you think there's any way they'll give you a contract after this, you must be off your head."

She sighed, looking miserable. "She thinks we're terrorists. She'll probably call the police."

Rafe didn't think so. "She knows better than that. She's not stupid."

"She said the designs showed where to attack the Parliament worldlet. She said they sketched out ideas for bypassing the security."

"And she was smart enough not to ask how we'd come across them, or what we intended to do with them."

His companion was a huddled ball of misery as they trudged along, following the bright green arrows through the darkening cold. He could feel unhappiness radiating from her.

"At least we know what these are now," he said, holding out the cylinder and the box.

It had taken Ahn no time at all to work it out. She took the back off the box, peered inside, shut it up again, handed the cylinder to Ginny, and pressed the button. The world went crazy. The inside of the old church became a wild jungle. Sounds and scents assailed Rafe. He couldn't see anyone else, the undergrowth was so thick. He shouted out in alarm and suddenly the world was normal again. Kelly Ahn's two children started crying and the nannybots whirled about them.

"It generates some kind of mass hallucination," Rafe had said, recovering from the shock.

"But not for you, eh?" Ahn had said to Ginny. Rafe looked at the cylinder in Ginny's hand as understanding dawned.

"You've seen these before?" he asked Ahn.

"Heard about them. Crims use them. Makes robbing a bank easy if everyone else is seeing things that you're not."

"We're not crims," Ginny had said.

In reply, Ahn had looked pointedly at the bulge in Ginny's overall where the handgun sat heavily in her pocket.

"I should go back and explain," Ginny muttered, trudging into the biting wind. "I should tell her everything."

"You'd only put her in more danger than she's in already."

They walked in silence. When they reached the building with their flyer on the roof, Ginny said she needed a pee.

"Well, there isn't anywhere." Rafe had grown grumpy and resentful from listening to her unreasonable whining and the unrelenting cold wind. "You should have gone before we left like I did."

"I didn't want to go then."

"Well good luck finding a public toilet around here. Just find an alley or something. I'm going up to get in the flyer before I die of exposure. You can join me at your leisure." He pushed ahead into the building, leaving Ginny standing in the street looking helpless.

The wind on the roof was stronger and colder than it had been at street level. Rafe broke into a jog at the sight of the flyer and the expectation of relief. He'd gone just a few paces when a man stepped out from behind a water tank and quickly moved to stand between Rafe and the quadcopter. Rafe stopped dead.

The stranger waited, keeping his eyes on Rafe. He was a young man, late teens maybe, but tall and broad. He had a look of contempt on his face and his eyes were still and calm. There was no shred of doubt in Rafe's mind that the man was there for him. His insides turned to water. His heart pounded in his chest. A footfall behind him made his head twitch round. A second man had appeared, as young as the first, but bigger, standing between him and the stairwell.

The fear made Rafe's head swim. "Oh Jesus," he said. A kind of prayer. He'd been hurt too much. He couldn't take it again. He held out his bag of documents. "Here. This is what you want." He threw it to the first man but it fell well short, sliding across the tarmac roof. "Just take it. I don't want anything to do with it. I won't write the story. I won't say a fucking word. Just… Just don't hurt me."

Still the two men said nothing. Rafe knew it was hopeless. They were going to beat him, kill him, make him tell them everything he knew, name everyone who had helped him. He looked about for a way of escape. There were two quadcopters on the roof now. His own and the one these men must have arrived in. Why hadn't he seen it as soon as he came out of the stairwell? How could he have missed a bloody great flyer?

He made an effort to compose himself. He was panting, he realised, every muscle taut. He needed to run. He couldn't let them catch him. His stomach was so knotted it hurt. The man in front of him took a step, then another.

And Rafe was running. He didn't remember starting but he was sprinting across the tarmac. He reached the knee-high wall that ran around the whole roof before he dare look around. The first man was vectoring across to cut him off and the second was following behind. He glanced over the wall at the wide street beyond and the dizzying, six-storey drop. He felt sick, hopeless. He stopped running and his pursuers slowed to a walk. He climbed up onto the wall. It was barely wider than the length of his feet. The empty space in front of and below him seemed to suck at him, making him teeter.

"Don't come any closer," he yelled, not daring to turn around, not daring to move at all. He could not hear their footsteps but the wind blustering in his ears made it hard to hear anything. "If you touch me, I'll jump." And he would. He meant it. *I should have died in Melbourne*, he thought. At the time he'd prayed for death, longed for release. Everything since then had been borrowed time. He looked up at the grey sky and thought about stepping out. It would take so little and yet would change everything so profoundly.

"Go ahead and jump you fuckwit," one of the men said. "Save us the trouble of pushing you."

"Shut up, dickhead," the other said. His voice was an angry snarl. This one was in charge and he didn't want Rafe swan diving onto the pavement. It did not comfort Rafe that they wanted him alive.

"Get down from there," the boss said. "We only want to talk to you."

"Don't come near me," Rafe shouted through clenched teeth. He was shivering in the wind and he didn't know how long he could stay up there on that wall. He didn't know what to do. If they touched him, he'd jump. He knew that.

"We're just here to warn you off," the boss said. He was trying to sound reasonable but Rafe could hear the lie. "You don't have to do this, mate. We're all reasonable men."

"Yeah, just keep your nose out of Consortium business," the second man said. "Then you can walk away with all your fucking body parts still attached."

The boss was not happy with the interjection. "Will you keep your fucking trap shut? Or do I have to cut your fucking tongue out?"

"I was just trying to–"

"Shut up!"

After that yell of rage, the boss seemed to need a few seconds to compose himself. Rafe didn't care. They were going to kill him. They'd try something soon and then he could jump and it would all be over. Everything would be over.

"Look, Rafe… That's a bloody stupid name if you don't mind me saying, mate."

"Up yours," Rafe said. "Go fuck yourself."

"We just want to talk, Rafe. We want to know what you know, who else is in on it, if you're working for someone, that kind of thing. Just a few questions, that's all. After that, you can go on your w–"

Rafe heard a quick rush of footsteps. *This is it. It's happening.* He closed his eyes, feeling his body sway.

There was a grunt and the sound of a weight falling. Then

a shot. He jerked, shocked. He hadn't thought that they might shoot him. He reached with his mind to where the pain must be and didn't find it. Would he be dead before he hit the ground? There were more steps. Someone running. Another shot. He turned to look and lost his balance, toppling over into the void, arms flailing.

Then Ginny caught him and yanked him back.

He twisted and fell onto the roof. Ginny let go of him and bent down, fumbling for the gun that was lying there. One of Rafe's attackers lay on the ground in a heap. Ginny lifted the gun in both hands, pointing it across the roof to the stairwell, and fired it twice. Twice more, he realised. Ginny had jumped those two thugs single handedly. He goggled at her, not yet able to take it all in. She cursed and turned to face him.

"Are you OK?" she asked.

"I… I…"

"He got away," she said, glancing back at the stairwell.

Rafe was still on the ground. He tried to move towards the fallen man but his arms were trembling and his legs wouldn't work. "Is he alive? Did you…?" There was blood pooling under the man's head, but not much. If she'd shot him in the head, surely there would be more.

Ginny walked over to the man, pointing her gun at him. "I don't know," she said, her voice shaky. "I hit him from behind. With this." She lifted the gun briefly. "I hit him as hard as I could. Would that kill him?"

Rafe nodded although Ginny wasn't looking at him. He tried to get up and this time found he could manage it. "They were from the Consortium," he said. He glanced back at the edge of the roof. Had he really been about to jump? It already seemed incredible.

Ginny put a foot against the man's shoulder and pushed

him. He stirred and groaned. Ginny jumped back, gun aimed at him, holding it desperately, as if it were a charm against evil. But the young man did not wake up. "He's alive," she said, almost a cry of triumph. "And I didn't hit the other one." She seemed to feel exonerated of some charge that Rafe had not made. She had fired four shots, two of them probably at close range, and had missed every time. It seemed to Rafe that the survival of either man was pure good luck. "We need to find out what the Consortium is," he said, trying to stay focused.

But first they needed to get off that rooftop. Every building, inside and out, every street, every field and farm had sensors of all kinds, all feeding their data into the local networks, all feeding the augmented reality that the world lived and worked within. Without doubt, the sensorium had picked up the gunshots, identified them for what they were, triangulated them, and fed the location to the local police. They could only hope that the nearest police officers were a long way off and would take a while to arrive.

"We could bring him round and ask him. Make him tell us," Ginny said, sounding queasy at the idea.

Rafe shook his head. No, he couldn't do that. Never that.

"Come on," he said. "Let's just go. We should just get out of here."

Ginny nodded and they moved away from the fallen man, watching him, moving slowly. When they were a few metres away, the hold he seemed to have on them weakened and they looked towards the flyer, began to hurry. Ginny made a beeline for it, her distaste for the machine seemingly over.

Rafe took a detour to his attackers' quadcopter, grabbing up the bag of documents on the way. Even latched, the flyer bore no markings, no company logo, no registration number.

He opened the cockpit and looked inside. It was bigger and more luxuriously appointed than the rental he and Ginny had hired. It smelled new. He poked around in pockets and cupboards but found nothing to identify its owners. He stepped out of it and saw Ginny sitting in the other flyer, watching him anxiously. The very least he should do was to disable the machine.

The wall that ran around the roof was brick with concrete coping stones on top. He ran over to it and pulled at the nearest coping stone, a flat slab of concrete as long as his arm but not very wide or deep. The crumbling mortar gave way easily and he soon had it free. He dragged it back to the quadcopter, it was too heavy for him to carry for more than a couple of seconds. He leaned it against one of the rotor cowlings to get his breath.

Immediately an alarm sounded from the machine and a loud voice in his aug said, "This machine is the property of the Rice Consortium. Any damage to this machine will be reported immediately to the police and could result in a criminal prosecution."

Rafe stood back in surprise and almost laughed out loud. After all his searching it had been that easy. A yell from Ginny made him look up. She was pointing the gun back towards the stairwell where the second of Rafe's attackers and two friends he'd found somewhere were emerging onto the roof. With an adrenaline fuelled heave, he lifted the heavy concrete block and let it fall onto the rotor, crushing several of the blades and knocking the plastic cowling sideways. There was no way they would be flying that quadcopter without a replacement part.

A shot exploded from the other flyer and ricocheted off the roof. He bent low and ran to join Ginny.

"What the hell were you doing?" she demanded as he climbed in. She fired the gun again, shooting across him. His ears rang and he yelled at the machine to get them airborne. The canopy began to close over them and Ginny yelled, "No! Don't close it or I can't shoot them."

"It won't take off if we don't let it close the canopy," Rafe said, feeling her fear, looking around for the three youths. They had spread out and were closing in on the flyer. Ginny fired off a last shot before the lid closed and one of the men twisted around and fell over.

"Shit! I hit one. Oh my God. Is he all right?" She looked like she might try to climb out to check on him. The flyer's struts lifted from their parked position and the rotors whirled into motion. He glanced out of the canopy at their pursuers. The shooting of one of them had sent the other two running for cover, but the wounded man was shouting from the ground and signalling towards the other flyer. Rafe prayed he'd done enough damage to keep it on the ground.

"He's all right!" Ginny shouted, clutching Rafe's arm.

"Like I give a shit. What is wrong with this bloody thing?" The rotors were whining and the flyer trembled. He could feel the machine coiling itself to spring into the air, but it didn't take off. He thumped the side of the cockpit and scanned through the virtual displays. Everything was fine, no warnings, no squawking alarms. Why wouldn't the damned thing move?

"Uh oh," Ginny said and he looked up. The two men at the other flyer had given up trying to make it start and were climbing out.

"Put the canopy up so we can shoot them," Ginny shouted.

Rafe shook his head. Sitting up there on the roof shooting

people while the police made their way to arrest them made no sense at all. He focused on the instruments again. Had the two thugs who'd jumped him sabotaged it in some way? Some insanely, improbably subtle way? He gritted his teeth. It had to be something he'd done, or hadn't done.

"They're coming," Ginny said. "What the hell are you doing? Take off! Now!" A young man appeared beside Rafe, pounding on the canopy with the pommel of a large hunting knife.

"If you think you could do any bloody better, just—"

He saw it. A small prompt saying, "State your destination," patiently waiting for him to tell it one. "Brisbane, for fuck's sake, you fucking stupid pile of junk. Brisbane. Take us to Brisbane!"

"Thank you," said the little prompt and the flyer whooshed up into the air.

—oOo—

They landed in Anzac Park, near Cal Copplin's home after Rafe had struggled with the flyer and it's handbook for most of the four hour flight home. Anzac Park was not a designated landing site and Rafe had to convince the vehicle they had a medical emergency before it would let him take manual control. Ginny had closed her eyes and whimpered as Rafe steered the aircraft down between the trees onto the grass. As soon as his feet were on solid ground again, he turned and kicked the stubborn machine and told it just what he thought of its design and its designers. Then they left it to ponder these home truths and walked back to Cal's apartment. As they came out of the little park, they heard its engines start up and turned to see the quadcopter rise up above the treetops. It made a beeline for the city centre and the Transit Centre roof where it had so wanted to take them and where Rafe suspected his attackers or their friends might be waiting.

They sat in silence, staring at the food cooling in front of them.

"I don't think we can stay here any more," Ginny said. Rafe nodded, not really paying her much attention. "I mean they're bound to come looking for us soon. They're bound to think of this place."

He nodded again. What he really needed to do right now was get back to Canberra. He had friends there and places to hide out. It had been bad enough when the police and the terrorists were the only people trying to catch him. Now there was a third group, the Rice Consortium – whoever the hell they were – and they not only seemed more efficient at finding him, but rather more direct in their methods of dealing with people they didn't like.

"That was a complete waste of a day," Ginny said. "We nearly got ourselves killed and I lost my big break with WorldEnough. And all for what? Just to confirm what we already suspected."

Rafe lost the thread of his thoughts and blamed it on Ginny's whining tone. What did she know about conducting an investigation anyway? Of course you verified your suspicions. You verified everything. That's how you knew you were writing the truth and not some load of old rubbish. He shook his head, irritated with himself. This wasn't a story – not any more – this was Rafe Morgan trying to stay alive.

"Can't the Sentinel help us?" Ginny asked. "I mean, they must have reporters in trouble all the time. Don't they have safe houses or private security or something? Why don't you call them?"

God! Was this woman stupid or what? "Because it's a bloody news feed, not the CIA. It's just a bunch of people, like Becky and Jan and…and me." He stood up, agitated. He wanted to be alone. He wanted to be safe. "I've got to get back to Canberra," he said. He pointed to the door. "Anyone could walk in here at any minute."

"That's great," said Ginny, also standing. "Yesterday you were doing your best to keep me here to help with you bloody investigation. Today you want to turn tail and run. Well what happened to 'The only way past this is through it'?"

"You don't understand." He tried to walk away from her but she followed him.

"Enlighten me then. How do you go from man of resolve to quivering jelly in twenty-four hours? I saw you on that rooftop today. You were going to jump. If I hadn't come to your rescue, you wouldn't even be here now. The bots would still be scrubbing you off the pavement. Now you think you're off to Canberra and leaving me behind. Well, think again Brainiac. You owe me." She poked him in the shoulder. "Do you hear? You owe me."

"What do I owe you? What the hell do you think I can do for you now?" She scowled at him, clearly ready to argue with anything he said. *OK, crazy lady, try this.* "The police don't want to catch us. If they did, they'd have us by now. My guess is they're hanging us out there like bait, waiting to see who snaps us up. The terrorists aren't after us either. For them we're just pawns – well, I am anyway. They want me to write the story." He waved a hand at the bag of documents. "They want me to put all that crap out on the Net. And it is crap, I bet. Hints and suggestions, a few names that everybody already knows, all pointing at some terrible plot that probably doesn't even exist. September 10 wants to use me for God knows what. That's their only interest in me. You, they don't care about at all."

Ginny's angry scowl had become a puzzled frown. "So who – ?"

"The Consortium! That's who your friend Dover Richards is working for. That's who's been tracking us." He corrected himself. "Tracking me. Again, you're a bloody irrelevance. The Consortium doesn't want me writing the story. This is all some kind of game between September 10 and the Rice Consortium, and I'm piggy in the middle, with the bloody police cheering from the sidelines. And you, you're just running around like some stupid mascot in a chicken suit confusing everything."

Ginny gaped at him. The hurt look in her eyes just made him more angry.

"You were a pawn once," he told her. "But now you're just noise on the channel. You should go home. I should go home." He stepped past her and began collecting up his things. Ginny remained where she was, staring at the wall. It was all so clear to him now. The only way he could be safe would be in a crowd. He had to get all of the September 10 documents into the public domain and then surround himself with people, night and day. He'd call Becky and get that organised. He needed people to meet him at the airport. Real, physical people. They'd only take him if he was alone. They wouldn't dare show up if he was with people.

"So you're just running away?" Ginny said. "You're just

turning tail and running?"

"Yes, I am. Goodbye."

"I didn't think you were such a coward."

He gritted his teeth. "Well you were wrong. I am. Yellow to the core."

She shook her head. Quietly, she said, "No you're not."

Anger boiled up in him. He threw down his bag and turned to confront her. "What the hell do you know? You saw me up on that roof. I was pissing myself with fear. I would have jumped. I would have." He choked up and couldn't say any more.

"I read about what happened to you in Melbourne," she said, her voice so gentle it felt like a knife in his chest. "I saw the clips of the police bringing you out of that man's house, the state you were in. I heard about what that psychopath did to you. It was a miracle you survived."

"What are you talking about?" He was remembering too, now. Why was she going on about it? What relevance did any of that have?

"I heard what the police said, afterwards, that you'd held out long enough for them to save that girl. That you'd sacrificed yourself and endured the most horrible mutilation…"

She seemed to be choking on her words too. But she couldn't see what he saw in his memories. She couldn't see him screaming and begging, thrashing like the wounded animal he had been, willing to say anything that would make the torture stop. Wanting to say it, pleading to be allowed to condemn and incriminate anyone and everyone to make that endless pain go away.

"I've heard you whimpering in your sleep," she said. He saw a tear roll down her cheek and realised he too was crying.

"I've caught glimpses of your scars. I've seen how you hide them, sensed your shame. But you were a hero. You held out long enough to save that girl. You did what almost none of us could have done."

He shook his head. It was all wrong. He'd held out at first, but he wasn't that Rafe Morgan any more. That man had died in that awful room. One of those cuts had killed him. The man who inhabited this mutilated body couldn't have held out for two seconds. He felt himself sobbing, felt himself sink to his knees, cover his face. That other man had held out and held out until the knives had shredded his resistance, cut out his heart, sliced his brain to sushi, and left him a snivelling, screaming creature, unable to comprehend how such pain could go on for so long, thinking of nothing but how to make it stop. In the end, not thinking at all, just longing for death to come soon.

He felt Ginny's hand touch his shoulder and he jerked away from it.

"Rafe, I didn't mean to… I was only trying to say…" She sounded shocked at what she'd done.

He rolled onto the floor, pulling his legs up into his chest, burying his head. He wanted her to go. He didn't want anyone to see him. He wanted to be alone with his pain, with the dreadful, unbearable shame of knowing himself.

—oOo—

When Rafe woke up it was dark. He was on the floor still but with a blanket over him and a pillow under his head. The floor smelled of dust and his shoulder ached where it pressed against the unyielding vinyl. He pushed himself off the ground into a sitting position. He felt hollow, as if the inside of his skull had been scraped out.

"Hi," a voice said from across the room. It was Ginny's voice but sleepy and soft. He could make her out in the gloom, curled up in an armchair with pillows and a quilt. "How are you?"

It wasn't a question that made much sense. "I don't know," he said. "What time is it?"

"Nearly morning. Do you want some breakfast?"

He nodded, then, realising she couldn't see him, said, "Yeah, that'd be good."

She got up and went to the kitchen, putting the lights on at a low setting. As she moved about, finding what she needed, he climbed to his feet and stretched the aches out of his body. The apartment was cold. The early hour and the dim lighting reminded him of something but he couldn't quite catch the wispy traces of memory. Then he saw it as clearly as if it had been yesterday, his father making sandwiches, chattering away in the kitchen while Rafe, just a small child, put his boots on. They were going fishing and Rafe was in a state of wonder at the strangeness of the experience, of this first glimpse into his father's secret world of men and their rituals.

"Last of the eggs," Ginny said, handing a plate to Rafe. The bacon wasn't burnt this time and smelled too good to be real. "Good job we're going today."

"You should come," he said, feeling awkward. "To Canberra." How did he get back from where he'd been yesterday?

"No," she said. Her tone said she'd understood something and knew what to do now. "I checked the flights. There's one to Canberra today. You should get that. It's two days till the next one."

They ate in silence for a while. Reluctantly, he asked, "What will you do?"

"I'll be fine. You're right. I'm not really in any danger. You just worry about getting yourself home and safe." She nodded at his bag in which the wad of documents still lay. "And make sure that gets out onto the Net."

He wanted to protest. She was treating him like an invalid. He could see it in her face. She knew now badly damaged he really was. Knew nearly as well as he did. Knew he could not cope with the danger that stalked him. Knew that just getting up in the morning and holding out until it was time to sleep was too much for him, that determination and bravado had only carried him a short way, and now he had no props. She could see that to lean on the people around him was all he could do to stave off a collapse that would soon come anyway. So, he didn't protest. He didn't take even the small risk that she might withdraw her collusion in his flight to safety. He let her give him what he needed and told himself it was all for the best.

He called his editor after breakfast, waking her from sleep, and explained that he needed her and anyone else she could rustle up to meet him on his arrival. "Yes, physically meet me," he told her. He got her promise in exchange for his own to explain everything in full as soon as he arrived.

Ginny called a cab to take him to the airport and went down to the street with him when it came. They stood beside it. He felt guilty and humiliated but forced himself to say, "It didn't change anything, you know, finding out about the Consortium. We already knew Dover Richards was from some other faction, that someone else, someone dangerous was taking an interest in what we did."

She nodded. She knew this too. She was still willing to let

him go, to get him safely home.

"We didn't know there were more of them," she said. "We didn't know what resources they had, or how hard they'd try to stop you."

He felt the panic rising in him at the mere suggestion of his continuing jeopardy. He should get in the cab and go. He glanced up and down the street but saw no-one.

"You should go," she said.

He nodded but still he did not move. He remembered the little black box and the cylinder and pulled them out of his pocket. He held them out to her. "Here. I'll feel better if you have them." She began to refuse but he took hold of her arm and pressed the gadgets into her hand. "Please." She looked unhappy, perhaps about his reasons for thinking she might need them, but she took them anyway. "It's not like they did me any good," he said. "The one time I could have used them, I was in too much of a panic to think of anything but running."

She stepped forwards and gave him a quick hard hug. When she stepped back, he smiled and nodded. Then he got into the cab and told it to go. He looked back after a while to see her still standing on the pavement, watching him leave, a small lonely figure in the bright cold morning.

Part 3

Chapter 13

Della Kubiak was at work when the doorbell rang. She worked as a middle manager for Chastity Mining PLC, Australia's largest mining company, and was wrapping up a staff meeting on the quarterly results. Her direct reports, their direct reports, and so on down to the lowliest staff members filled a small auditorium. Over two hundred faces gazed up at her as she stumbled over her sentence and investigated the interruption.

It was her apartment doorbell, which was weird, especially since she had set the apartment never to interrupt her at work except in exceptional circumstances – like if the place was burning down or something. Or if it was a close personal friend. There in the virtual pop-up she saw Ginny standing in her hallway, looking around nervously.

Barely missing a beat, she told the apartment to open for Ginny then turned to smile at her audience. "So, to cut a long quarter short, we did well. Most of you are on track for healthy Christmas bonuses if we can keep up the momentum until the end of the year. I need to shoot through right now, so I'll leave Chui Yi to deal with any questions you might have. Have a great weekend and I'll see you all on Monday."

She left the podium mouthing a silent apology to her

surprised deputy, and went straight back to her tank. As the lid came up, she found Ginny standing over her, looking sheepish.

"I need somewhere to stay for a few nights, Del. Any chance I can crash here?"

She looked her friend up and down. Ginny seemed OK, apart from her anxious expression. She noted the travel bag on the floor behind her. "Of course you can stay."

"I don't know," her friend said, as if she were already reconsidering. "I should probably explain it all to you first, then let you decide."

Della grinned. "Ah, Ginny Galton, Woman of Mystery. I suppose you've been consorting with terrorists again. Well, whatever it is, why don't you take a seat and I'll get us a cup of coffee. Then you can buy me dinner – there's a great little place in Paris I've been dying to try – and tell me what kind of mess you're in this time. I've got a guest tank in the spare bedroom and the bots are filling up the drips even as we speak."

Ginny smiled weakly, which was not a good sign, then moved in for a hug. "I knew you'd be just what I needed," she said.

"And what's that exactly?"

"Sensible," said Ginny. "In your own slightly crazy way."

—oOo—

The restaurant was a seedy little place in a tiny street behind the Rue des Théatres, in a version of Paris a good hundred years older than the real one. There were just ten tables in the whole place, and only half of them were occupied. An overweight, middle-aged woman in a floral dress saw them to their table, making no attempt at pleasantness. Della found the simple wooden chair rather more comfortable than it looked – thanks to the magic of virtual reality – and ordered for both of them in French from the one-page menu. She smiled at the couple at the next table, a quiet man with a moustache and a loud woman in a hat. A standard poodle sat beside the woman on its own chair. She fed it morsels of food with her fingers and cooed over it.

"Nice," said Ginny in a tone that suggested she thought otherwise. "A personal recommendation? Or did you read about it in the Kennel Club Magazine?"

Della winked. "Just wait, the food is supposed to be fabulous."

Ginny smiled sweetly. "Well Lassie seems to be enjoying it."

"Never mind the other diners, let's hear the rest of the story. You were just up to the part where Detective Chu kicks in your front door and you swoon onto the sofa."

"If you're not going to take this seriously…"

"Ginny! Lighten up! You've been acting completely stonkered since you arrived. Of course I'm taking it seriously."

Ginny regarded her steadily. "I don't think I'd ever been so scared in my life, Della. I thought Dover Richards was coming in to get me."

"The creepy one you quite fancied when you first met him."

"The one who murdered Gavin."

Della raised her hands in surrender. "OK, I'll stop being glib. Just tell me the rest of the tale."

With a sigh, Ginny continued, talking non-stop through three courses and a couple of after-dinner liqueurs. Della, who had started off believing her friend was dramatising herself and making a great deal out of very little, grew increasingly astonished as the tale unfolded. If half of what Ginny said was true, she had been through an adventure such as Della had never heard of in real life. The fight on the roof in Stanthorpe shocked her so much she thought Rafe's consequent breakdown perfectly reasonable, even if he had started out mentally hale and healthy.

"You actually shot that man?" she said as the coffee arrived.

"He was only wounded," said Ginny in her defence. "I had to shoot or they'd have killed us both."

Della noticed their grumpy waitress was hanging around close to their table and wondered if she might be a real person and not a construct as she had assumed. She made a small gesture of caution to Ginny and nodded towards the woman. "Let's go for a walk along the Seine," she said.

They got up and Della paid the bill.

"You should let me," said Ginny, dismally.

"This place might look like a dump," said Della, not caring if the nosy waitress heard. "But the prices are top of the range." Seeing her friend's glum expression, she added, "Come on Gin, you're a struggling artist and I'm a rising star in the corporate firmament. I make – what? – ten times what you do? Twenty? I'd tell you my actual salary only the French proletariat would have me swinging from the nearest lamppost before I'd got all the zeroes out." She was glad to see a small grin on Ginny's lips.

They teleported straight to the river, appearing close to Notre Dame on the Quai de la Mégisserie, and linked arms as they ambled downstream, past the shops and cafés towards the Jardin des Tuileries.

"Do you think Rafe's right?" Ginny asked. "I mean, about me being in no real danger any more?"

Della thought about it for a minute. She didn't like the sound of this Rafe bloke at all. His prime motive in everything he'd done seemed to be his own self-interest. In fact, Della could see several reasons why the various parties would want to hurt Ginny – or at least keep an eye on her. Yet her friend was so anxious. Even here, she was looking around all the time, checking everybody they saw on the street.

"I'm sure you're worrying too much about it. Besides, the plebiscite is tomorrow and, if they get a 'yes' on that, the Government says it will have the vote in Parliament within a few days. After that, it's all over, isn't it?"

Ginny nodded. "That's what I thought." It seemed to give her no comfort though. "Whatever they're going to do, it should be before the vote. And Rafe said he'll put the S10 documents out on the Net as soon as he gets to Canberra. There's nothing I could add to that, even if I wanted to. Even if I went to the police, all I could tell them is to go and look at Rafe's documents. I'm not a threat to anybody now, am I?"

Della squeezed Ginny's arm. "Stay with me until the vote is over. Then you can go back home without having to worry."

"But what if the Consortium thinks I'm part of the S10 plot? What if the police think I'm with S10 – or the Consortium?" She pressed her palms into her forehead. "It's driving me nuts. I can't think straight."

"Hmmm, well, two bottles of French wine might have something to do with that."

But Ginny was not to be jollied out of it. She looked around again. "Can we go back?" she asked. "I feel too exposed out here."

Reluctantly, Della agreed and called up a portal that would take them back to their tanks. But Ginny caught Della's arm and stopped her. "You don't have to let me stay," she said. "Now you've heard the whole story, you know what a risk you're taking. I'd understand if you told me to sling my hook."

Della could hardly believe her friend was being so melodramatic. Ginny had always taken life a bit too seriously, of course, but there in the yellow lamp-light of that quiet street, she had the tortured expression of a 2D movie heroine caught up in one of those inexplicable old plots about virtue or family honour. Could she really be so scared? Did she really feel so helpless? It prompted a question that had been in her mind for several hours now.

"Ginny, why don't you just go to the police and tell them everything?"

Ginny looked confused, as if Della had missed the whole point of what she'd been saying. "Because I don't trust them to be on my side. From their perspective, I've been a courier for September 10, I've consorted with known terrorists, I've failed to report a death, I've shot a man, I'm in possession of an illegal firearm..." She paused for breath. "They might just arrest me, Del. They could easily do that. And then they could hold me indefinitely without access to a lawyer. They could even torture me if they wanted to. I'd be crazy to risk all that on the slight chance that they might be able to protect me from untagged ghosts who can come and go without the police knowing." She stared into Della's eyes as if looking for an acknowledgement of the peril they were both in, but clearly did not find it. "I should go," she said. "It was stupid of me to come here and put you in danger like this, only..."

"Yes?"

"Only there's something I wanted your help with, something you might have the right connections to help me find out."

"The Rice Consortium," Della said, leaping to the obvious conclusion.

Ginny nodded. "I've tried every search I can think of but I can't find much. It's a real company. It has a sort of minimal worldlet that's all corporate colours and discrete logos and doesn't even say what it does. I thought maybe you might know people, or people you could ask, anyway."

"And this is the group that sent people to grab Rafe? Don't you think it would be better to just leave them alone? If they find out someone's trying to find them, wouldn't that just be like poking a dangerous animal with a stick?"

Ginny sighed and looked at the ground. "I know. And I shouldn't ask you to help. I just need to know. I just need…" She looked up suddenly, her gaze intense. "Something bad's going to happen. S10 or the Consortium, or somebody is planning something terrible. People might die. I'm not a hero, Del, but what if I'm the only person who can do something about it? How could I live with myself afterwards if people died and I'd just stood around and let it all happen? I wouldn't have come here, I wouldn't ask you to help if I didn't think there was so much at stake."

There were tears in Ginny's eyes and Della pulled her friend into a hug. "It's all right, hon. Don't worry about it. I'll help you. Of course I will. Nothing terrible is going to happen, you'll see. I bet the police have been onto these drongos all along. They'll keep everyone safe, you'll see. And, meanwhile, you'll stay with me and we'll have a good time and forget about terrorists and murderers and secret plots."

She felt Ginny's head shake against her shoulder and pulled back to look at her. "Well, we'll give it a go, anyway. At the very least we can get in some quality girl time while society falls in ruins about our ears."

Ginny grinned, despite herself. "But you'll ask about the Consortium?" she said.

With a sigh, Della agreed. "Whatever you need, hon. Just think of this as a short vacation. I'll do all the detective work for the next few days. You just kick back and relax. OK?"

Ginny's voice was wistful. "Sounds wonderful."

"It's agreed then. Come on." She took her friend's arm and steered her through the exit that led to the real world.

Chapter 14

"She's scared stiff," Della insisted. The broad, handsome man sitting opposite rolled his eyes, just a fraction, but enough to give away the fact that he was losing his patience.

"She's in no danger," he said again.

"Detective Chu, you're missing my point."

They were in the Federal Police Building in Sydney, a surprisingly dull and ordinary worldlet, Della thought. Weren't the Feds supposed to have renovated all their worldlets recently? She vaguely remembered an exposé she'd watched about cost overruns and management incompetence. If this was all they got for their millions, they had been seriously short-changed.

"Ms Kubiak, we all have Ms Galton's safety as our number one priority. Nothing bad will happen to her."

"She was almost killed just a couple of days ago."

He compressed his lips, obviously trying to keep his temper in check. "I explained that. She and that reporter surprised my people in Brisbane. They weren't expecting them to take off in a quadcopter. It took our officers on foot a while to locate a suitable vehicle to follow them in."

"Meanwhile they get jumped and almost murdered."

"As I said before, now that Ms Galton is staying with you, we don't expect her to go flying off without you telling us where she's going."

"I don't like spying on my friend."

"Even if it's for her own protection?"

Della scrunched down in her seat, feeling cornered. Of course she wanted to help Ginny, that's why she'd been willing to meet Detective Chu when he called that morning, but what he was suggesting seemed all wrong.

"Tell me again why you don't want me to tell Ginny about this?"

Chu gave a barely-suppressed sigh. "Ginny's had a bad experience with the police. That man, Dover Richards, impersonated one of our officers and gave her quite a fright it seems. Her companion, Rafe Morgan, is one of those anti-establishment reporters who has a very jaundiced and paranoid view of what we do. I doubt that she trusts us any more." *Well that's true enough*, Della thought. "In fact, the fact that she hasn't been in touch tells me she's as scared of us as she is of September 10. I don't want to alarm her further and run the risk of her bolting."

"But you could track her through her tag, surely?"

"Of course, but who knows what mischief she might make for herself before we caught up with her? The incident in Stanthorpe you just mentioned ought to be proof enough that we're not infallible."

"And you're keeping her under surveillance because you think she might be contacted by these terrorists, September 10?"

"It's vital we get our hands on those people as soon as possible, Ms Kubiak. We have no other leads. This is the only way."

"What about the Rice Consortium?" She had already given Chu a summary of all that Ginny had told her on the previous evening.

Chu shook his head. "It's a red herring. They're a legitimate business. We've already checked them out."

"What kind of business?"

"Some kind of lobby group."

"So why were those thugs flying around in a Rice Consortium quadcopter."

Chu regarded her steadily. He seemed angry, probably resentful of being cross-questioned by his would-be informant. *Well that's just tough*, Della thought. *If he wants my help, he can damned well work for it.*

"We checked that too," he said, slowly. "The Rice Consortium flyer just happened to be on the roof that day because one of their employees was visiting the town on business. They were very upset that Mr Morgan damaged it but we persuaded them not to prosecute him, or Ginny."

"Why?"

"Because it is in our interest to keep both of them in play. There is more at stake here than the vandalism of corporate property." He paused. "I have the feeling I have not convinced you to help us, Ms Kubiak."

Della found the man's excessive politeness and his overly formal speech irritating, but he was wrong. She was completely willing to help and didn't need convincing. Cooperating with the police seemed to be the only sensible thing to do. She had already told Detective Chu a lot of what Ginny had told her and would continue to report on Ginny's plans and activities. It was the only way to keep her friend safe. It would be idiotic and reckless not to help the police. All the same, she did not like the idea that Chu was keeping her friend 'in play', using her as a lure to draw out the terrorists.

"Ginny's worried you'll arrest her," she said.

Chu seemed to find the idea funny. He laughed out loud and said, "Don't worry, I certainly won't be arresting her."

"That's good to hear. I wish I could tell her."

"You can, once this is all over. It won't be long."

She nodded and they both fell silent. Chu seemed satisfied at last that Della was on his side. He broke the silence by asking, "Where does she think you are at the moment?"

"I told her I had to pop into my office for a while to check on a few things. She knows I'm a workaholic."

"That's good. Maybe you can invent some crisis, or an urgent piece of accounting that will require you to drop by every now and then. At least once a day would be good."

Della nodded and stood up to leave. "Yeah. No worries. I should be off."

He stood too and held out a hand. "And you'll call if anything comes up? Anything at all?"

"Of course." They shook hands and Della left by the nearest exit.

—oOo—

She didn't go straight home but, instead, went to her office. She really was a workaholic and the chance to extend her absence by another half hour to get some work done was too good to miss. After the daggy drabness of the police station, the offices of Chastity Mining seemed unusually smart and modern. Display surfaces everywhere responded to her presence and updated her on critical business indices, intra-office communications, and news.

She got stuck into her work immediately but within a few minutes her attention began wandering. A few minutes later, she set her work aside and sat back in her chair staring at the ocean. When she wasn't entertaining clients or meeting colleagues, her office configured itself as a kind of high-tech beach shack. Bleached wooden planking, the sounds of gulls and distant breakers, and the smell of the sea, provided an incongruous background for the banks of virtual displays that hovered around Della's high-backed leather chair. With the screens pushed out of the way, she had a view through the open door past her wooden verandah to the ocean and wide, blue Caribbean skies.

"I always say–"

Della jumped and swivelled the chair to face a tall woman with angular features who had just walked in behind her.

"Sheila! I thought I was here on my own. Just a sec." She popped up a display to reset the décor to office normal, but the tall woman stopped her.

"No, leave it. It's nice. I have my own office set to Gstaad, skiers whizzing past all the time, wooden chalets and fir trees." Sheila was CEO of the company and could pretty well suit herself in such matters. Although she was just three management layers above Della in the company hierarchy, it might have been three thousand as far as actual status went. "I always say," she went on, "working weekends is a sign of poor delegation skills."

Della laughed politely, assuming it was a joke and not an admonition.

"Your figures for last quarter were really very good," Sheila said and Della tried not to look amazed that anyone at Sheila's level would notice anyone at Della's. She immediately felt stupid, realising that Sheila must have pulled up her division's performance figures, probably had them on display from the minute she saw Della working, along with peer comparisons, market averages, and year-on-year trends.

"I'll see if we can do even better next quarter," she said, playing along.

"Good onya. I'll set a flag so I don't forget to check up on how you did." She laughed as if she'd just made a big joke. Della tried to look pleased, despite the sinking feeling. It was, of course, an opportunity to shine, and be noticed. That was the right way to look at it. Yet the timing wasn't great, what with all this business with Ginny at the moment.

"I suppose it's no big deal, coming in here all hours with no family at home to worry about," Sheila said. So the woman had pulled Della's personnel file too. "Still, even single people have to make sure they get their work-life balance right. Don't you agree?"

"I just popped in to check on how a few things were going. I won't be staying long."

"Make sure you don't. It's all too easy to burn yourself out in this business. And how is everything going?"

Della glanced at her displays. "I could do with a better exchange rate against the Yuan, but the year's going well against plan." This would be the perfect opportunity to mention the new nickel dredging project in the Torres Strait, she told herself, prime the pump a bit so it's already on Sheila's radar when the approval request hits her desk. Instead, she found herself asking, "Do we have any dealings with the Rice Consortium?"

Della's heart skipped a beat as her CEO's face fell and her body stiffened. Sheila stepped closer, standing over Della. "What do you know about the Rice Consortium? Where did you hear about this?"

"I–" The woman looked really angry. Had Della stumbled onto some terrible company secret she shouldn't know about? Could she bluff this out, find out what was going on? She would never have brought it up but it had rankled with her that Detective Chu had so obviously lied about the Consortium and their attack on Rafe and Ginny. She said, "I heard about them. From a friend. They seem to crop up a lot lately. My friend suggested I try to make contact to see if there were any business synergies. She seemed to think there might be. So I just wondered whether we already had a relationship with them."

Her boss underwent a swift transformation from anger to cautious suspicion. "Your friend isn't with Chastity then?"

"No, she's…in the worldlet services business." Sheila nodded as if that made sense. Della risked a gentle push. "So are we in bed with them?"

"No, we are most definitely not. Whatever your friend may think, the Rice Consortium is not a company we would ever do business with."

With Sheila's emotional state rapidly swinging back towards anger, Della's instinct was to shut up and back off but, for Ginny's sake, she tried to look innocent and asked, "Why? What's wrong with them?"

"Never you mind. All I'll say is this. They approached us about a year ago. We did the usual due diligence, and something came up."

"They're some kind of lobbyists aren't they? What was it you turned up? Bribery? Blackmail?"

"Frankly, it's none of your business. That's what it is. I don't want to hear them mentioned again. And if they ever approach you again – through friends, or any other channel – you report it to me, straight away. Yes?"

"Er, yes, of course."

Without another word, Sheila turned and left, leaving Della wishing she'd kept her mouth shut.

—oOo—

"But that's great news," Ginny said, when Della related the details of her roller-coaster meeting with her boss. "Now we just have to get hold of that report Sheila had done on the Consortium and we'll know what they're into."

"Yeah, right. I'll just nip along to the CEO's office and ask for a copy. That'll get me back in Sheila's good books."

Ginny winced. "I'm sorry, Del. She's probably forgotten all about it by now though. I'm sure it'll be all right." Della did not feel reassured. "But, look, Sheila got a report, but she didn't actually compile it herself. That would have been done by someone else. Who does that kind of thing, your legal department?"

"Accounts, most likely."

"Right. Accounts. So that's where we need to go to get the file."

"Unbelievable! I've just trashed my reputation with my CEO over this and now you want me to break into our Accounts Department database and steal a highly confidential report? I'd never work again if they caught me – and that's *after* I got out of jail."

Ginny chewed her lip and looked around as though searching for some way past the problem of getting her friend arrested for larceny, yet still acquiring the file she wanted. It took her about ten seconds before inspiration struck and her face lit up. "Rafe!" she said.

"Rafe? You mean your emotionally unbalanced reporter

friend who goes to pieces at the first sign of danger? He's going to burgle my company's file system?"

"No, of course not, but I'll bet he knows someone who can."

Della took a deep breath. It wasn't much more than an hour ago that she had promised a Federal Police officer that she'd keep him informed about what Ginny was up to. How could she possibly tell him something like this? Even conspiring to commit an offence was an offence. And she would be an accessory before the fact, or something. She should quash the idea immediately. But Ginny was so excited by the prospect and was thanking her for being so brave with her boss and getting them this brilliant new lead. Della just didn't have the heart to do it. On the other hand, she was pretty sure that the fragile Rafe would bottle out of the proposed burglary, so the whole idea would fall at the next hurdle.

"All right, let's talk to Rafe then," she said. From Ginny's surprised expression, her friend had obviously expected more of a struggle.

"He said he knew computer experts," Ginny said. "I bet he knows all kinds of shady people. He's got that air about him. Looks like he's always doing dodgy deals with underworld types for juicy bits of information."

"Sounds charming."

"Yeah, but useful, I reckon. Let's go see him."

Ginny had actually taken a couple of steps towards the guest tank before Della called out, "Whoa. When did you turn into Action Woman? Some of us haven't even had our breakfast yet. I think I'm going to need a full stomach when I meet this seedy reporter of yours."

So they printed some toast in Della's top-of-the-range

autochef and Della nibbled at a slice while Ginny wolfed hers down and waited impatiently for Della to finish. When Della could stall her friend no longer, they got into their respective tanks and turned up at the offices of the Sentinel.

"I'll see if Mr. Morgan is in," an animated receptionist told them with a bright smile. The construct went through the motions of picking up an old-style phone and murmuring into it. Cute, but Della wasn't in the mood for being entertained.

"Just tell him we're not going away until he sees us," she snapped. "Or maybe he'd rather we went to talk to the police?"

"Mr. Morgan will see you now," the receptionist said in a sing-song voice, smiling cheerfully. It indicated a door and Della strode off towards it with Ginny hurrying to keep up.

"What's put you in such a grumpy mood?" Ginny asked.

"I'm always grumpy when I'm conspiring to break the law."

Ginny looked shocked, as if it hadn't occurred to her that her friend might resent being dragged into all this. She put a hand on Della's arm and said, "I'm sorry Del, I didn't mean to—"

Della cut her off. "Let's just get on with it, shall we?"

She threw open Rafe's door and marched in. A scruffy-looking man in his forties regarded her from a smart leather chair in a smart, white office. The office was so out of keeping with the way the man looked and dressed, it emphasised his crumpled, careless appearance. *Like a chimp in an operating theatre*, she thought. She studied him for a moment as Ginny said hello and introduced everybody.

The Twenty Per Cent Rule was a law passed in the early days of ubiquitous augmented reality and applied to virtual reality too. It said that no-one could alter their appearance by more than twenty per cent on any particular attribute. You could be taller – but only by up to twenty per cent. You could be slimmer, younger, have bigger eyes, longer legs, a squarer jaw, bigger breasts, anything you liked, but only by up to twenty per cent. It meant people were always rather more beautiful than they really were, but not so much more that you didn't get an impression of what they were really like. If Rafe Morgan looked this shabby in VR, he must look a complete wreck in reality.

"I don't want to see anyone," Rafe said, looking at Della. "I don't want anything more to do with it." He turned to Ginny. "I thought you understood."

"Ginny needs your help with something," Della said. She was already predisposed to dislike this man. As she saw it, he had used Ginny and then ditched her when it all got too much for him. "All we want is a name and you can go back to your nervous breakdown or whatever your problem is."

"Tough guy," he said with a sneer.

"Don't make me come to Canberra and beat the snot out of you," she said, sneering right back at him.

Ginny stepped forward, looking alarmed. "Rafe, I just need a name. You said you knew computer people. Good ones. I…" She hesitated. "I need to break into somewhere and look at a file. You're the only person I know who might have contacts like that. It's just a name. Then we'll leave you alone."

He frowned at her. "What the hell are you doing, Ginny? I thought you were going to keep your head down until all this is over."

"I can't do that, Rafe. I need to try to stop it – whatever it is. You're a journalist. Don't you want to know what's going on?"

Rafe looked away. "Curiosity killed the cat."

The sheer shiftiness of his gesture and tone made Della suspicious. "Did your feed publish those September 10 documents?" she asked.

He didn't answer at once and Della saw Ginny's mouth fall open in dismay. "Oh, Rafe!"

"Becky wouldn't go for it. We had a discussion and the conclusion was that if S10 wanted us to publish them, it was probably a bad idea."

"The plebiscite vote is today," Ginny said.

"So you've handed everything over to the police?" Della didn't believe he had for a moment and Rafe's glare confirmed it.

The journalist stood up and gesticulated. "We don't even know what all that stuff means. It could have been deliberately leaked to mislead us, to implicate innocent people. September 10 are not the good guys."

"Mate, you're just full of shit," Della said, and, to Ginny, "Come on. This bloke's as much use as tits on a bull." It seemed like a good opportunity to get Ginny away and put a stop to the whole break-in plan, but Ginny stayed where she was.

"Never mind the documents," she said. "There's still time, anyway. The plebiscite is only to give the government a mandate to bring its legislation forward. We just need to make sure the right people get to see the documents. Isn't that right, Rafe?"

The journalist tightened his jaw and turned away. To his back, Ginny said. "All right. Just give me a name, someone who can get this file for me. I won't even say you sent me."

Rafe didn't move as the seconds ticked by. Then he made a few, rapid hand gestures as he worked with a virtual display Della could not see. A business card appeared in his hand and he gave it to Ginny.

"Thank you," Ginny said, accepting the information transfer, and, with a glance at Della, she made for the door.

"Ginny?" Rafe said, as they were leaving. "I'm sorry."

Chapter 15

"Let's take a walk," Della said and asked the teleporter for the Enchanted Forest.

"Seriously?" Ginny asked.

"Ah yeah, it's where I always go when I need to do some serious thinking."

"It's a bit pricey. There are plenty of open source forests you know."

"Ah but they're not like this one. We should get in costume too." She called up a menu and selected a couple of outfits. "Don't worry, it's all on my account." For herself, she chose a Sleeping Beauty outfit straight out of the ancient Disney movie. For Ginny, she selected a fairy godmother dress complete with sparkles, tiara, and magic wand.

Ginny lifted the voluminous skirt of her dress and examined her glittering high-heeled pumps. "Not exactly walking boots," she said.

"Like it matters. You look lovely. Come on."

They stepped through the portal into the lushest, greenest forest imaginable. Exotic blooms the size of dustbin lids caught sunbeams from the high leafy canopy above them. Brightly-coloured birds flitted through the undergrowth, and a group of dappled deer looked up from their browsing at the far edge of the clearing and, seeing it was only them, returned to their meal. A stream gurgled out of sight and a pond nearby had water lilies with smiling frogs sitting on their lily pads. As Della watched, a dragonfly brushed the surface of the water as it swooped by, setting the air tinkling with a delicate arpeggio.

Ginny burst out laughing. "Oh my God! This is so kitsch!"

"I find it quite relaxing. Just try to enjoy it instead of looking at it with your jaded designer's eyes. Look. Watch this." She raised an arm and put out a finger, as if pointing to something. After a moment a tiny blue bird fluttered down to land on it, singing its little heart out.

"Oh now that's cute." Ginny put out her own finger and soon had her own little bluebird. She stroked its head and it rubbed itself against her hand.

Della smiled, seeing her friend's critical attitude evaporate. She lifted her finger and the bluebird flew away. "Let's go that way," she said, indicating a grassy track between the trees.

They walked along in silence for a minute or two. They passed a gingerbread cottage on their left and, to the right, distant, snow-capped mountains with a pure white, many-turreted castle could be glimpsed through the trees. As they walked, Ginny's dress rustled and brushed across the grass. She looked quite striking with her hair up and the wings of the high collar framing her face.

"Nice, isn't it?" Della said.

"It's amazing. Is that a unicorn?"

They both stopped to admire the mythical beast as it stooped to drink from a forest stream.

Della took a deep breath and said, "I know Rafe gave you a contact, but I don't think you should use it. In fact, I think you should drop the whole thing. Rafe's bottled out. Those documents are never going to be published and they're never going to the police. He's too scared." Ginny didn't say anything but carried on walking, her head bowed in thought.

"Which leaves you on your own, with no evidence of anything, some half-formed notion of what this is all about, an illegal firearm, at least three organisations probably watching you, and a crazy plan to burgle my employer."

Ginny glanced around. "I don't feel comfortable talking about this in here."

Della felt a twinge of irritation. "Who's going to be monitoring us? The police? ASIO? So what? They're on our side – or they would be if you'd go and tell them what you know."

"You know I don't trust them."

"But that's just–" She stopped herself. No point in calling her friend names, however much she deserved it. She tried a different tack. "All right, what do you expect to find in an internal report on the Rice Consortium? What would make it worth the risk of finding?"

Ginny stopped walking and threw up her arms. Tiny stars trailed from the end of her magic wand. "I don't know. There must have been something juicy in there to make your boss react so badly. Whatever it is, maybe it will lead us on to other things, give us some clues so we're not completely in the dark."

Della shook her head. "It doesn't sound like much to risk us both going to prison for."

"Look, when I told you about leaving that package for Gavin…" For an instant, Della thought, *Who the hell is Gavin?* It all seemed so long ago. "…you were all concerned about how innocent kids might pick it up and find something in it that might hurt them. Remember? You poured guilt on me by the bucketful. You were all, 'Oh, think about those poor children! How could you, you evil bitch?' Well, nothing's changed. These people – S10, the Consortium, whoever – they're planning something that's going to hurt people. Innocent people. Why aren't you worried about that?"

Della couldn't help smiling at Ginny's impression of her. Even so, she thought her friend was being wilfully obtuse. "It's different now. You know it is."

"How? How is it different?"

"Oh, come on! Back then we thought maybe there was some kind of petty crime going on – drug dealing or something. Now we've got a dead terrorist and gunfights on rooftops and sinister people tailing you. Don't you think you might be just a teensy bit out of your depth?" One of the little deer came over and nuzzled at Della's hand. She snatched the hand away and snapped, "Not now, you stupid bloody animal." Wide-eyed with alarm, it turned and bounded into the forest. When she looked back at Ginny she found her friend staring at her with a sad expression.

"It's OK, Del. I understand if you don't want to get involved. I just get a bit carried away."

"Ginny, it's not that, I–"

"No, really, it's all right. Look, we've never been all that close. Not really. Not like I can turn up on your doorstep with some crazy story about terrorists and ask you to risk everything to help me work it out." Della began protesting but Ginny cut her off again. The whole scene, with them in their flouncy dresses and big-eyed animals watching them from the cover of that ridiculously lush forest, made Della wish she'd just taken Ginny back to her unit and they'd done this over a cup of coffee in the kitchen.

"I'll move out to a hotel or something. I shouldn't be asking you to break into your own company's accounts. You shouldn't have anything to do with this. I don't know what I was thinking. It's much better if I do what I have to on my own and don't drag you into anything illegal."

Ginny attempted a reassuring smile but Della just stared. She couldn't get past the part where Ginny had said they weren't that close. "We've been friends since uni," she said. "All those nights when we got pissed and bitched about blokes and how you were going to do great things and set the world straight. Remember? With Kate and Maggie and that creepy girl from the Genetics department with the animated tattoos. What was her name?" Ginny smiled sadly but said nothing. "You're my best friend, Ginny. You were then and you still are. How can we not be that close?"

Ginny struggled to find the right words. "I didn't mean it like that. I just… It's… You were always the sensible one."

"Not that again."

"I know I say it a lot but you are. Look at me. I'm a failure. I had big dreams and ridiculous ambitions, but I never did anything right. I never took the right courses, focused on the things I wanted, pushed my way into the right circles, seized the opportunities that came along, made openings for myself. Now it's all too late. I've frittered away whatever talent I have on bloody soundscapes and corporate morons who'd be just as happy with computer-generated rubbish, and now I've got no work, no money, and no prospects. Kate's the same. She was going to be this big civil rights lawyer but she's a junior solicitor in a grubby little firm of ambulance chasers. She hasn't even done any *pro bono* work in years. You're the only one of us who did just what she said she would. You're the only one who actually succeeded."

Della gaped in amazement. "I'm a middle manager in a massive mining conglomerate! That's your idea of success, is it?"

"No, it's yours. I remember you telling me right from the start that what you wanted was a secure, solid career, a steady climb within some major corporation, good money, a comfortable lifestyle, a good pension and an early retirement. I actually laughed when you told me. I was so up myself, so full of pretentious crap about art and music and creative freedom."

Della did remember, she remembered the envy she felt over Ginny's effortless talent, and how happy she'd been to have such a circle of exciting, fascinating friends. Della had never been the sensible one, she'd been the frightened one, the one who dressed up her feelings of inadequacy with harangues on stability and a life of quiet, productive contribution. Even back then she knew she was a complete fraud.

"I like your soundscapes," she said, quietly. "I sometimes take people to the National Museum and make them listen and I tell them my friend did that."

Ginny blinked but said nothing. With a small, shy smile, she said, "Last year, I took a tour of the Kimberley bauxite mines, just to see one of your division's big projects. It was completely awesome. I hardly dared speak to you for a month afterwards, I was so impressed."

Della felt her throat constrict. She stepped forward and took Ginny into her arms and held her tight, grinning, even as her eyes filled with tears. They hugged in silence as the forest creatures came out of hiding and smooched and fluttered around them.

"So, no more talk of moving to a hotel?" Della said,

holding her friend out from her. She choked up again at the sight of the tears on Ginny's cheeks, the quick flash of gratitude in her eyes.

"I shouldn't ask you to—"

"You see, that's where you're wrong." A wave of lightness surged up through Della's body making her feel almost giddy. "This is important, and you need my help. For once in my life, let me do something crazy and stupid in a good cause. I'm fed up of feeling ashamed of myself."

Chapter 16

They stepped out of the teleport onto bare rock. Grey cloud roiled in a threatening sky and a cold wind whipped at their cloaks and hair. Behind them the sky was vast and empty. The ledge on which they stood ended abruptly, exposing the gaping, monstrous space between the ragged peaks of lesser mountains. Ahead, a staircase thirty metres wide, cut through the basalt cliff, rose towards a grim stone castle, piled in countless buttressed walls and soaring towers to scrape at the base of the lowering cloud.

"If he thinks I'm walking up all those bloody steps, he's got another think coming," Della said, raising her voice above the clamouring wind. "Hey! Sorenssen! What the hell is this?"

Ginny looked troubled. "Maybe this was a bad idea. I'm not sure this guy can be quite right in the head – what with the costumes and the castle and everything."

Della had been thinking the same thing. The journalist's computer specialist friend might be the genius Rafe thought he was, but that didn't stop him being not the full quid. They'd called to set up an appointment and Sorenssen's personal assistant – a construct in the form of a gnarled and toothless old man in a hooded cloak – had set up the meeting. When they arrived, the old man simulation greeted them in a room that looked like an ancient crypt and told them they must appear in costume for the "audience" – as he put it.

Della had almost baulked right there when she saw herself and Ginny in their outfits. Fantasy Classic, the style was usually called – thigh-boots, leather straps everywhere, swords, wristbands, and big hairdos were the basis of the look. Ginny's outfit was, essentially, a white bodystocking and featured a short, low-cut golden breastplate. Her own comprised a tiny loincloth and a matching tiny bra and little else. Frowning in the mirror at her outsize breasts and muscular thighs, she growled, "This definitely violates the twenty per cent rule."

Ginny looked at her anxiously.

"Oh, don't worry. I'm not backing out. If this Sorenssen creep likes his visitors to look like porn stars, why should I care? As long as he delivers on Rafe's promises."

And now they were standing on a wind-scoured mountaintop with their cloaks snapping like flags.

"Sorenssen!" Della tried to keep herself from getting angry and upsetting Ginny, but this was all too much. "If you don't–"

Suddenly the old man PA was with them. He was stooped and clung to a long staff as gnarled as he was as if it was all that prevented the wind from blowing him over the cliff. "My Ladies," he said, bowing low. "If you will come closer, I will take you to my Lord." Della and Ginny exchanged glances but stepped over to the old man. "Please," he said, "place your hands on my staff."

Della took a firm grip of the shaft, glowering at the PA, and Ginny tentatively followed suit. Light filled the air, so intense it washed out all vision, then cleared slowly.

The two women were in a large stone chamber – inside the castle, Della supposed. Straw rustled beneath their feet as they turned. Torches guttered in brackets on the walls and pillars, casting a shifting, uncertain light on the high, vaulted ceiling. The old man simulation backed away from them. Guards in armour and helmets eyed them from the dim edges of the room, firelight glinting on their breastplates, long pikes in their gloved hands. At one end of the room, on a raised platform, a giant of a man lounged in a massive wooden throne. He was dressed in furs and leather and sported a bushy red beard and long, braided red hair. His bare arms were muscled beyond credibility and his blue eyes regarded the two women from beneath heavy brows. At his feet lay two lionesses, also watching the women.

"You Sorenssen?" Della demanded, stepping forward. She felt annoyed almost beyond restraint at this childish show. It was a trend becoming more popular all the time, especially among the young, to build elaborate worldlets on fantastic themes and inflict them on everyone who called. It was a trend Della hated. Even by modern standards, this one was way over the top.

The giant spoke. "I am Odin, King of the gods of Asgard."

Della strode up to him on her newly-acquired long legs and glared into his too-blue eyes. The lionesses shifted and grumbled. "Odin, eh? Well, I was expecting a scrawny computer geek with acne and a swagful of nervous habits. Men hvis du virkelig er Odin, jeg tror vi kom til feil sted."

"Er…" said the king of the gods.

"It's Norwegian, you fuckwit. Call up a translator. Or, better still, cut all the crap and let's talk business."

"Er…" he said again.

213

Della lost patience. She turned to Ginny. "That's it. I reckon I've had enough pissing about in this galah's masturbatory fantasy. Let's go and find someone a bit more mature to talk to."

"Jeez, talk about not getting into the spirit of the thing," said Sorenssen. His appearance hadn't changed, nor had the bass rumble of his voice, but his tone certainly had. Della eyed him with a sour expression. "A lot of people find all this really cool," he said.

"Well, a lot of people don't. Have we finished playing now?"

Sorenssen sighed heavily and rolled his eyes. "Sure. Whatever. What did you want to see me about?"

Della glanced at Ginny, giving her the floor, and walked a few paces away.

"Did Rafe tell you why we're here?" Ginny asked the sulky giant.

"Not really. He said you needed help getting hold of some information."

"Well, that's true. But the information is in someone else's file system."

Sorenssen sucked his teeth. He looked across at Della who stared back at him with such contempt that he quickly looked away. "Whose data do you want me to steal?" he asked.

"It's a corporation. A big one."

"Industrial espionage?" he asked, in a tone that implied such an act was both boring and tacky. Perhaps feeling he had the moral high ground, he turned back to Della. "Another mining company?"

"Can you do it?" Ginny asked.

"Of course, but can you afford me?"

Della almost snarled, looking far more fierce than the two

big cats. "Our friend, Rafe, said you'd do it as a favour. He said you owed him one." She saw the giant quail, so she pressed on. "He told me he knew certain things, things you wouldn't like to be made public." For a moment, she enjoyed watching the man's fear of whatever Rafe had over him wrestle with his desire to make them pay through the nose. "Was he wrong?"

Sorenssen forced an unconvincing smile. "Of course, I'm always happy to help an old friend." The smile dropped. "But then we're even, right? You tell him that."

"Tell him yourself. Now, can we dump all this crap and talk business?"

—oOo—

In the flesh, or, at least, within a twenty per cent approximation of it, Sorenssen was a short, overweight young man barely into his twenties, sporting a neatly-trimmed beard and a smart suit from a bygone age. Della and Ginny were back in their own bodies and their own clothes. The loss of her spectacular physique made Della feel small and dowdy. A fact that irritated her enormously.

They were in a large sitting room with white walls and white furniture. A picture window ran the whole length of one wall revealing a wide balcony and a view across a mountainous, crenelated shoreline. The fjords, Della guessed. This might be another room in the young man's idiotic castle. The scale and elaborate detail of this worldlet suggested lots and lots of money.

She felt Sorenssen watching her, waiting for her to be impressed. Instead, she eyed his choice of wardrobe. "Nice suit, fantasy boy. I thought we'd finished playing games."

"Fuck you. You want to talk business? This is my business suit."

"Maybe you don't quite understand what grown-ups mean when they say 'business'."

For the first time, Sorenssen looked angry instead of just petulant. "No, you don't understand. You think this is all a game, just play-acting." He waved his arm to indicate the castle and perhaps the world beyond. "Well, that's because you're old. That's because, for your parents, augmented reality meant a geotagged app on their smartphone." Della had no idea what that meant, but she did remember her gran talking fondly of smartphones and a time when computers were actual objects that sat on desks. "They filled your head with the idea that the world out there is somehow more real that the world in here. Well, I've got news for you, Methuselah, it's not. This is where we live and work. This is where the economy happens. This is where we meet people and fall in love and raise our kids. This is where our friends are, where our lives are. One day we'll work out how to move in here permanently and we can forget about our useless meat, and the stupid twenty per cent rule, and tags, and tanks, and topping up our drips. Then we'll spread our wings and fly. Your generation is the last one that will ever pine for the 'real thing', or look forward to a heaven beyond this life. For the rest of us, life is a beautiful, infinitely pliable thing, and heaven is a place right here on Earth."

Della was gobsmacked by the young man's outburst. She drew a deep breath and opened her mouth to tell him just what she thought of his solipsistic, transhumanist clap-trap, but Ginny took Della by the elbow in a firm grip and pulled at it. She smiled at Sorenssen and said, "Could you just give us a moment?" She led Della aside. She didn't speak, but shot

Della an expression that said, "WTF?"

"What?" Della asked, defensively, knowing full well what was bugging Ginny.

"Can you stop baiting the guy, please? I know he's a jerk, but I need his help."

Della drew a long breath. "He really gets up my nose."

Ginny shook her head, amused. "You must be an absolute tartar at work."

Della bristled. She could be a bit tetchy, sometimes. "I don't tolerate fools wasting my time. That's all."

"But you'll tolerate this one, just for a while, yeah?"

"All right, but if he tries any of that double-D tits stuff again, I'm going to take my fantasy sword and hack him to pieces with it."

Ginny smiled. "I thought it was fun. You looked amazing."

"So did you. I'll show you the recording when we get home."

"You're recording this?"

"Of course. So is he, I'll bet. The pervert."

Ginny put up a hand as if to halt a resurgence of Della's anger. "Tolerance, remember?"

"We'll see."

They went back to join Sorenssen.

"OK, here's the deal," Della said, settling into one of the white sofas. "We want you to break into the accounts department of Chastity Mining and to take a copy of a due diligence report on an entity called the Rice Consortium. Don't leave any traces, give the report to us, and that's the job finished."

"Can't do that."

Della's face froze. "You said you could."

"I can break in, find the report and get out without a trace, but if you want a copy of the report, they'll know. If it's important, there'll be a quantum watermark. Any copying will disturb it and they'll be able to tell. You know? Like quantum entangled transmissions. You intercept one single bit and they can tell. Same principle."

Ginny sounded dismayed. "So you can't get it for us?"

Sorenssen sighed. "Here's the thing. If you don't want me to leave a trace, there are certain things I can't do. I can't take a copy. I can't remove it from the file system. I can't destroy it. I can't alter it in any way."

"So what can you do?" Della was struggling to keep herself from walking out.

"Just one thing. I can read it. Even then, I have to use their own systems to display it to an authorised user."

"If you can read it, why can't you just record what you're seeing?" Ginny asked.

"Because recording software is too easy to spot." He looked meaningfully at Della. Then carried on explaining to Ginny. "Worldlets are intellectual property. Even the cheapest rubbish is designed to prevent itself from being recorded. Something like a big mining company's HQ would spot a recorder in an instant. Don't forget, when we're in here, we're just running programs within virtual environments. They've all got security layers that check out and veto any software they don't like. No-one wants a worldlet they've paid a fortune for being copied and sold as a cheap Nigerian knock-off."

"But you could get around that," Della said. "You got around the twenty-percent rule, and, when we first arrived, your tag was saying 'Odin, Father of the Gods', not 'Peter Sorenssen, Loser,' as it does now. If you can do all that, why can't you run an invisible recorder?"

Sorenssen opened his mouth, then closed it again. "It would take too long to explain. Trust me, it's hard."

"So where does that leave us?"

Sorenssen looked from one to the other, dragging it out. "Either you drop the whole thing...or you will have to come in with me and read it directly from the display."

Della stood up and walked away, too agitated to stay still. She heard Ginny ask, "But if the worldlet can detect recorders, won't it be able to detect us?"

"Sure, but the system won't mind because it will think we're legitimate Chastity Mining employees."

"But our tags…"

Della spoke up. "Obviously tag data isn't as secure as us old folk believe it is."

—oOo—

"Do you know what the third biggest cause of death is for under-twenties?" Della asked as they chewed on printed steaks.

Ginny shrugged. "Drugs?"

"Nope. Thrombosis."

"Oh my God. Really? But they put additives in the drips to avoid that, don't they? And the tanks monitor you."

"Yeah. They feed tiny amounts of aspirin into your blood unless you stay in for more than twenty-four hours, then it switches to warfarin. But there's only so much the tanks can do. Some of these kids stay in their tanks for two or three days at a stretch. Sometimes longer. Top of the range models have good medical systems that alert you if they detect blood clots, and parental overrides to limit their use, but we're talking lots of money. The kind of tanks poor kids use don't have medical monitoring at all, and the poorest families are the very ones that spend most time unlatched. It's a big problem."

Ginny looked a little queasy and Della supposed she was thinking about her own tank and its limitations. Della had never seen it, but she guessed the tank she had in her spare room was several grades better than Ginny's.

"Sorry," Della said. "Not really a topic for mealtime." But she couldn't stop thinking about it. Kids in tanks, choosing to be there rather than in the world, unlatched and unchained, living their comic-book fantasies. Sorenssen's outburst had upset her. It had actually scared her. Was this the world they were building? A world where kids died in their tanks, immersed in pleasant deceptions, preferring to live and die as gods and heroes, than to step out into the real world even for as long as it took to stretch their legs?

She recalled Ginny's story of visiting Cal's house, and Tonia's, of riding through the streets on a bicycle, riding in planes, staying in hotels. "Everything is so daggy out there!" Ginny had said, apparently amazed by the revelation. "It's all so scruffy and neglected when you turn your aug off. I suppose that's why we all stay latched." Della tried to remember when the last time was that she had looked at the world – even her own apartment – with minimal aug. She couldn't. She remembered the last time she had left her apartment. It had been two years ago, when she got her last promotion and moved out of her old one-bedroom place and into this new one. She had made the whole trip latched. Why wouldn't she? She grunted with surprise to realise she had never seen what her unit actually looked like.

"Maybe Sorenssen is right," she said. "Maybe we're all,

gradually disengaging from the world, slowly disappearing into our own minds."

Ginny looked at her for a long time then said, "Which way did you vote?"

After meeting Odin, Father of the gods, they had taken a few minutes to vote in the plebiscite. Oddly enough, Sorenssen had reminded them before they left. "Vote 'No'," he'd said, earnestly. "Keep artificial reality real." Della had treated his injunction with sneering contempt. As if she'd listen to a dickhead like that. But Ginny had questioned him closely about it, listening carefully to his reasons. Of course, she would, being so tangled up with September 10 and the cyberterror legislation. To Della's ears, the boy's maundering about trust and government sounded like he'd been reading too many S10 slogans and not actually thinking about the true purpose of the legislation, which was to keep people safe from lunatics like the ones that had nearly killed her friend.

"I voted 'Yes', of course."

Ginny nodded, looking troubled. "Yeah, me too."

—oOo—

Della met Inspector Chu at the usual pavement café the next day. The news feeds were full of the plebiscite: a sixty-eight per cent vote in favour of the new legislation, lower than the polls had suggested, but a decisive victory for the government. Talking heads from the Cabinet were already promising that the Government would press forward with all speed to fulfil the wishes of the people, to honour its new obligation, exercise its overwhelming mandate, and bring the legislation before the lower house in a matter of days. It gave Della a queasy feeling to think the terrorists would be watching these same feeds, perhaps saying to one another, "OK, the time has come to act." It was some comfort to know the police were across it, keeping tabs on what was happening, but Chu had always seemed a little too relaxed about it, and he had lied to her about the Rice Consortium.

Seeing him lounging in the café, dressed in jeans and a T-shirt, blatantly checking out a curvy, long-legged waitress construct, did little for her confidence.

The slogan on his shirt said, "Big Brother has better things to do than watch you." She nodded towards it as she took her seat. "Cute. You undercover?"

He grinned. "It's Sunday. Even cops get a day off." There was something different about him. He seemed cheerful, more cocky.

She ordered a coffee and the leggy waitress construct simpered at Chu, no doubt sensing his interest. "Two hundred years of the struggle for women's rights," she said, "and we still get this shit everywhere we go." It didn't usually bother her but her transformation into a comic-book goddess yesterday still rankled.

Chu kept grinning. "Hey, if you like, we'll call over one of the waiters and he can flex his biceps at you. If you want equal treatment, nothing's stopping you from having it."

"Yeah, I know the argument. We all have the right to behave equally badly."

He shrugged. "Anyway, she's a construct. Where's the harm? Don't tell me you've never taken a construct to bed."

"I didn't come here to talk about my sex life, Detective." Which begged the question of what she had gone there to talk about. Sorenssen had called that morning to say he'd reviewed the security set-up at Chastity and was ready to go when she gave the word. The imminence of the intended crime had panicked her. She'd called Chu without thinking and set up the meeting, intending to tell him everything. But, since then, she'd had time to rethink her intention. Did she really want the police to know she was about to commit a crime? That Ginny was? Surely the police would have no option but to stop them, or inform Chastity, or something? Did she even want Chu to know that she was helping Ginny dig into the Rice Consortium when it was clearly something he'd tried to steer her away from?

"So?" Chu asked. Again there was that difference in his tone. Until now, he'd been ultra-polite. Now there was a kind of insolence in his tone. It was as if something had happened to change his whole attitude. It made her wary.

"So, there isn't much to tell. We went to see that reporter, Rafe Morgan, yesterday, but it looks like he just wants to drop the whole thing and hide under a rock." That much was true, and if the police had been tracking Ginny, they'd know where she'd been. "Then I took Ginny out – to take her mind of things."

"That's it? That's why you asked to see me?"

"You said I should report regularly."

"Yeah. If something happens. Are you sure that's all?"

Della couldn't blame him for being suspicious. She decided a sudden change of mood might provide a smokescreen. "Hey, I don't exactly enjoy spying on my friend, you know, even in a good cause. I'm not asking for thirty pieces of silver, but you could at least show a little gratitude. Or are you pissed off because I interrupted your day off? What's the matter with you today, anyway? Did you win the lotto last night? You sound like you couldn't give a stuff one way or the other."

He laughed. "Yeah, something like that. You're pretty

223

sharp. I–" He stopped talking and stared, wide-eyed over her shoulder. "Shit." He jumped to his feet, knocking his chair over and pulled a gun out of the back of his jeans. Della watched him raise the weapon, open-mouthed before turning to see what he was so scared of.

Standing in the doorway of the café was a tall, handsome man, square jawed and broad shouldered. He turned towards them at the sound of Chu's chair clattering across the polished wood floor. Immediately, he reached into his jacket, almost certainly for a gun. Explosions crashed overhead and Della had instinctively curled up and shut her eyes before she realised the sound had been Chu shooting at the newcomer. There were more shots, joined now by screams and smashing crockery. She forced herself to open her eyes.

The café had become a disaster movie. Tables and chairs were thrown everywhere and people were screaming and yelling and running for their lives. The man at the door was standing like a statue in the chaos, firing back at Chu. She turned to the policeman but he had gone. She spotted him sprinting down the street, gun in hand and, even as she watched, the other man pushed past her, throwing furniture aside, and raced off in pursuit.

Her heart was hammering and her breath came in ragged gasps. The two men disappeared around a corner and the panic around her slowly abated. People were talking loudly, excitedly. A woman was sobbing. Someone shouted, "Call the cops." People were looking at her. An anxious voice said, "She was with one of them."

Frightened and dazed, Della stumbled clear of the wrecked café and opened a portal. "Hey, you! Wait a minute!" a man shouted. Without hesitating, she stepped through and was gone.

—oOo—

She spent the next hour on the beach, a lonely stretch of broad white sand in the far north of Queensland, the ocean churning and roaring on one side and pandanus trees on the other, fringing the low hills and rain forest beyond. She walked barefoot through the surf, trudging for several kilometres along the gently-curving shoreline. Far ahead of her, everything was shrouded in spray. After a while, her heartbeat slowed and her thoughts began to unscramble themselves.

Della knew who the stranger had been: Dover Richards, the man Tonia had said killed her brother, the man who had pretended to Ginny that he was a policeman, the man who had tailed Rafe. According to Ginny, Richards probably worked for the Consortium. And Della had just seen him walk into a crowded street café and try to shoot a federal police officer.

Just reviewing the bare facts of it started Della's heart pounding again. She splashed on through the cold water until she was calmer.

She couldn't tell Ginny. The fact that she was there in that café meeting Chu was a betrayal she couldn't admit to. So what could she do? Go to the police? Perhaps, but Chu was the police. One way or another, they'd know by now. And if Richards had shot the cop, there would be a dozen people from the café happy to point her out as having been involved. If Chu was injured or dead, the police would be coming to her soon enough. If not, then Chu could contact her if he liked, but she wouldn't be meeting him again. It was pretty obvious that Richards was hunting him down and the safest place for Della to be was as far away from the inspector as possible.

And wasn't that weird? The criminal hunting down the cop? Is that how things worked these days. Had criminals become so powerful that they could attack cops on their day off in a public place, in broad daylight?

And why hadn't Richards shot her? She had been with Chu. She might have been another cop for all Richards knew, although – and the memory filled her with shame – an exceptionally cowardly one. But Richards had run right past her. He'd had plenty of opportunity to shoot her but he had ignored her completely.

And the guns…

She had no doubt they were deadly. Guns were used in all kinds of interactive adventures in VR. People played out every kind of battle from the Civil War to imaginary space wars. The guns they used wouldn't hurt a fly – just knock you out of the game. But she knew that the police and criminals had guns that would hijack a worldlet's software and deliver dangerous feedback through a person's neural implants. The gun and the bullets – like everything else when you were unlatched – were merely metaphors. They helped the gunman direct the software to the target whose cognitive implants they intended to fry. She'd seen a documentary about it once. Worldlet builders were forced to include mandatory security layers to prevent such attacks – except by the authorities – but criminal hackers could always get around them, and so many proprietors failed to keep their worldlet security up-to-date. The documentary had shown people with severe brain damage, living their whole lives in hospice worldlets, needing twenty-four-seven care.

It could have been me.

She stopped walking, waiting for her breathing to settle, before moving on.

So the Consortium was hunting the cop who was keeping an eye on Ginny. They probably knew where Ginny was. They probably knew all about Della. She felt panic rising in her. What the hell were they playing at? And what was she going to do, if even the cops couldn't keep her safe?

She didn't like the fear. She didn't like being helpless. She felt a sudden irrational resentment that her CEO knew something about the Rice Consortium that she wouldn't tell. Della's life was in danger and no-one seemed to care. It hadn't seemed quite real when Ginny had told her about it. It had been behind glass, somebody else's problem. Now she had seen too much of it, all first-hand, hackers changing their identity and appearance, gunmen shooting at the police. It felt as if everything she had known and trusted had been a lie. Like the wet sand beneath her feet, shifting and oozing and sucking her under…

She realised she had stopped again and was staring blankly into the distance. She shouldn't be doing this, she told herself. She should get back home, talk to Ginny, make plans. A small jolt of fear hit her as she imagined herself – her real self – supine and helpless in her tank, and Dover Richards standing over her. She started walking again, agitation overcoming inertia. The security on her unit was minimal. A lock on the door, that's all. But people didn't waste time and money making their physical homes secure. What would be the point? They contained very little worth stealing. Everybody's true wealth was on QNet, these days. That's where you made your money; that's where you spent it. If you wanted art or fancy gadgetry, you got it for your virtual world, not the real one. The criminals knew this. There were no burglars any more – except in VR.

She opened a portal so she could teleport back to her tank, but she hesitated. What if he was there? What if he was just waiting for her to come out? She looked around at the endless beach, the vast empty ocean. What if he stepped out of a portal right there? She would have nowhere to hide, nowhere to run.

"I can't live like this!" She shouted it at the blue dome of the sky, but the crashing waves made her shout a tiny thing, and the blustering wind took it and tore it to shreds. She had to go home, no matter who or what waited for her there. She wanted to be angry, so angry she would spit in the eye of the Consortium and its murderous thugs, but all she had was fear.

And money. She could hire protection. You could get robot guards off the Net – not exactly legal, but who gave a stuff? She could put in a fancy security system. She could go away – physically – to Europe or the States, somewhere far away, while all this sorted itself out. She could pay that creep Sorenssen to change her identity, keep her hidden. She could–

But what about Ginny? Again resentment welled up in her. It was all Ginny's fault. She'd told her to take that damned package to the police. But no, she'd had to do what Cal asked her. That was Ginny's trouble. She'd always been so eager to please, so accommodating and appeasing. Well, no wonder with a family like hers. Anybody would grow up warped in a home like that. It was no wonder she didn't have a career or a bloke. She was so busy doing what everyone else wanted she had never made a stand for what she needed. And now she'd landed herself in this mess, all for the sake of some man who – surprise, surprise – was just using her all along.

She walked away from the ocean towards the line of

pandanus trees, where the sand was dry and hot, and sat down, not wanting to stay, but unable to make the decision to go home. At least here she was out of it all for a while. Well, she could pretend she was, anyway.

Ginny and Sorenssen were expecting her to join them later to burgle the Chastity offices, but Della knew now that she couldn't do it. If Ginny found a way to reach the Consortium, she would go there. She would do whatever she could to uncover their nasty little secrets and expose their plans. They wouldn't like that. They'd try to kill her. And they'd probably succeed. What could Ginny do against them? Poor, sweet, gentle Ginny?

The touch of tears on her cheeks made Della realise she had started crying. Ginny was her best friend, the only friend she had these days, once you discounted all the acquaintances at work, the over-friendly vendor reps who wanted so much to be her mate, the people she had known and once been close to but with whom she had been too busy to stay in touch. And now she was going to let Ginny down. She had to. She wasn't some kind of hero from an interactive. She was just an ordinary person, a manager in a mining company. She juggled figures and negotiated contracts. She wasn't fearless and brave. She couldn't face down terrorists and killers…

She stopped and blinked in surprise.

But Ginny could. Poor, sweet, gentle Ginny could do all that. And she didn't even have to. No-one was making her. No-one was even suggesting that she should. She had already faced the kind of danger that had made a quivering wreck out of Della, and she was going back for more, deliberately putting herself in harm's way just because she thought it was the right thing to do.

Since when had meek and mild little Ginny been such a

hero? Where had all that courage come from? It disturbed Della that they had both been tested in the fires of deadly danger and, while Ginny had come out tempered and hardened, she herself had turned into a molten puddle. That wasn't Della's conception of the two of them at all. Ginny was the weak one, the one who always gave way, and let people walk all over her. Della was the strong one, the one with the will to succeed and the backbone to make it happen. Could she have been so wrong about all that?

"You're the sensible one," Ginny had so often told her. And it was true. All her life she'd made the right decisions, weighed costs and benefits, evaluated the risks and made the sensible choice. She'd been proud of that. It had made her a solid achiever, a person of substance. But maybe sensible just meant 'safe'. Maybe her whole approach to life was based on an underlying cowardice, an inability to take risks, a fear of failure. Of course, Ginny had her hang-ups, lots of them, but maybe Ginny had been the brave one all along.

She sat on the beach and thought about her life and her friend, her fear and her options as the sun passed its zenith and began its descent. In the end, she knew barely more than when she started. But she was sure of three things; she was not going to Chastity with Ginny and Sorenssen, even though she would not stop them; she was going to tell Ginny all about Inspector Chu, however bad it made Della look, Ginny had a right to know the police were already taking action; and she was leaving town that very afternoon on the first flight to anywhere that was a long, long way from Sydney.

She got up and teleported home. Her eyes were tightly closed as the lid of the tank lifted, but nothing happened, no-one spoke. She peeped out at the empty room and almost sobbed with relief.

She unplugged the drip from her catheter and rushed out to find Ginny, but her friend wasn't there. The guest tank was empty. The whole unit was empty. She tried to call her but Ginny's phone was redirected to her message service.

At a loss, she sat down and tried to work out where Ginny might be. There was no sign of a struggle. The door had not been kicked in. She jumped up and went to the guest bedroom. Ginny's things were not in the wardrobe, and her bag had gone.

That's when Della noticed the piece of paper on the bed. It wasn't real paper, of course, but another of those endless metaphors, a private message, geotagged to the bed, looking like a folded sheet of paper.

"Dear Del," it said. "I've gone with Odin, Father of the gods, to do that bit of business we had planned. I hope you won't be too cross that we left you out of it. I think it's for the best. You've been a true friend to me when I needed it most and I will always be grateful but I can't impose on you any longer – and who knows how this might all end? Take care of yourself. I'll tell you what happened soon, I hope, when it is all over. 'Til then, love, Ginny."

Part 4

Chapter 17

Ginny looked around the office as if the desks and coffee machines, potted palms and corporate artwork might just explode in her face.

"Try to act natural," Sorenssen said. "You're Katia Dobric, accounts manager, and you have every right to be here."

She looked down again at her large breasts and tight pencil skirt. "There wasn't a single woman in the whole accounts department who didn't look like a dominatrix, I suppose? You just picked this one at random? You know I can hardly walk in this thing? If we have to make a run for it, I'm going to look like a complete drongo teetering along in double time."

"You look fantastic. I don't know what you're complaining about. You're lucky you don't have to look like this." He made a gesture to show her his own stolen identity, an overweight, middle-aged man with receding hair and heavy jowls.

"Yeah, well, I'm sorry the company didn't hire more Norse gods to run its accounts department. You're sure this bloke will have the right clearances? He doesn't look much."

"No probs. He's the head honcho."

They crossed a space littered with sofas and low tables.

Around it were individual offices. Bland muzak was playing at a level that made it easily ignorable, but Ginny clenched her teeth anyway, annoyed that Della's company was so cheap as to use out-of-copyright rubbish like that. Ahead was a broad corridor with plush carpet. They had studied a map of the office together in Sorenssen's castle before setting off but it had not helped her much. Luckily her partner in crime seemed to remember the layout – more or less – because they could not use the worldlet's nav system without tipping off the security monitors that there were strangers in the building. The doors in the corridor were labelled with the names of the most senior accounts staff. The last one they came to belonged to Gerry Frink, Head of Accounts.

Sorenssen pushed the door open and strode in, with Ginny mincing along in his wake. They both stopped dead at the sight of a slender young woman staring at them from a desk opposite the door.

"Hello," said Sorenssen, recovering first from their three-way surprise. They were in a private secretary's office, Ginny guessed. A door to the right of the desk stood ajar, revealing a far larger office beyond.

"Hello," said the woman. She took a long look at Ginny – or Katia, as it must seem to her – and a hint of a frown crossed her face.

Sorenssen stepped across to the inner office door and pushed it open. Ginny walked past him into the room, painfully aware of her outsize tits and bum as she wiggled past the secretary. Whether Sorenssen had noticed it or not, Ginny could see just what the woman was thinking.

"We don't want to be disturbed," Sorenssen said in a firm voice and closed the door on her.

"You can't leave it like that," Ginny told him as soon as

the door was shut. "She thinks we've come in here to have sex. She's probably got her ear up against that door right now – metaphorically speaking. Christ! For all we know, those two have got a thing going on. She might do anything."

Irritatingly, Sorenssen waved her anxieties away with a dismissive sneer. "She'll sit and stew for half an hour first," he said. "By then, we'll be long gone."

"You hope."

With a sigh, the young hacker went to sit in the accountant's chair. "You stand by the door with a vase and clobber her if she comes in," he said. "I'll be over here doing something useful."

Ginny scowled at him, lips pursed. If it would have made the least impact, she would have clobbered him with a vase. She watched him pulling up displays and moving information around with quick, precise gestures. Well bugger this, she couldn't just stand there while that woman decided what to do. "Sorenssen, call me back in when you've got the file." Before he could argue, she opened the door and went out, closing it behind her.

The secretary, Shelise Kwang, according to her ID block, stood up and came over to meet her. She seemed to be labouring under some strong emotion but Ginny could not say what. She stood right in front of Ginny, too close for comfort, staring into her eyes. They were about the same height, although the other woman was of a slighter build.

"What's going on?" she asked, almost demanded.

Ginny tried to sound casual. "It's just Gerry. Some kind of flap about the payroll." She wished Della were there to come up with something plausible.

The woman blinked, but maintained her self-control. "When I saw you come in here with him, I thought…"

Ginny wasn't exactly used to office politics, she had always worked for herself, but she was fairly sure that this woman's behaviour was far from normal. What on Earth had she walked into.

She almost jumped when Shelise raised a hand and touched Ginny's cheek. "I know what he's like, the fat pig. I'd die if you ever…" She moved forward and kissed Ginny on the lips. Ginny fought the urge to jump back but hyper-sensitive Shelise must have noticed the way she stiffened.

"What's the matter?" she asked, stepping back to study Ginny's face.

Ginny grabbed the woman's hands and held them. "Nothing's wrong…darling. But Gerry's just through that door. He could come out at any minute."

Shelise yanked her hands free. She raised her chin in a defiant gesture. "So? It's not a crime to love someone, even in this awful place. You're the one who's always saying I'm too timid. You're the one who said we should shout it from the rooftops." She turned away. "Or have you changed your mind?"

Ginny raised her face to the heavens and cursed her luck. Then she cursed Sorenssen. If he hadn't been such a pervert, he might have picked her an identity that wasn't going to get them both arrested. She took a breath and moved up close behind Shelise, slipping her arms around her and pulling her close. "Don't be silly, darling. You know I love you." She nuzzled the woman's neck and kissed it. At first, Shelise resisted, not pulling free but standing rigid and unyielding, but as Ginny continued to murmur reassurances, the other woman softened and melted. Eventually, she turned in Ginny's arms and made a small, coy smile.

"So you still love me then?"

"Of course I do. And to hell with Gerry."

Shelise laid her head on Ginny's shoulder. "I'm such an idiot. Only you're so beautiful and so hot and I know all the men fancy you and I can never really believe someone like you could love me."

It was breaking Ginny's heart to listen to the poor woman pouring out her insecurities. Yet she daren't say too much to her. One wrong word could give away the whole impersonation. So, instead, she found Shelise's lips with her own and kissed her.

It was a tender, consoling kiss, meant to say more than words ever could, and it seemed to work because, in moments, Shelise was kissing her back. And the kiss escalated quickly from tender to passionate.

Ginny had rarely kissed a woman. There was a girl at school once, and Deborah Beals at university. She and Debs had spent the whole of one hot summer night together. But Ginny was basically hetero and had never felt the urge to experiment farther. Even so, she felt herself responding to this woman's keen desire, enjoying the press of body on body, the hands that caressed her buttocks and breasts so eagerly. She opened up to the embrace and let her own hands explore the other woman's delicate curves, let her mouth and tongue return the woman's passion. By the time she felt Shelise's fingers against her belly, sliding down the tight fabric of her skirt towards her crotch, she was so caught up in the fever of the moment that she moaned in anticipated pleasure.

And that's when she realised Sorenssen was standing in the doorway watching them. She disentangled herself from Shelise in a rush, trying to regain her dignity. Damn that boy! How long had he been watching?

"Mr....er..." she said, trying to stay in character but

completely forgetting Sorenssen's alias.

He grinned. "Katia, would you mind coming in for a moment, there's something I need you to look at. That is, unless you'd rather continue what you were doing."

Ginny felt herself redden, not just from embarrassment, but from anger at the stupid boy. She turned to Shelise, who had hurried back to stand behind her desk. The secretary fidgeted with a small ornament, a twitch of her head betraying the anger she too must be feeling. Yet, even after so short an acquaintance, Ginny was sure Shelise's anger was directed inwards, not at Sorenssen. She said, "Shelise, why don't you go home? Call me this evening. I'm going to be busy with this payroll thing for ages now."

Shelise seemed confused. Perhaps she was not used to the beautiful Katia being so assertive. Perhaps she was having even more trouble with the abrupt emotional switch than Ginny was. She looked at Sorenssen, who said, "Yes, off you go, Shelise. I won't be needing you."

Without waiting to see how she responded, Sorenssen went back into his office. Ginny gave Shelise what she hoped was a reassuring smile. "You know, probably everyone will just forget all about it by the morning," she said, and followed Sorenssen into the office.

When the door was closed behind her, Sorenssen leered and said, "Nice diversion. I wish I'd got it recorded."

"Up yours, Sorenssen. That poor woman's going to be a mess when she finds out the real Katia and Gerry don't remember a thing about all this. Did you find the file?"

"Of course." He flipped a display so that she could see it.

She pulled up a chair and began flipping through the pages of the report. It wasn't long. When she'd read it through once, she started again from the beginning.

The Rice Consortium, the report's author had written, was a legitimate company with the financial backing of several very large, very high-profile Australian corporations and high-net-value individuals. Its purpose was to lobby in favour of the proposed cybersecurity legislation. But the compilers of the report had been instructed to dig as deeply as possible, and had been given a very large budget to do so. They had recruited the services of specialist private investigators who found that there was no evidence of any lobbying activities whatsoever by the company. They also found – and this must have been what had shaken Della's CEO so much – that several of the Consortium's owners and chief operating executives had connections to organised crime. They didn't actually say 'Tong' or 'Mafia' but there was no doubt there were large and powerful criminal organisations behind the Consortium.

"You read this?" she asked Sorenssen.

He gave a quick nod. "Looks like you're screwing with the Mob."

There were names and contact details for several key Consortium personnel. Too much detail to remember. "You're sure we can't record any of this?" she asked and felt relieved when Sorenssen confirmed it was impossible without discovery. That was it then. End of the road. She could maybe make an effort and commit some of these names to memory, maybe even a Net address or two, but there was no point. She was not going to beard a bunch of gangsters in their lairs or burgle their homes looking for evidence. There was a limit to how far her nerve would take her and this was it.

She nodded towards the display. "Is that all there was?"

Sorenssen shrugged. "There were notes, records of travel

and meetings, payments to various people for services. Loads of stuff really, but that's the report."

"OK," she said. "Tidy this up and let's get out of here."

Sorenssen smirked. "If you're quick you might catch the hottie out there before she leaves, get a bit more girl-on-girl action going."

"You're a disgusting creep. When we leave this place, I hope I never see you again."

"I'm just saying, while you've got that great body to play with, why not have a bit of fun?"

She turned away from him, too angry to respond. The mere presence of that emotional imbecile made her want to scream. She noticed her hands were shaking and she clasped them together to hide it from Sorenssen. She felt terrible about having deceived Shelise, not to mention confused and conflicted about how much she had enjoyed what they'd done. That, together with the fear and relief she had felt on discovering the Consortium was a front for organised crime, had left her emotions in a mess.

"I'm leaving," she said, turning to face him with as much composure as she could muster. "There's no point in me hanging around. Thank you for your help."

But Sorenssen did not seem to be listening. He stared into the displays, head darting from side to side, hands flicking and stabbing. She didn't like the tense expression on his face.

"What is it?" she asked, but she already knew.

"An alarm," he said, his attention focused on the displays.

"I don't get it."

"They're coming?" How long did they have? What could she tell them when the security guards or the police burst in? Could she keep Della out of it?

"I – I don't know. It's not…" He dodged around in his

feverish interaction with the systems. "I'm trying to divert…"

"Maybe we should just run." She could feel the panic taking hold. What was the boy doing? They should leave, surely?

Abruptly, he stepped back from the desk. "Shit!" He looked at her and she could see his shock and fear. "It's not the Chastity systems. Somebody planted a tell-tale on the file. Somebody else." The way he said it made her insides turn to liquid. The only other people who might be interested were the Consortium.

"We are so rooted," he said. "They scanned the office. They found us. They know who we are. Who we really are." He blinked once, blank-faced. Then he ran.

Ginny tried to grab him as he passed but he shook her off, threw open the door and bolted out of the office, heading for their exit portal. It was the trigger for Ginny to panic too and hurry after him, weeping with frustration at the tight skirt and heels that slowed her to a teetering hobble.

—oOo—

She burst free of the tank like a diver coming up for air, tore off the drip and scrabbled for the gun she had hidden in the bedside drawer. It was not until she had the weapon in her hands and it was pointing at the hotel-room door that her breathing began to steady and her brain began to work again.

The Mob was after her. The Mafia. The Triads. They knew her. They'd caught her spying on them. They were coming for her. She had to get out of there and hide.

She began dragging things out of cupboards and shoving them into her bag, everything made harder because she daren't put down the gun, not even for a moment.

Where could she go? Where could she hide? Another hotel? There were so few in Sydney a child could find her in a two minute Net search. An empty house, then? A derelict. There must be lots of places like that. But where would she find one? Where would she start looking? She knew Brisbane well enough, but not Sydney. Dare she call Della and ask for help? No. They could be monitoring her calls. A thought struck fear into her. They might even be able to track her tag. But, surely, only the police could do something like that? Even if that were true – and she doubted now that there was any privacy or security for anyone any more – the Consortium would need just one corrupt cop in their pocket and they would know exactly where she was. For a moment, she thought about going bush. Out in the vast interior of the continent were those wild places Rafe had spoken of that had little if any QNet coverage. But how would she live? What would she eat? How could she even get there?

The police, then. She had to go to the police. It was her only hope. She pulled Detective Chu's ID out from her contacts and set up the call, still her finger hesitated over the call button. Which was worse, taking your chances on the run with gangsters trying to kill you, or giving yourself up to the Feds and having them ship you up north to an offshore "processing centre" where you could be held indefinitely as a suspected terrorist?

She could see Chu in her mind's eye. Tall and strong, with dark, gentle eyes, she couldn't help but trust him to treat her well. And he had been so kind to her that day she had flipped out and fainted. It was that memory more than anything that made her press the call button.

He seemed surprised to see her. "Miss Galton. What can I do for you?"

"I – I think I'm in trouble. I mean real trouble. Some people are after me." It was only when she said it to Chu that it struck her that the Consortium might always have been after her. That, perhaps, discovering their underworld backers didn't really change a thing. Maybe she was in no more danger today than she had been yesterday. "I have things I need to tell you," she said, "about some terrorists and a criminal organisation." She steeled herself. "And about some things I've done and seen in the past few weeks."

Chu regarded her as if he couldn't quite make up his mind how to respond. Cautiously, he said, "We should meet. Physically. Why don't I come to you?"

"I don't know if I'm safe here."

"I'm not far away. I won't be long."

"You're in Sydney?"

"We both seem to be travelling a lot lately. Just wait there. I'm on my way."

She ended the call and sat down on the edge of the bed. Waves of exhaustion swept through her. At least it was all over now. Whatever her fate, it was no longer in her hands. Chu would take her away somewhere, she supposed. There would be questions, even accusations, but at least she would be safe. She let her eyelids close. The gun in her lap seemed to weigh a ton. She could just go to sleep. She thought about calling Della and telling her, but decided it was best not to involve anyone else. She lay back on the bed, not bothering to move the bag next to her. She should probably tell Sorenssen that she'd contacted the police, but she was still angry with him and, when the crunch came, he had just run off and left her. Well, she hadn't expected anything better of him. It occurred to her that, in her own panicked flight, she had not even glanced around to see if Shelise Kwang had still been there in the outer office. That poor woman. She remembered Shelise's lips against her own, the feel of her arms pressing their bodies together. It was such a shame Sorenssen had interrupted them, spoilt that blissful, delicious moment...

Chapter 18

She woke to pounding, hammering fear. Her heart lurched as she half-fell off the bed, remembering the gun, groping for it. It was the door. Someone was banging at the door. She shook herself. It must be Chu. She must have been asleep. She hurried over and peeped through the spyhole. There was the detective with two other men behind him. She shoved the gun in her overall pocket and yanked the door open.

"Thank God you're here," she said. She rushed back to the bed and grabbed her bag. "Where are we going? Do you have, like, physical offices or something?" She turned to find Chu standing close behind her. The other two men had closed the door and were standing inside, watching her. Chu held a gun, pointed at her chest.

She tried to speak but could not. Her brain just would not send the signals. Her mouth opened and closed as everything she thought she understood whirled into a cloud of confusion and refused to reassemble itself. She sat down on the bed, not even looking at Chu. What was the point? This was the end. It was all over.

"You're with them," she said, surprising herself. "The Consortium." She looked up at him, anger beginning to seep into her awareness. The big man with the gun, the room itself, began to slide away. Could she believe anything she thought she knew? Was everybody lying? How could she know what was real? "Are you even a cop at all?"

"I'm just going to ask you a few questions, then we can all be on our way."

"You're not going to kill me?"

The momentary hope was dashed when he said, "Of course not," and she could hear the lie in his voice.

"First, you can hand me that gun you carry. The one you used to shoot our guy in Stanthorpe."

Again an instant of wild hope. If she could draw the gun and shoot him… But the chances of success seemed tiny and the chances of him shooting her seemed enormous. She nodded. A kind of grief crept over her, an overwhelming sense of loss and regret. She was about to die. Ludicrously, she thought about the Old Vienna contract for UnReality. It was the last soundscape she had written. It would be her legacy. It was a bitter, bitter thought.

"The gun, please, Ginny." She snapped out of her reverie and reached into her pocket. "Slowly and carefully," Chu said. She nodded, the hard metal of the weapon under her fingers. She reached farther so she could pull the gun out by its barrel, so there would be no mistake, and her fingers found something else. She pushed her hand right down into the pocket and found the smooth cylinder, the little black box.

"What the fuck?" Chu yelled, looking around wildly. One of the men at the door shouted "Hey!" and drew his gun. Ginny rolled sideways, dragging her bag after her, and crawled towards the door.

"I can't see anything but fucking jungle," the guy at the door yelled.

Chu fired two shots at where Ginny had been. "Don't let

her get out," he shouted.

Ginny saw the guy at the door raise his gun and point it at Chu. "Is that you shooting, Chu?" He looked scared and his aim wandered around uncertainly.

"Nobody fire!" Chu yelled, seeming to realise the danger they were all in.

By the time Ginny reached the door, one of Chu's guards had stepped away from it, but the one with his gun drawn blocked her exit. She pulled out her own gun and pointed it at his chest. It would be so easy to kill him. He didn't even know she was there, blinded and deafened by the aug illusion she was transmitting. It was too easy, a horrible, cold-blooded execution. She couldn't do it. Even to save her life, she couldn't kill a man like that.

Furious with herself, she looked around for inspiration. She could hit him with something maybe, but the hotel room had no handy sticks or lamps, just a too-heavy chair across the room near Chu. She backed up against the wall. How long would this effect last? How long before one of them accidentally touched her and grabbed her? She pointed her gun at Chu. Maybe she could shoot that lying bastard even if she couldn't shoot a stranger. Or maybe she didn't have to.

As quickly as she could, she crawled across the floor to the bed and curled up beside it on the far side from Chu. Then she fired a shot past Chu into the far wall.

Chu cried out in surprise and turned to face her. His friend at the door, shouted and fired a shot indiscriminately into the room. The other guy drew his own gun and started shooting too.

"Stop fucking shooting!" Chu screamed.

But the others didn't have his self-control. They were both completely spooked. "She's not going to pick me off like a fucking target in a shooting range," the one by the door shouted and fired all around him. "I'm not just going to let her kill me."

Chu took aim and fired at where the shots had come from. It took him four shots before he hit the man in the hip and sent him reeling off across the room to fetch up against a small desk, still shooting. By then, the other was shooting back at Chu. Her ears ringing from the fusillade going on all around her, Ginny crouched low and ran for the door. Chu was still bellowing at his men to stop but they had each clearly decided that they'd rather kill everyone else in the room than die at the hands of an unseen enemy.

She slipped through and into he hallway, still staying low but pausing at the other side of the wall. She knew the range of the device must be at least fifteen metres. That was about how far away the children had been from Rafe when Kelly Ahn had used it in Stanthorpe, and they'd obviously been affected too. That meant she had at least that far to go before the men in the hotel room could see again. There was a stairway to her left. If she took that route, she'd maybe make it to the bottom before the pursuit started. It wasn't much of a lead and the men following her were bound to be very motivated after what she'd just put them through. On the other hand, if they did catch up with her, they wouldn't be able to find her.

As long as the battery held out.

She ran. She almost killed herself racing down the stairs too fast and crashing into the wall on the first landing. Ignoring the pain in her shoulder and the way her legs threatened to buckle at each reckless leap down multiple steps, she careened on down to the lobby and the street exit, slamming into a robot luggage trolley and heaving at the sluggish automatic doors. She fumbled and dropped her gun, snatching it up with a sob, and then she was out and pounding along the pavement.

She couldn't even tell if her aug hallucination was still protecting her. The streets were empty except for the ubiquitous robot trucks. She rounded a corner and kept running. The terror of pursuit was rapidly being quenched by the physical impossibility of sucking in enough breath to keep going at that speed. When a stitch hit her like a knife between the ribs, she swerved into an alleyway and hid there, clutching her side and screwing up her eyes against the pain. She couldn't go on. She had to rest and get her breath back. But she could watch the street. If Chu and his men came after her, at least she'd be able to tell whether they could see her or not when they came close enough.

She poked her head around the corner and there was a man running towards her. Just one man, tall and lean. She waited, with her heart thumping and her breathing still laboured. At about twenty metres he staggered and almost fell, coming to a halt with his arms out as if he'd been struck blind in mid-stride.

She could see him quite clearly. It wasn't Chu or one of the others. It was Dover Richards.

With a gasp of surprise, she drew back and leaned against the cool brick wall. How many of them were after her? Could she ever escape them? She peered back at him. He was talking to himself – presumably on the phone to someone – and he sounded cross and impatient. He raised his voice and she heard him shout, "…the whole damned city if you have to! Just get it done!"

He wasn't coming closer and she felt quite safe for the moment. No-one else appeared as he stood there, looking around at the dense jungle that surrounded him as if he'd like to tear it all down with his bare hands.

"Ginny," he called and she jumped. "Ginny, turn that bloody thing off. It's me, Inspector Richards. I'm here to help you. I know you can hear me. I know you're nearby. Please, Ginny. I want to help you."

So, he still thought he could fool her by pretending to be a cop? Well, why not? Chu had managed it. She had a vision of them both, back at Consortium HQ, laughing together over what a gullible, trusting fool she had been. Now she was stuck again. It sounded like Richards knew the kind of device she was using, knew its range. He began edging his way towards her, arms out ahead like an insect's feelers. He was going slowly but his sense of direction was better than she would have liked. She had a minute, or maybe two, to think of something. She could shoot him, of course. The gun was still in her hand. But she already knew she couldn't do that – even to Dover Richards. She put the gun away and pulled the black box and the cylinder out. The box was hiding her, but it was also giving her away.

She closed her eyes and cursed herself for an idiot. The answer was obvious. She put the box down by the corner of the alley but kept the cylinder. She stepped away from it into the street. Richards was still blinded but she could see him as clearly as ever. She crossed the street to the other side and stood behind a parked truck. If the battery suddenly failed, she didn't want to be out in the open. She scouted about for a way to get clear, preferably back the way she had come, so as to confuse her pursuers. She could stroll right past Richards and leave him groping his way up the street. The idea that she might stroll right up to him and punch him in the teeth was almost irresistible. But she needed escape more than she needed retribution. She saw the route she would take, a half-block beyond Richards and a right turn into a side street. He started calling out to her, pleading with her to be sensible and let him find her. She would be gone and far away before he realised she was even missing.

And then Chu appeared in the street. Ginny clutched the side of the truck and tried to melt herself into it. The man who had just tried to kill her was limping and trailing blood. His face was grey and his eyes burned. His gun hung at the end of his arm like a weight on a pendulum. He stopped when he saw Richards and must have realised from the man's behaviour that he was caught in the aug illusion. Chu himself was still clear of it. Ginny saw a grim smile spread across her would-be assassin's face.

"Tagger!" he shouted. "She's mine!"

Richards showed no sign of hearing him, deafened as he was by the jungle noises in his aug.

Tagger? She remembered Chu himself explaining that taggers were police officers from the Department of Missing Persons. But if Chu thought Richards was a tagger, that meant he too had been taken in by Richards' cop impersonation.

Chu raised his gun, slowly, as if it weighed a ton. Ginny noticed blood on the man's hand, blood that had run down from a would on his arm. The gun wavered but Chu was still smiling, taking his time with the shot. He raised his other hand to support the weight of the gun. *But if Richards and Chu weren't on the same side…*

She pulled her gun and aimed it at Chu. If she shot Chu and Richards survived, might he be willing to help her? Might his own agenda, whatever it was, be to keep her safe from the Consortium? If she didn't shoot Chu, right now, Richards would be dead and she would never know. Without being aware that she had made the decision, she squeezed the trigger a the gun jumped in her grip.

A chunk of brickwork exploded from the wall beyond where Chu stood.

Her would-be victim flinched and ducked, but still had the presence of mind to swing his weapon around to point at her. *I really need to learn how to shoot one of these things*, she told herself and pulled back behind the robot truck. *Now what?* Now Chu knew just where she was and could see her. She had to get away, but how?

She jumped as the truck's engine whined into life and then stood unbelieving as her only cover pulled away from the kerb and drove off down the street.

"That was a clever trick, back there in the hotel," Chu said. He seemed completely unconcerned that she might shoot him. She supposed he had made a realistic assessment of her skill with a handgun. "I'm going to look like a complete arsehole when I go back and report on all this." His smile returned. "But at least I'll be able to tell them you're dead."

"Why are you doing this?" she said, her voice had a pleading, whining tone she didn't like to hear. "I don't know anything about the Consortium. Not really. I'm no threat to anybody."

"You keep poking your damned nose in our business though. And that has to stop."

They were a long way apart – twenty metres at least – each pointing their gun at the other. Could Chu really shoot her dead from that far away? Could he still hit her if she was moving? She could run past the hallucination device and keep going. Chu wouldn't be able to get past it. He'd have a receding target to aim at. It must give her a better chance than just standing there like a practice target.

"You wanted to ask me some questions," she said, stalling while she plucked up the nerve to run. "Why don't you ask them now and you'll see I don't know anything."

He laughed. "Like I give a fuck what you know. It won't matter a damn when your dead. All I care about is paying you back for what you just did."

"But the Consortium cares. Won't they be–"

Some small movement, some shift in his stance gave him away. Ginny threw herself into a flat-out sprint across the road, back towards the black box in the alley. She heard the crack of Chu's gun as he fired. Then she heard it again. Then three more shots in rapid succession. How could she still be alive? How could he miss her?

She stole a quick glance over her shoulder and what she saw made her stumble and almost fall. Chu had dropped to the ground, flat on his back, arms and legs spread. And there was Dover Richards down on one knee, his own smoking gun in a two-handed grip, still aiming at the dead man. She staggered to a halt as Richards turned to face her. Her heart was knocking so hard in her chest she could feel it rocking her body.

He could see her. The device had stopped working.

Richards had her in his sights for a moment then he lifted the barrel up and away, took a long breath, and pushed the gun back into its shoulder holster.

"Are there any more of them chasing you?" he asked, sauntering towards her as if nothing had happened.

Ginny pointed her own gun at him, her hand shaking. "Stop. Don't come any closer. Who are you? I mean really. Who are you working for?"

He didn't stop. He strolled right up to her, his handsome,

cocky smile unwavering. "Do you have a license for that thing, Virginia?"

"I said stop!" She shouted so loudly, it surprised even her.

The smile fell away, replaced by an angry frown. "Put the gun away right now and we can talk. Otherwise, I'm going to take it off you and arrest you for discharging a weapon in a public place."

"So you really are a cop?" There seemed no other reason for him to keep on acting like one.

"Yes, I am."

"That's what he said." She waved her gun towards Chu's dead body.

The instant she did so, Richards stepped up to her, grabbed the gun and wrenched it out of her hand. He put it in his pocket but didn't step back. "That's better," he said.

Ginny nursed her twisted fingers and scowled into his grinning face. "You can drop the act now, I suppose. Even if you are a cop, you're in somebody's pocket. Who else is interested in the outcome of the cyberterrorism vote? S10 maybe? No, you killed Tonia's brother, didn't you? Another terror group then. Or maybe you just sell your services day-by-day to the highest bidder." She watched his face keenly for any tell-tale sign, but all his expression showed was bemusement.

"Where did you get that augblaster?" he asked, ignoring her accusations.

"That what?"

"The device you used to bamboozle me a while ago. Who gave it to you? Where is it?"

"It's a stupid device. It gives you away as much as hides you. And it has the battery life of a Nigerian housebot. You're welcome to it." She glanced over to the alley where the little

256

box was lying on the ground.

"The battery's fine," he said, sauntering over to pick it up. "I called in a little drone to hunt it down and zap it with a microwave pulse." He wiggled the box between his long fingers. "These little buggers are a damned nuisance but they're easily disposed of once you get a drone onto them." He slipped it into his pocket and held out a hand to her. "The other piece, please."

Ginny took the cylinder from her overall and passed it to him. He pocketed that too and went over to Chu's body. He frisked it quickly and expertly and came away with nothing but bloodied hands, which he wiped on Chu.

"This fella's got two holes in him that I didn't make. Did you do that?"

Ginny shook her head, turning away from the sight of Chu's bloody remains. "There are two more, in a hotel room back there. I didn't shoot them, either." She felt a lightness in her head and chest, a giddiness that made it hard to stand. She walked over to the nearest building and leaned against it, bending forward as her stomach and throat tightened against the nausea.

Richards was beside her in a moment. He put an arm around her back and held her firmly against him with a hand on her ribs. "I'm fine," she said, but couldn't deny that she felt better to be supported. He was as strong as he looked and she knew he wouldn't let her fall.

"Let's go find somewhere to sit down," he said and led her back up the street.

After a few paces, the nausea and giddiness began to ease and she squirmed free of him, regretting her lapse into weakness. "Just keep your hands to yourself," she said, pulling away.

He grinned at her but said nothing. From the icons in her aug, she could see he was talking to someone on the phone. Whoever it might be could well be a matter of life or death to her, but, for the moment, the fight had gone out of her. She was tired and her mind was empty. She would have given anything to be back in her unit in Brisbane, to take a long shower and curl up in bed.

"Here we go," Richards said and steered her towards a concrete staircase outside an old brick building. She sat down and he sat nearby. She could still see Chu's body from where they were.

"I wish I could get a cup of coffee," she said.

"That's the trouble with reality. It's so primitive."

She glanced at him to see if he was mocking her. Of course, he was. He was a man with just two modes, mocking and bullying.

"Feeling better?" he asked, and even his concern had a taunting edge to it. She didn't bother to reply. "Good. Now tell me where a nice, law-abiding citizen like you got a gun and an augblaster."

"I found them?"

"OK," he said in a tone that said let's play games then. "Where?"

"In Cal Copplin's unit. I stayed there a couple of days."

"I know. We searched that unit when he went missing and didn't find anything."

"You obviously didn't search very carefully."

He considered that for a moment. "What else did you find?"

"Some papers." What harm could it do to tell him?

"Papers?"

"Yeah. Real paper, with ink on."

"Where are these papers now?"

"Rafe Morgan has them. He was going to make them public but he bottled out. Rafe said they were software specs. Stuff like that. They didn't mean anything to me but they were to do with security in the Parliament worldlet."

Two police vehicles came hurrying into the street, the robot delivery vans scuttling out of the way to let them pass. They pulled up beside Chu's body and a small fleet of drones lifted off the roof while several uniformed police officers got out.

"Excuse me," said Richards and sauntered off towards them. It took Ginny several seconds to realise she was free to run if she wanted to, but it seemed pointless. Even if she could get away, where was there to run to? She watched Richards talking to one of the uniform cops. After a while, he held out Ginny's gun and a small bot came from one of the police cars and took it off him, dropping it into the evidence bin in its chest. Then he handed the bot the augblaster and the cylinder. He pointed down the street towards Ginny and a couple of drones left whatever they were doing at the crime scene to buzz over and scan her. Eventually, Richards sauntered her way again. More police cars and an ambulance had arrived before he got back to her.

"That should look after itself for a while," he said. As he spoke, another vehicle came from up the street and rolled to a stop beside them. Richards opened the door and invited her in. "Why don't we go and get that coffee?"

They went to a café by the harbour called Reality Bites and found a table outside. The Opera House shone in the bright sunlight, looking smaller in real life than Ginny remembered it from VR. The Sydney Harbour Bridge, blue-grey and freshly painted, turned a dirty, rust covered brown when she minimised her aug. The sky, however, remained just as blue and the water sparkled just as brightly, even though the ferries and the pretty sailboats disappeared.

She looked around at the clientèle of the little café and didn't much like what she saw. Perhaps Dover Richards saw the grimace she made because he said, "The only people who come to real cafés these days are weirdoes who don't like aug, bored rich people who want to try something different, and cops and crims who need to meet where no-one's monitoring them."

"I've got a client who still likes to have face-to-face meetings," she said, although it probably wasn't true any more that UnReality was her client. "Couple of weird kids. Give me the creeps."

Richards gave a negligent shrug. "It's an acquired taste."

"See any fellow cops here? Or any fellow crims?"

He smiled. "A few."

"Look," she said, annoyed at his deliberate ambiguity. "I need to talk to you about—" He stopped her with a gesture as a little robot rolled up to the table and he gave it their order. She pursed her lips and waited. "About Della," she said when the bot trundled away.

"What about her?"

"I need to know she's safe."

He gave her a look full of disdain. "You don't mess around with what you're mixed up in without putting yourself in danger. You should at least know that by now."

"That's why I want to be sure she's safe. I'll cooperate. I'll do whatever you like. Just promise me she'll be OK."

He seemed amused. "You're bargaining now?"

"You're supposed to be a bloody cop. Why don't you just do your job and protect her?"

He gave her a long, steady look. "Tell me more about these papers that Rafe Morgan has."

"I'm not saying anything until you give me some kind of assur—"

"Oh for God's sake! Your friend's safe. No-one is the least bit interested in your friend. Can we just get on with this?"

People at nearby tables glanced over at them hearing Richards' raised voice, then quickly looked away. Ginny felt her heart skip. Maybe Richards was a cop – he must be, she supposed, having seen him working the crime scene near the hotel – but that didn't mean he wasn't also a hired killer in the pay of the Consortium, or, more likely, some other group. She reminded herself that he was armed and she was, effectively, his prisoner. All the same…

"And what about Sorenssen? What's happened to him?"

"The geek's dead. We didn't get to him in time."

"Dead?" He was just a kid, a stupid kid who liked to play games. And now he was dead? Dead because Ginny had asked him to help her? Because she had pushed him into it?

The robot rattled up to the table and deposited various cups and plates in front of her. She watched it, unable to grapple with the massive, unwieldy fact that she had caused Sorenssen's death. *I didn't even like him*, she thought and the idea seemed to accuse her.

When the robot left again, Richard's said, "So tell me about the papers."

How could he expect her to talk about papers? "Ask Rafe. He's got them all. I'm sure he'll give them to you."

"Rafe's disappeared."

"What?"

"Tag went offline about the same time you were burgling Chastity Mining. Tagger who went to find him says it looks like he was snatched."

"Snatched? You mean, like, kidnapped?"

"Yeah, kidnapped. Or he ran off and fixed it to look like that. And no-one found any paper documents at his unit or anywhere else he might have been."

"Oh my God."

"So you didn't know anything about that?"

"Me? How would I know he'd been kidnapped?"

"You tell me."

"Wait. I just remembered. His office. He had whiteboards full of stuff he'd copied from the documents, plus all kinds of timelines and ideas and stuff from analysing them. Everything from the papers is on those whiteboards."

Richards made a call, communicating silently with someone while Ginny waited. When he hung up, he shook his head. "They found whiteboards, all right, lots of them. But they'd all been scrubbed. Forensics is going to take a look at his office systems to see whether they can reconstruct anything. The thing is, that will take time, and we don't have much time left, do we?"

"What do you mean?"

"I mean this is all connected to the vote, isn't it? September 10, the Consortium, whoever else might be involved, they're all fixated on this bloody cyberterrorism bill."

"Have they said when the vote will be?"

"You haven't heard?"

Ginny didn't like his tone. It suggested he thought she was pretending to be ignorant. And that scared her. Until that moment, she had thought Richards at least trusted her. Now it seemed he saw her as complicit with one of the parties in this business. He couldn't think she worked for the Consortium, surely. They'd just tried to kill her. But maybe killing one of your own was common among gangsters. So he must think she was S10, a terrorist. Her heart sank. It was just what Rafe had warned her about.

"I haven't had much time for watching the news," she said, her voice weak.

"Tomorrow." He watched her face as he said it. "Tomorrow morning at ten AM."

Ginny knew nothing about parliamentary procedure but at the very least it seemed like indecent haste. A question tickled at her mind. "I can see why S10 wants to stop this bill, but what's in it for the Rice Consortium? They seem to be trying to stop S10 from stopping the vote. But they're crooks, organised crime, surely the government can use the new laws against them too. They should be working with S10, not against them."

Richards leaned back in his chair and took a sip of coffee, still watching her as if trying to understand the game she was playing. "We don't even know what S10 is planning."

"They're going to break through the security of the Parliament worldlet. That's all I know. Once they're in, what can they do? Trash the place? Paint slogans? Make a public statement?"

In an instant, Richards' cynical expression vanished. He sat forward and put down his coffee, slopping it into the saucer. "How about kill every single Member of Parliament? It's the perfect time. They'll all be there. No-one will be allowed not to attend for a vote like that."

"Kill them? How? It's not real. It's just a worldlet. How do you kill someone in a worldlet?"

Again, he looked at her as if she might be trying to mislead him, as if she had to be pretending to be so ignorant. "The same way you kill any piece of software attached to a network. You send it a virus. It's how our guns work in VR. They trigger a piece of code that downloads itself to the perp's cognitive implants and makes the implants scramble the user's mind. It's like inducing an epileptic fit. It isn't meant to kill when we shoot people in VR, but it can do, sometimes. Thing is, it wouldn't take much to create a metaphorical bullet – or bomb, I suppose – that killed people every time. Is that what September 10 is planning? Is that what they've been cooking up?"

Ginny could see he really thought she might know. She drew back from him. "You think I'm involved. You think I want to kill all those people."

"Well, do you?"

"Of course not. I'm not a monster."

"How do I know what you are? Consortium enforcers were trying to kill you not long ago. Why was that?"

"Because I'd been spying on them, trying to find out who they were."

"Stealing Chastity Mining's corporate data with your radical hacktivist friend Sorenssen?"

Ginny could feel her heart racing. This was going badly. Richards seemed to be able to put an unpleasant spin on everything she'd done. "My radical what? He's just a kid with grandiose ideas and a fixation on big tits."

"That's not what his records say. He's flagged on a number of terrorist watch lists."

"You're joking."

"Do I look like I'm joking?"

For a moment his hard eyes seemed to pin her against her chair. She didn't know what to say, how to defend herself. She wished Della were there. She thought about asking for a lawyer. But Richards seemed satisfied that he'd scared her enough. He sat back with a grin and picked up his coffee again. "Either you're the most useless terrorist I've ever seen, or you're one hell of an actress." He took a drink and shrugged. "Either way, doesn't matter much."

Because she was his prisoner. Because he would take her away and lock her up and expert interrogators would come and force her to confess to things she hadn't done.

She looked away from his unkind eyes and her gaze fell on the blue waters of the harbour. Such a beautiful day. Such a beautiful place. A breeze carried the smell of the ocean to her and she saw it in her mind's eye, stretching on forever. She almost wept at the thought of that wild, empty place, all that freedom.

She wondered where Rafe had gone. He'd fried his tag and gone underground, hunted now by people like Dover Richards, people who were Rafe's greatest nightmare. How would Rafe survive on the run, jumping at shadows, whimpering with fear in the night? Did he have friends who would help him, or would he head out into the bush and live out there like a hermit?

"OK, Virginia, let's be going," Richards said, standing up. "Under Section 3 of the 2052 Security of the Commonwealth Act, I am exercising my right to detain you for questioning. Please come with me."

She didn't move. Couldn't move. "I – I'd like to call a lawyer," she said. People around them were staring. One man got up, looking nervous, and hurried away.

"Your detention is subject to judicial review at the end of

each fortnight, at which time the Magistrate will decide whether to allow legal representation." He sounded as if he was reading from a cue card, which, of course, he probably was.

"Don't do this," she begged him. "Please. You're making a mistake. I'm not a terrorist. I just—"

He put his hand on the butt of his firearm and it wiped all thought from her head. He would shoot her right there in the street if she didn't do what he said. She could hardly breathe and her arms trembled as she pushed herself up.

"Don't even think of running," he said. "I'm a quick draw and a very good shot." He stepped around the table and took hold of her upper arm. "This way. Back to the car."

His grip was firm, his hand large. He loomed over her, the sheer size of him that close made her quail. Struggle and flight were impossible. There was nothing she could do except let him lead her away, lock her up, and leave her to the mercy of a system that had already made up its mind about her. She stumbled through the bright, sunny streets not knowing what to do, her thoughts a buzzing confusion of fear and despair. *I should look at the sky*, she told herself. *And the water. Oh God, what will they do to me?* But the sky was just a blue sheet, the water a dazzle of sparkles. Nothing seemed to have any depth or meaning except the hand that held her and urged her remorselessly forward.

The car wasn't far away. Parking in major cities had not been a problem for many years. The sunlight flared on the vehicle's solar panels as they approached and she blinked away the afterimages. A strange voice said, "Let go of the woman, tagger, and put your hands on your head." Her heart skipped. She tried to turn to see who had spoken but Richards' grip tightened on her arm, preventing her. "If you want to die," the voice said, "you just go on reaching for that gun."

Ginny felt Richards relax. She gasped with relief at the realisation he had decided not to put up a fight. He took his hand off her arm and she turned to face whoever had ambushed them. So did Richards. With a jolt of horror she saw the monsters that were pointing guns at them. And, even as her heart thudded in fear, the hideous creatures resolved into what they really were, three men wearing pig masks.

"Friends of yours?" Richards asked, his voice relaxed and full of its usual disdain.

Ginny couldn't speak. Not friends. She didn't have any friends who wore masks and pointed guns.

"Step away from the woman," the lead pig-man said. His two companions stepped away from his side and moved to flank Ginny and Richards.

"I'm a federal officer," Richards said. "And this woman is my prisoner. I've already called for backup, so you should either start running or surrender your weapons."

"Shut up and do as you're told. If I have to, I'll blow your head off."

"What's so special about her?" Richards asked, not moving.

It was the same thought that had occurred Ginny. Fair enough, the Consortium had tried to kill her when they found her snooping on them, but to risk snatching her from police custody like this just didn't make sense. What could she possibly know that would be worth taking such a risk for?

The pig-man leader didn't answer. He held his gun out at arm's length and aimed it directly at Richards' head. With a gesture of submission, the tagger stepped away from Ginny. The pig-man nearest him, moved in close and pulled

Richards' gun from its holster. It made Ginny feel helpless and vulnerable, as if the cop had somehow been protecting her and now she was at the mercy of these strangers. But that wasn't the reality at all. Her head swam. The police might have thrown her in jail forever, tortured her as a terrorist even, but the pig-men might do anything. Her heart was beating so fast it seemed to be impeding her breathing.

"Who are you?" she asked, but the words were a whisper. Darkness was gathering around the edges of the world, gravity was fading and she felt she might lift off the ground. She heard the sirens of approaching police cars. A swarm of the little orange police drones she'd seen at the crime scene buzzed around them. It all seemed to be happening in a dream, far away.

"Get her into the van before she falls over," someone said. "I'll fix the drones." Two men grabbed her, one on each arm and hustled her to a van. As they went, little orange drones rained down from the sky and clattered to the pavement. One of the pig-men stood on one and it crunched like a big insect. She was lifted, pushed. People crowded around her in the gathering darkness. The van's engines whined into life.

Chapter 19

Ginny woke on a sun-lounger by a pool. Her eyes were still closed but she could hear the splash of a swimmer, the tinkling laughter of a young woman, smell the chlorine, feel the texture of a towel beneath her fingers. She felt warm sunshine on her body, saw pink light through her eyelids. From the warm breeze that touched her bare legs and arms, she guessed she was wearing a swimsuit.

She tried to open her eyes but didn't have the strength, tried to move, but her body would not respond, could not respond. *Drugged*, she thought. Although she had never been drugged before and didn't know how it might feel, she just knew it was true.

It was nice by the pool. She was warm and relaxed. Light, subtle melodies wove through the pink light like swallows in the sky. It made her think of that nice Mr. Mendelssohn. *So nice to be drugged by the pool*, she thought. *It's the nicest possible way to die.*

When Ginny woke again, nothing had changed but the mood. She snapped open her eyes and sat up. She was still on a sun-lounger, still by the pool, still warm, still in a swimsuit, but any idea that her situation was in any way pleasant had gone.

"How are you feeling?"

Her head whipped around to face the man standing beside her. For a moment, she squinted up at him, his face silhouetted against the bright blue sky. Then her eyes widened. "Cal?" It was Cal. Definitely Cal. She jumped up from the lounger and almost fell over, but Cal caught her and kept her steady.

"Cal, where are we? I think they drugged me. Who are they? What do they want us for?"

Cal smiled. It was a sad smile. He felt sorry for her. She wanted to hug him for the sympathy in his smile. "It's all right, Ginny. Everything is all right. You don't have to worry. You're safe. We're both safe."

"But..." She looked around, trying to make sense of it. The pool was large. A handful of people splashed and played in it. Beyond it were lawns and beyond those, trees and distant hills. Behind her, past more lawns, a gigantic mansion in brick and stone filled the whole view. She turned back to Cal. "We're unlatched." It was obvious, all this space, the palatial building, the perfect weather. "What...?"

"Sit down," he said, gently. "Let me explain." He still held her arms and guided her down safely. He sat on the lounger next to hers. "First of all, I want to apologise."

The word slapped her on the face, snapping her out of the torpor she'd been in. She pulled back from him. "You set me up, you bastard. You made me think you liked me. You...you..." She wanted to say he'd trifled with her affections but the words were just too corny to utter. "Then you sent me to deliver your bloody package to that crazy terrorist bitch. Because of you, the police have arrested me and the Consortium has tried to kill me. Twice! What the hell did I ever do to you? Why pick on me? And what the hell are you doing here, sitting by a pool like some bloody banker who just swindled a billion dollars, when you're supposed to be dead or something? And do you know that September 10 is using the information you gave them – most of it delivered by me, I'm guessing – to kill the entire Australian Government?"

She took a breath and it gave Cal a chance to butt in. "You've got it all wrong, Ginny." He reached out a hand to soothe her but she batted it away. She stood up, roughly forcing down her automatic feeling of self-consciousness at being dressed only in a swimsuit.

"Don't tell me I've got it all wrong. I'm the one whose been running for my life, scared to death, with people shooting at me. I've been hiding out at my parents' house, and Della's, and camping out in your old unit like a bloody squatter. People have died, Cal. Some stupid bloody kid who I had blackmailed into helping me, who deserved a good slap, I'll admit, but not a bloody gangland execution. And Tonia's brother, your alleged friend, Gavin. Who shot him, I'd like to know, because I really don't think it was the police? Do you? And Rafe Morgan nearly died too, the poor bastard. So don't tell me I've got it all wrong. I think I know exactly what's going on here, and who's paying your bills."

Cal looked gratifyingly contrite. "I didn't mean for you to get in so deep. I didn't want you involved at all when the time came, but things got a bit out of hand for a moment and I had to improvise. I'd spent weeks getting you to the point where you would do me that little favour and, even though…" He took a deep breath. "Even though I'd changed my mind and wanted to keep you out of it, that damned tagger, Dover Richards, was on my tail and there wasn't time to start over again with a different woman."

He stood up, slowly. She could see he was being careful not to appear in any way threatening. Even so, the gap between the two sun-loungers was not big enough and she fought the urge to push him down again. "Do you mind giving me a little more space?" she said in as cold a tone as she could manage.

He didn't move. "I thought, if you'd just listen to what I have to say, we could be friends again."

The effrontery of the man! "There was a time when being half-naked in a place like this with you would be something I'd fantasise about. Now the reality just turns my stomach." She saw him wince and, despite all the reasons she had for trying to wound him, she still regretted it. *Because you're just an appeasing wimp*, she told herself. "All right then, explain yourself. Go on. I'm listening. Tell me why you're working for the mob. Tell me why you think it's OK to screw with innocent people's lives."

He studied her for a moment, as if trying to decide whether to give it a shot, then he said, "You can get changed in there." He indicated the row of changing rooms along one side of the pool. "They have en suite showers if you want one. I'll meet you back here and we'll go up to the house. Then I'll explain everything."

With a last scowl at him, she set off for the changing rooms, but stopped after a few paces. "And where's my body? You know, the one your thugs kidnapped and drugged. Where am I?"

He looked abashed. "It's in an old warehouse in Canberra."

"What?"

"It's OK, I've got a couple of guards watching over you. I just thought it would be better to bring you to where I am."

"You took me to Canberra?" A shocking thought occurred to her. "What day is this?"

Again, he looked uncomfortable. "It's Monday. Morning. You were out for quite a while. My, er, thugs overdid the sedatives."

Her fists clenched and she felt her lips twitch into a snarl. She really, really wanted to hit him. "And the vote?"

"In about two hours."

She turned away and stomped off to the changing rooms. It was a *fait accompli*. There was nothing she could do now. It was all too late. Whatever was going down at the Parliament worldlet was beyond her control. Probably, it always had been. It was up to the police to do whatever they could. She saw Dover Richards in her memory, a gun at his head, looking dumbfounded and helpless, and decided that there was nothing the police could do. Nothing anybody could do now.

—oOo—

They sat together on a terrace outside the magnificent mansion. Not just its size but the elaborate detail proclaimed it to be a very expensive piece of real estate. Ginny looked across the perfect lawn, her eyes drawn by a sudden mewling sound, and saw a pair of peacocks strolling away among the shrubs. She and Cal sat in deeply-cushioned wicker armchairs among side tables and footstools. A young man in a servant's uniform approached – a construct, judging by his striking looks and physique – and asked if they'd like tea brought out. Cal nodded and the servant stepped quickly away.

Cal seemed to be waiting for the right moment to speak and not finding it, but Ginny didn't care. She was thinking about her father and mother. Since she'd stayed with them, she hadn't so much as called to see if they were OK. Her father had the loss of his job hanging over his head and her mother, she knew, would struggle to cope with his unemployment, probably doubling the burden on him in the process. And Ginny had been flitting about like a kitten, pouncing at shadows, telling herself she was saving the world, and it had all been a complete waste of energy. In the dismal anticlimax of her futile efforts, she could hardly believe what a self-aggrandizing fool she'd been.

"OK," said Cal. "It's like this. After the war, most European economies moved towards a kind of tepid socialism."

"What?"

"I'm explaining."

"I don't want to hear the social history of Europe. Just tell me what you've been up to."

"I think I should set it in context."

"Well, I don't. Just get on with it."

He stared at her like a dog whose bone she'd taken away. "You sound like you hate me."

"Oh, really? Now why would that be?"

He sighed. "All right. I'll start somewhere else. Fifteen years ago, I was a young Turk. I was The Man, the go-to guy if you wanted advanced IT. I was just a kid, mid-twenties, but I had a rep that was solid gold."

She turned away and watched the peacocks. What did she care? Let him ramble.

"That was back in the UK. I was approached by some people. Important, powerful people, from the Government.

They wanted to talk to me about something they called the Virtual Curtain. I'd heard rumours. Everyone in my business had heard them. It was wild, paranoid stuff that the conspiracy theory worldlets were full of, and people like me only took half-way seriously after five pints on a Friday night. These people, in their dark suits and club ties, wanted to know if I could build one for them."

Ginny said nothing. She supposed he was waiting for her to ask him what a virtual curtain was, but she didn't care enough. After a while, he went on.

"The thing is, when QNet replaced the old Internet, a lot of things became possible that weren't possible until then. The bandwidth was way beyond anything anyone had imagined before for a start. Security was better too. And it was cheap. So cheap that it brushed aside the old technologies in just a couple of decades. It meant that everything was on QNet. Everything. There was no need for any other kind of network. Augmented reality was a natural application. Sensor strips were stuck up in every home, every street, every public and private space. Farmers put them in their fields, airports floated clouds of microdrones in the air above them, conservationists stuck them on every tree. Soon aug was an indispensable part of all our lives. If you weren't latched, you were lost, helpless, unable to function in society.

"But QNet gave us much more than that, the massive bandwidth made nationwide access to virtual worlds a piece of cake. People had already started using cognitive implants in a big way to make the most of the aug. The tagging laws were starting to be debated. It only took a little extra in-cortex digital enhancement and the world was ready to unlatch, to live their social lives almost entirely in VR. Do you know that, in Australia today, ninety-nine-point-nine per cent of all business and social interaction takes place in virtual worldlets? It's the same in every developed nation."

Ginny felt his voice as an irritation between her shoulders. "Is there a point to all this?"

"Oh yes. Definitely. Let me ask you when was the last time you saw a real news presenter?"

"What do you mean?"

"It was probably in your childhood. All news feeds have artificial constructs to do the presentation. And why not? It's a simple enough task, and you have the advantage that you can make the construct as beautiful, engaging, trustworthy, and with as much apparent gravitas as you like. Most individuals who run info worldlets use constructs to deliver their content too. Gets around the twenty per cent rule. The thing is, a construct will say whatever you feed it, with absolute sincerity and an open, likeable manner. There's no way for you or me to spot the lie any more. Never was, really, ever since the big corporations took over the broadcast media. So, tell me, how do you know the result of the last election?"

Ginny ignored him, sure that this was yet another rhetorical question. Yet she was no longer uninterested. Some feeling about where this was going unsettled her. What he was saying sounded a lot like the September 10 slogans Rafe had shown her.

"I'll tell you then. You know because you saw it on a feed. Maybe you got it from several feeds. And they all said the same thing because they all got it from the same source, and you – and they – simply trusted that the source was authoritative. And why would they publish something that was incorrect, or a deliberate lie? Sooner or later the truth would come out and they would be discredited and lose subscribers. Ultimately, the courts and the government would arbitrate on what the truth really was.

"But what if the Government itself, the Electoral Commission, say, was lying? What if the Government was allowed to lie by law? What if it could tell you anything it wanted, change any source, falsify any feed?"

He paused, waiting for Ginny's reaction. At last she saw just where he was going. "It's the cyberterrorism bill, isn't it? That's precisely the power it gives the Government, the ability to lie to us about anything it likes, perfectly legally. That's why some people think it's so dangerous, because the Government could lie to us and say it is in our best interests."

Cal was shaking his head. "Not just lie, Ginny. Because of the way we live, because of our dependence on aug and VR and QNet, they can change reality. They can shape the truth to be anything the want it to be. The last checks and balances would be gone. Everything we know would be theirs to remodel and rework into any form that suited them."

Her chest tightened as unease morphed into anxiety. "But that's just alarmist nonsense. The Government wouldn't do that. We elect them. We can say what they do."

"We elected them last time, but what about next time. Where will the election results come from? Who will check and verify them? How will you know what really happened?"

She didn't want to hear this. She didn't want to believe it. "You're being ridiculous. What you're suggesting could never happen. People wouldn't let it happen."

"It will happen. It's going to happen today. Ask me how I know."

She shook her head, not daring to let herself acknowledge the answer she had already guessed. She stood up and walked a few paces away from him, looking rigidly at the horizon.

After a moment she realised he had joined her.

"Those men in their dark suits called it the Virtual Curtain. They said America already had one. China already had one. Half of Europe was planning one or building one. I was so naïve back then I thought the reference was to the Iron Curtain, some kind of national firewall, but it wasn't: it was to The Wizard of Oz. They were to become the wizards, pulling the levers and turning the knobs behind the curtain while the rest of us carried on in ignorant bliss."

She glanced at him and saw that he too was staring at the horizon.

"When I realised just what they wanted me to build, I was appalled. Stunned. But they were persuasive. They offered me the Earth. They made it sound as if only by doing this could the nation survive in a world where every other government was sleek and efficient and unencumbered by democracy and the need to appeal to the lowest common denominator on every issue. In fact, the few thousand people behind the curtain, the people with their hands on the levers, people like me, they said, would enjoy a true democracy. Like in Ancient Greece, every one of us would be part of the decision making process. There would be no political parties, no corrupt representatives, no compromise candidates. Each of us would vote on every issue if we cared to. Direct democracy. Great Britain would become a modern Athens."

"And the helots and slaves?" she asked.

He sighed. "They didn't dwell on that part. They planned to let the rest of the country have its parliaments, its institutions. Everything would be the same as before as far as the great mass of people were concerned, only, once the curtain went up, the decisions people made would sometimes be based on false information. Their perception of reality would be changed to ensure they did what they were required to."

"It's impossible," she said. "You can't control everything. There are too many voices to silence them all. People would see the inconsistencies."

"No, not really. The systems we built had hooks into the whole of the national QNet and every channel in and out. They're big systems. I had a huge team and a massive budget and we worked for five years building it. The software monitored every single communication in real time and made sure everybody saw just what we wanted them to see. If someone wanted to say there was a discrepancy in the nation's accounts, we let them, but the message everyone heard was that there was *no* discrepancy. And if that puzzled whoever said it, when they reviewed their own message, it looked exactly as they had intended it. There's no shortage of computing power. Even the binary quantum computers we had back then could filter and fudge billions of messages a day. With modern computers, it's a piece of cake."

Ginny still struggled to accept what Cal was saying. The USA was being run by despots from behind a virtual curtain? And the UK? And God only knew where else? That couldn't be right. Could it? Then she remembered Rafe's office and all his whiteboards.

"The legislation didn't pass in the UK. It didn't pass in the US either. Or in China, or anywhere else. It was always voted down. No government has ever been given the power to do what you're saying. None of this is real. The whole thing is a lie."

She stared at him, hard. "What the hell is your game? Why are you trying to make me believe all this?"

He turned towards her, almost reached out to her, but

held back. "I want you to know the truth. After I'd built their damned curtain for them, full of the pompous crap that naïve young men are always so full of, I expected to be one of the new Athenians, making my country a better place because I'm so bloody brilliant. But, when the curtain fell, I found myself on the outside." He smiled as if it were a fond memory.

"I kicked up a hell of a fuss. I threatened to expose them, reveal everything. But, of course, I couldn't. Nothing I could say would ever be heard by anybody at all. My own software put me in an informational vacuum chamber. It didn't matter how loud I tried to shout, only silence came from my mouth.

"I was furious. I felt cheated. Knowing that I was living in a web of deceptions where nothing I saw or read or heard could every be trusted, drove me wild. Worse still was the thought of those people on the other side of the curtain, the wizards, the Athenians, enjoying fabulous privilege and complete power.

"There weren't many countries left that had not yet drawn their own curtain on reality. I knew that from my five years on the inside. In fact, Australia and India were the only advanced democracies still free. I applied to emigrate here and, for some reason, they let me go. Glad to be rid of me, maybe. That was ten years ago. Since then, I've been working to make sure that, when the curtain falls here, I'll be on the right side of it this time. My friends in the Consortium will see to that."

Ginny had gone past confusion and anger to a cold, clear-headed suspicion. She only had Cal's word for how much time had passed, and now here he was spinning her a fantastic yarn about how he had been working to corrupt the Government. She could see only one reason for any of it and that was to stop her doing something or warning somebody.

She looked back at the enormous house and wondered if there were portals in there she could use to escape. She had already tried summoning her own but it hadn't worked. She was a prisoner there, but there had to be a way for her to get free or else why was Cal trying so hard to distract and mislead her?

"I knocked on a few doors, made a few discrete enquiries," Cal was saying, "and pretty soon I was talking to all the right people. Ten years ago there was a Labor Government in power and they didn't want to know about seizing control – even though the rest of the world's governments were a sham and they knew it. So I worked with the opposition. They were keen as mustard. They wanted to take power and to make sure they held onto it forever. My experience in the UK was very attractive to them but I did more. Much more. I organised the Rice Consortium, brought in all the biggest corporations, and a select group of Australia's richest and most powerful people."

"And none of them knew that organised crime was behind it all," Ginny said, to keep him talking while she tried to work out an escape.

He looked sheepish, but, she thought, a little pleased with himself. "Yeah, that was unfortunate, but I needed some muscle on my side. I knew I couldn't trust the Government. If I didn't want to see a repeat of what happened in the UK, I had to make sure there were people on my side who were even bigger and scarier than the people we voted for. By the time the Government cottoned on to the real nature of the Consortium, it was too late for them. Anyone in the inner circle who didn't want to draw the curtain with my guys in tow, might just disappear. So might their families. It gives me a lot of influence to bargain with."

"But it kind of makes a nonsense of your New Athens bullshit doesn't it? Sounds like you drove a container-load of snakes into your Garden of Eden."

His body stiffened. A dark cloud passed across his expression. "It's a compromise I had to make. It'll work out in the end. Crooks are just businessmen really. They'll act in their own best interests. Just like the pollies will. And now, they all have a common interest."

"So it amounts to this: you've arranged for a bunch of self-interested arseholes to take over the country and run it for their own profit and that's OK with you as long as you're one of the arseholes? Feel free to point out all the flaws in my summary."

His face set in a scowl. "You've got ambitions. I remember you telling me about some orchestra you admire, how you've had this dream that one day they'll perform your music at the Opera House, serious music, the kind you've always wanted to spend your life writing." He looked away in frustration. "I was hoping you might appreciate what I'm offering to you here. We'd live like kings and queens. We'd have our very own continent that we could do with as we please."

"We?"

He stopped dead and she saw the anger drain out of him to be replaced by sadness. "I—" he began but seemed overwhelmed suddenly by a wave of hopelessness. "I tricked you into liking me. I played you. I needed someone to be my courier and take documents to S10, someone to draw attention away from me. Those idiots were my bogey man. I set them up, got everybody looking their way while my team implemented the software we'd need to make it all work. I wanted the police and security forces chasing them while I got on with building the systems we'd need to make it all work."

He paused again, looking into Ginny's eyes. "The thing is, it didn't go exactly as planned. I – I developed feelings for you. I got to look forward to our meetings. It got so I wasn't having to fake being interested." He stepped forward and took her hands in his. "Ginny, I fell in love with you. I didn't mean to but it just happened. That's why I need you here with me when the curtain comes down. That's why I'm telling you all this. That's why it's breaking my heart that you don't understand, don't see the possibilities."

Ginny blinked several times before her thoughts began moving again. "Love?" was all she could say. Cal nodded, with a sad puppy look that infuriated her. "You set me up, you lied to my face, you're planning some kind of terrorist attack, you kidnapped me and you're holding me prisoner, and you are fucked up enough to tell me you love me? Well I'd hate to see how you treat the people you're merely fond of."

He continued to look into her eyes, searching for something. Then, with a sigh, he gave up and turned away saying, "It was just a stupid dream I supp–"

In that instant he vanished. Everything vanished. The world became dense, suffocating blackness.

Chapter 20

Ginny came to inside a tank. The dim light, the dashboard displays were all familiar yet different from any tank she knew. So, somebody else's tank then. She felt muggy as if she'd slept too long, and her arm, as she moved to find the release button, weighed a ton. *Drugged again*, she thought, and she cursed Cal. The fridge-door suck of the seal breaking and the crack of light that appeared all around her meant the tank was opening even though she had not yet told it to.

"Ginny?"

Rafe Morgan peered in through the widening gap, looking concerned. She stared back at him and all she could think to say was, "You disappeared."

He helped unplug the drips from her catheter block and fussed over her as she struggled to sit up and swing her legs out.

"What day is it?" she asked, her brain slowly coming back to life.

"Day? Monday?" He peered into her eyes. "Have you been in there long?"

"What time?" She could have checked the clock in her own aug but she'd asked before it occurred to her.

"Nine twenty-five."

She glanced at her clock. Nine twenty-five AM. Still thirty-five minutes until the vote.

"What's going on, Ginny? Why are you here?"

Good question. She looked around. The tank was against one wall of a large, half-derelict industrial space – an abandoned factory maybe. Sunlight came in through tall windows and from a large steel roll-up door thirty metres away that had been raised to about man height. With a shock of recognition, Ginny saw two dark heaps on the ground near the door resolve into two human bodies – men in dark overalls. They looked dead and the pool of blood beside one of them added to the chilling impression.

She couldn't take her eyes off the dead people. "Did you do that?" It was a stupid question. Rafe couldn't have killed anybody.

"That would be me."

She turned towards the voice and saw Tonia Birchow, crazy bitch terrorist, walking towards them from the interior of the building. She had a gun in one hand and a grin on her face.

"If this is some kind of nightmare," Ginny told the smiling apparition, "I want to wake up now."

"She's been drugged, I think," Rafe said to Tonia. There was a familiarity in his tone that suggested they had become friends, or at least that they had been working together.

"Tell her how we found her," Tonia said.

"Cal told you to come here," Ginny said. It was the only possible explanation. No-one else knew where she was.

Rafe and Tonia exchanged glances and Rafe said, "He sent me a message. He told me all about his role in the Consortium. He said a lot of other stuff too about some kind of coup he's part of. He says they're taking over the country."

He paused, as if waiting for Ginny to confirm or deny Cal's insane story, but she said nothing. "He said I'd find you here and I should come and get you out."

Ginny glanced at Tonia. "And everybody's favourite psycho bitch? Where does she come in?"

Rafe looked nervous. Ginny reckoned he was probably worried about Tonia taking offence. Ginny was past caring about things like that.

"Tonia's been helping me with a new identity," Rafe said. "The Consortium turned up again. I nearly didn't get away. I contacted Tonia and she's been helping out." For the first time, Ginny noticed that Rafe's data block gave someone else's name and details. Tonia too was somebody else today.

"Why would Cal...?" Ginny began, but she thought she knew. They'd stood on the terrace together and he'd declared his love. It was probably the most bizarre and surreal thing that had happened to her since the whole affair began. Her astonished rebuff had been reflexive. The guy was clearly as mad as a gumtree full of galahs. Then, his ludicrous offer of a lifetime of unimaginable power and wealth having been turned down flat, he had no further use for her. So he called Rafe to come and pick up the trash.

It made a kind of sense, but something nagged at Ginny. She shook her head to clear it and almost toppled over as the world swam out of kilter. There was a problem with the timing. Something about the –

"Oh my God, the time!" She stood up. The vote was just thirty minutes away. She grabbed Rafe – partly to stop herself falling over. "Where are we? No, that doesn't matter. We need to get to the Parliament right now. We've got to stop it."

Rafe shook his head. "It's all right. There isn't any

September 10 bomb. Not as such."

"Never was," said Tonia.

"No?"

Rafe looked to Tonia to explain but the woman walked off towards the two dead men by the door. "She told me all about it," he said. "I seem to be on the inside, now that I have nowhere else to turn." He sounded bitter about the loss of his former life, but Ginny had never noticed that he had been particularly happy with it. "Cal joined them. You remember we saw all that in the documents? He told them he could get them access to the Parliament worldlet so they could sabotage it. He gave them designs and access codes but he always held back, they never quite had everything they needed. That's what was supposed to be in the package you delivered: the final pieces."

He watched Tonia as he spoke. She was frisking the dead men, taking things from their pockets and tossing them aside, examining their weapons, obviously intending to keep them.

"Meanwhile, Cal had been persuading her to release some stuff to the press. To me. Junk, really. Suggestive, but nothing too incriminating. It was meant to get the cops in a lather about an S10 attack, raise the profile of the group, and make sure that, whatever they did, would have maximum publicity. At least, that's what he said. Tonia said she feels now that he was just playing her, putting S10 up as a distraction for whatever he was planning."

Ginny looked at him sharply but he was still watching Tonia. "You don't believe all this rubbish about taking over the country, do you? That's just…"

"I don't know. It makes more sense than anything else right now. I think Tonia believes it. She's been acting pretty weird since I showed her Cal's message."

Ginny had no idea how you'd tell if Tonia Birchow was acting weird. Nevertheless, it unsettled her that both Rafe and she were taking Cal seriously.

"So there's no bomb?" she asked, getting back to the point. She had to be sure because, if they just sat there talking when they could have done something, a lot of dead people would be on her conscience.

Rafe didn't seem too interested. "They weren't planning to blow anything up, just disrupt the vote, show what they can do. I've met a few of them lately. They're not crazy killers like everyone thinks. They're more like protesters, you know, activists. They bring down comms networks, mess up Government websites, that kind of thing. She says they've never killed anyone. The Government just lies about them, or has ASIO blow things up and then blame them."

"And you believe her?"

"Yes, I do. She's not so bad when you get to know her."

"But she killed those two guys, right?" Tonia had finished with the bodies and was standing beside the roller door, checking the area outside.

"It was self-defence. If I'd come here by myself, those two thugs would have jumped me. If Tonia hadn't spotted the ambush, I might be dead by now."

The big door began grinding and squealing itself shut and Tonia walked back towards them.

Ginny felt a tightening in her chest, a growing excitement. "Could they still do it?" she asked.

"Do what?"

"Disrupt the vote."

"I – I suppose, but it would be suicide. Cal set them up. The cops have got all the papers I had. They've talked to you. Security around the Parliament must be massive by now."

"But what if you're right and Cal really is planning a coup?"

"So what?" Tonia said, joining them. "Politicians, big business, and organised crime have always controlled the country. What Cal's been working on is just a formalisation of the arrangement. It just means they can do their deals and make their plans behind the cover of this 'virtual curtain' of theirs without having to worry about snooping journos or cops." She looked at Rafe. "Not that the media and the cops haven't always been in their pockets."

"No, but surely this is worse," Ginny insisted, realising as she spoke that she too was starting to believe. "We don't live so much in the real world as we used to." She remembered Sorenssen saying, *They filled your head with the idea that the world out there is somehow more real that the world in here.* She said, "It's easier to trick us now, easier to mislead us, feed us any old reality that they want to. People would believe it. I would believe it." *Would have believed it.*

"Oh wake up, Ellie," Tonia said, growing heated. "You've been swallowing their crap all your life. Nothing will change, even if it's true."

Ginny's heart almost stopped when she saw the defeat in Tonia's eyes. It scared her more than the thought of a world under the control of a corrupt elite. "You've given up," she said. "You think Cal's curtain is coming down and you're finally beaten."

Tonia snarled back at her. "Well, he's right. We've been following this across the world for fifteen years now, trying to wake people up to what's been going on as country after country went dark. Nobody listened. Everyone is so fucked up with their designer worldlets and their cybersex and their Apple iTanks, they don't even want to listen. Did you ever listen? Did you ever wonder what the hell S10 was doing? No, of course you didn't. The Government said we were crazy terrorists and that's all you needed to know. Well, it's one thing fighting when there's the possibility of change, another thing when that possibility has gone."

Ginny fought the turmoil inside her head, the acknowledgement of her own dumb complicity, the shock that some people – successive governments too – must have known for so long but had done nothing. "But there is still something we can do," she said.

"Like what?"

"Like disrupt the vote. Use your tech and stop the vote."

"Are you nuts? We'd never get past the security. And if we did, it only delays things. It just gives them more reason to vote the legislation in."

"I know. I know. But a delay buys us time. It buys us a bit more freedom. It keeps that opportunity for change open just a little while longer. Isn't that worth a try?"

Tonia turned her back and walked away a few paces. Ginny turned to Rafe. "Are we just going to let this happen? Rafe? We might be the only people who can stop this. Tell her. We've got to use that thing of hers to stop the vote."

Rafe fell into some kind of internal struggle between his fear and what he knew to be right, watching Ginny with a pained expression. She turned away from him in disgust.

"It's a virus," Tonia said. "It's a good one but all the smarts are in the software that gets through the worldlet's defences to deliver it." Her voice was steady and calm. Too flat, Ginny thought, as if the woman had been drained of emotion. "We can only make it work if we're inside the Parliament worldlet itself. The public gallery would be fine. That was the plan. But there's no way we can get inside.

They'd spot us."

Ginny felt her excitement grow. "How long do we need?"

Tonia shrugged. "There's a set-up sequence, then it worms its way through the security levels, then you have to give it a go command. Thirty seconds? A minute? Our tech guys had to hack it around a lot. The designs Cal gave us were incomplete but we made it work despite him. We didn't spend a lot of time on a nice user interface."

"OK. Let's go."

Tonia didn't move. She aimed a mocking grin at Ginny. "So now our Ellie is a fearless rebel leader."

Rafe spoke up. "All that is necessary for the triumph of evil is that *good men do nothing*." He didn't sound very happy about it.

"Are we safe here for…" Ginny checked her clock. "…ten more minutes?"

Tonia shrugged again. "It's not like we have any other option."

"What about the…the virus thing?"

"Already loaded into my implants. They won't detect it."

"Right." She steeled herself and lay down on the dusty concrete floor. If someone did come after them while they were lying there unlatched, they might all die in that dismal place. "I'll meet you both at the public gallery. There must be a foyer or something. Then we'll go in separately and meet up again inside."

Tonia shook her head, perhaps a reflection on Ginny's off-the-cuff plan. She looked grim. "The most stupid thing I ever did was to get my brother killed. This is nothing by comparison, right?"

—oOo—

Ginny stepped out of the portal into a crowd of people. She was inside a large building like the foyer of a cinema or concert hall. Occasional sets of double doors punctuated a long, white wall and people were drifting in an out through all of them in dribs and drabs. It all seemed very informal. There was no obvious police presence. She looked around for Rafe and Tonia but could not see them. There were far more people there than she had anticipated and it might take a while to find her companions and move into the public gallery.

"You've missed most of the debate."

The voice at her shoulder made her freeze.

"But then I don't suppose you're interested in that part, are you, Ginny?"

Dover Richards loomed over her as she turned to face him, standing too close and looking angry.

It took a moment for her heart to slow down and her breathing to come under control. She saw a comms icon appear briefly beside his head, meaning he had probably called for backup.

"You don't know what's going on here," she told him. "And I don't have time to explain it to you." Richards was such a pig-headed, arrogant man, she doubted she could convince him if she had a week. "But we have to stop this vote, right now."

She could see the confusion in his eyes. Maybe he could see the certainty in hers.

"We?" he said. "You mean you'd like me to help you disrupt the proceedings of the House of Representatives?"

She could see he was stalling her until his backup arrived.

She thought about running into the crowd. She'd stand a good chance of eluding him for a while if she could get away from him. And it would create a diversion so Tonia and Rafe could get in and load the virus. Yet she couldn't help trying again to persuade him.

"It's Cal Copplin. He's behind all this. Well, lots of it, anyway. He set up the Rice Consortium. They're a group of big-shot business types backed by organised crime, and they're working with the Government to take control of the country."

Now he really did look puzzled. "Last time I saw you, you were being kidnapped in Sydney and bundled into a van. Now you turn up here rattling on about some kind of conspiracy theory. Either your kidnappers gave you some powerful drugs…" He pondered for a moment. "…or you really are working with September 10 and you really did come here to blow up the Parliament." He grinned. "Like Guy Fawkes."

Ginny forced herself not to look around, even though she desperately wanted to know if Rafe and Tonia were there. As long as they were free there was still a chance. She needed Richards to think she was alone.

"What are you doing here?" she asked, the question suddenly occurring to her.

"It seemed the logical place to find you and your friends working your gunpowder plot." He looked smug. He'd played a hunch and caught her and now he could amuse himself with stupid jokes at her expense.

A flick of his eyes told her his backup had arrived. She had to act. Ducking low, she sprang past him, parting the crowd with her arms like a diver, pushing against heavy bodies to lever herself away from Richards and his men. With a hand on a man's shoulder, she leapt into the air, scanning the crowd for Tonia and saw her in a doorway, twenty metres ahead of her.

"Everybody inside!" she shouted at the top of her voice. "There's a bomb in the foyer!"

She continued her dash towards Tonia, shouting more encouragement to the crowd as she went. Other people began to run. Men shouted. A woman screamed. People began to pack the doorways, blindly doing what Ginny was yelling at them to do, trying to get into the Public Gallery, away from the bomb. She kept making her way towards Tonia, who had disappeared from view – hopefully into the gallery – but the crowd around the door was dense now and she could barely make any headway. She struggled with all her strength but her own frantic attempts to get through the door incited everyone around her to greater heights of panic and she was soon stuck in a flailing scrum of people fighting and elbowing each other to escape the lobby.

A big hand grabbed her shoulder from behind, bunching up her blouse in a powerful grip, almost strangling her as it yanked her backwards.

"Don't try to run, or I'll break your fucking neck," Richards snarled. She felt his breath hot against her ear. His strength was appalling, overwhelming. He spun her to face him and she quailed at the fury in his eyes. He dragged her – one pace, two – out of the thick of the crowd. Desperately, she kicked at his shins, but if he felt it, he showed no sign. Through clenched teeth, he said, "Virginia Dalton, I'm arresting you on—"

He grunted as something collided with him at high speed, knocking the air out of him and sending him flying away from Ginny. It took her a moment to see that Rafe had barrelled into him, knocking him into a group of frightened people. The group collapsed around the struggling pair in a confusion of flailing limbs and toppling bodies.

People close to Ginny were starting to wink out of existence as they did what they should have done all along – hit their panic buttons and teleport back to the safety of their tanks. It cleared a path to the door and Ginny took it, bolting into the darkness beyond the foyer, leaving Rafe to struggle with Richards on the floor.

She stopped just on the inside to peer out from the shelter of the door frame. Richards had Rafe face-down and was roughly applying cuffs to his wrists. Unlike real cuffs, they immobilised the journalist completely. Another metaphor. Rafe lay still, his forehead against the parquet, his eyes closed. Ginny thought she could see utter defeat in his posture, yet she was elated by the courage he'd shown in attacking the big policeman. She felt proud of him, like a mother whose little boy had finally stood up to the bullies.

She ducked back behind the door frame. Richards had been joined by four others and he was directing them to check the Public Gallery entrances. His own attention focused with laser precision on the door she had run through. She had seconds to find Tonia before Richards would be inside with her.

She scanned the gallery. It was a vast space, an oval platform of tiered seating above and surrounding the floor of the Chamber. She saw the Speaker at the head of the Chamber and the rows of green leather benches running in parallel to the left and right of him down to the half-circle of cross benches at the opposite end. The Chamber was packed, the benches full of raucous politicians, clamouring to shout down their opponents. Up in the Public Gallery, another kind of bedlam was under way with confused and distressed people demanding to know what was going on and whether they were safe. There were ushers and security personnel, besieged by frantic spectators, some of whom had fled into the gallery after Ginny's fake bomb alert, and others who had been inside already when the commotion erupted. The politicians below were oblivious of the fuss, the gallery not being visible in their part of the wordlet.

Tonia was the one person still in her seat. The one unperturbed individual in the whole mêlée. Ginny moved towards her at once. Tonia had her head down and moved her fingers in the air above her lap, clearly engrossed in a virtual display only she could see.

"Haven't you done it yet?" Ginny demanded when she was close enough to be heard. "They're right behind me." A call for order from the Speaker silenced the shouting down below and, just as Tonia looked up at her, Ginny heard him guillotining the debate and calling for the vote.

"It's all fucking stuffed up," Tonia said through clenched teeth. The frustration in her voice needed no further explanation. "Get me another minute," she said. "One more minute." They both knew they had less time than that. The division bell would sound soon and the MPs would vote, not by walking through doors as they would once have done, but by pressing voting buttons on their private interfaces. It would all be over in seconds.

"Stay where you are. Put your hands in the air."

Tonia bent again to her work as Ginny slowly raised her hands and turned to face Dover Richards. He had a gun aimed at her chest and a look on his face that just dared her to do something stupid. Other security people were moving in all around her.

"Tonia," she said, urging the woman on.

"Birchow!" Richards shouted, apparently noticing the woman for the first time. "Hands above your head, right now!" As he swung the weapon to point at Tonia, Ginny lunged at him.

It was suicidal. She realised it only after she began to move. She saw Richards turn his eyes her way. She saw the puzzled creasing of his brow. Even he could not understand why she was throwing her life away to give Tonia just a couple of seconds more. His gun swung back towards her. Just a flick, really, moving just a few degrees to line up with her onrushing body, yet it seemed to take forever, plenty of time to realise what she'd done, to realise that she had no regrets. She thought about Rafe, so brave in the end, about Tonia, the evil bitch desperately trying to save them all, and Dover Richards, the cop, the good guy, doing the right thing but getting it so terribly wrong.

Then the muzzle flashed.

Chapter 21

Ginny clutched her chest and gasped for air, eyes staring. Above her she saw a low ceiling. Her gaze shifted left and right. She was on her back, on a bed, her own bed, in her own unit in Brisbane. She looked down at her chest. There was no sign of trauma. No blood. No hole. But, then, there wouldn't be, would there? With a start she saw she had on pyjamas. Not her own – she didn't even own any pyjamas. These were pink silk, as light as cobweb.

There were too many questions for any of them to demand an answer above the rest. She swung her feet to the ground and sat up. She felt fine. No pain. No dizziness. She looked at her bare feet, feeling that something was wrong for an inordinate amount of time before she realised she had been given a pedicure. A shiver of fear swept across her skin. She had no memory of having had a pedicure. It was something she would never do. She didn't even own a pedicure machine. Absently, she reached down to touch her toenails and saw that her fingernails were also perfectly trimmed and lacquered.

The horrible thought that she might not be in her own body, drove her from the bed into the bathroom to stare into the mirror. She almost sobbed with relief to see her own face staring back. She went back to the bed and sat down again.

She struggled to make sense of it. Someone had brought her back to Brisbane from Canberra, given her a manicure and a pedicure along the way, dressed her in silk pyjamas and laid her on her bed. She jumped up again and ran to the lounge room. Everything looked normal. She popped up a display on one wall and checked the date. Three days had passed since the date of the vote.

The vote!

She put up a news feed and scrolled back three days. The headline, "Major Upset for Government" was at the top of the most-accessed list. She ran the clip.

"In a major setback for the Government, today," the presenter said, "the House of Representatives voted by an overwhelming majority to reject the Liberal Party's Cyberterrorism Bill, with over a hundred Liberal Members crossing the floor to vote against it." Ginny watched in astonishment as various pundits were called on to voice their opinions. She couldn't take it all in. The pyjamas, the toenails, the vote… There seemed such a vicious wrenching of reality going on that everything felt out of shape. She shuddered, feeling menaced and dislocated.

She requested follow-up stories and, from two days ago, found the headline, "Double Dissolution Likelihood Rocks the Country."

"Prime Minister Jason Dougherty stunned the country today when he made this announcement outside his Kirribilli residence." The feed cut to the Prime Minister, looking tired but resolute, saying, "Yesterday's surprise decision in the House has come as a severe blow to this Government and to me, personally. I invested a lot of personal capital in ensuring the Cyberterrorism Bill would succeed and its failure leaves me no option but to resign as leader of the Liberal Party and as Prime Minister. The no-confidence motion tabled by the opposition has found support with a great many of my colleagues, many of whom I consider close friends. It is with some bitterness that I acknowledge that my own leadership has failed my party and failed the Australian people."

Ginny watched as a tear rolled down the man's cheek. The presenter came back on. "Political analysts are unanimous in believing that a successful vote of no confidence in the Government will mean a dissolution of both Houses, with all seats in the House of Representatives and the Senate to be contested in a general election. Australia has not had a double-dissolution since–"

Ginny paused the clip and sat back on the sofa, blinking at the presenter's perfect features. *When was the last time you saw a real news presenter?*

She felt her stomach knotting. She scanned the news feeds for the past three days, then did a general search. There was no mention anywhere of a terrorist attack at the Parliament worldlet. Nothing at all.

Had it even happened? Part of her could swear she had been there, fighting to stop the vote, just minutes ago. Yet here she was, looking at the evidence that three days had passed since then and no-one had mentioned what had happened in the Public Gallery. And the toenails... And the pyjamas...

Her mind wandered off into a fugue of aimless speculation and random thoughts. In the end, all she could think was that she should call her parents and Della to check that they were all right. And that she was hungry, starving hungry.

She turned to the kitchenette and stopped dead. A vase filled with long-stemmed red roses stood on the counter. She stared at it for several seconds, afraid to go near it. On an impulse, she turned down her aug to minimum. It was still there. Real roses in a real vase. She could not remember ever having seen real cut flowers before. Slowly, she moved closer until she could reach out and touch the cool, velvet petals and smell their thick, rich perfume.

Cal, she thought. *This is all Cal's doing.*

She stepped away from the roses, frightened by what they might mean. She wanted to see Della. She wanted to talk to somebody, tell somebody, have them tell her she would be all right. She hurried out to the bedroom automatically seeking her tank so she could get out of there. She glanced at the news presenter's face, still frozen on the big wall display. She was a beautiful woman, intelligent and serious, but with just a hint of humour about the eyes and mouth. She was a woman you'd like to get to know, a little bit intimidating, perhaps, but someone you could imagine being friends with.

No, not a woman at all. A construct.

She heard Cal's voice in her memory. *You can make the construct as beautiful, engaging, and trustworthy as you like.* With a gesture she killed the feed. Her messages replaced the image. There were lots of them, many were from Della, there was an odd one from Bernard Recszyk, Director of the Australian Chamber Orchestra, which was a puzzle, and one from her bank requesting an urgent interview, which was not. There were also several from her father. Her stomach lurched, imagining the bad news he'd called to share. Instead of viewing any of them, she carried on to the bedroom. She had reached out to open the tank's lid before she jerked back her hand in shock.

It was not her tank, not the battered second-hand unit she'd bought two years ago with her first UnReality pay cheque. This was a brand new top-of-the-range model that probably cost more than she could earn in two years. She couldn't believe she hadn't noticed it when she'd first woken up, but she'd been a little distracted at the time. What else might be different in her apartment that she hadn't seen yet?

She rushed about her two small rooms, checking everything, but the only difference she found was in the kitchenette. A fabulously expensive food printer stood where her old microwave had been, the cupboard below and the fridge beside it were stuffed with goopacks to go in it. Her stomach growled at the thought of food but she kept away from the printer as if it were a dangerous animal.

She thought about leaving her unit, just to get away from whatever it all meant, but the idea of being outside, alone, with nowhere to go was too much to bear. So she lay down on the bed, eschewing the new tank, and unlatched.

—oOo—

When Della came out from her office into the Chastity Mining foyer, Ginny thought her friend looked worn and stressed, although on the surface her expression was one of astonishment and joy. She ran straight over to Ginny and grabbed her in a ferocious hug.

"Oh my God, Gin, it's been five days! Where have you been?"

Ginny clung to her friend for the length of a long, calming breath.

"I – I don't know. I mean, some of it I know. Some of it maybe I just dreamed. But the last three days... And look." She pulled back and showed Della her fingernails.

Della frowned, clearly concerned at Ginny's incoherence.

She said, "Your father called me yesterday, several times. He's been trying to reach you. I had to talk him out of calling the police. Maybe I should have let him."

Ginny didn't want to deal with that now. "It's probably his job. He probably wants me to help him deal with Mum. I'll call him soon."

"You ran off," Della said. "We were going to–" She glanced around and lowered her voice. "You know what. But when I came home you were gone. Did you do it? Did you find anything? Of course, it doesn't matter now, I suppose. Maybe it's best if I don't know."

Did any of it matter now? "You heard about the vote?"

"Heard about it? It's on all the feeds. No-one's talking about anything else, what with the election and everything. Who'd have thought, after all you went through? And S10 and Detective Chu and the Consortium, and all for nothing. No terror attack needed. They just voted against the bill and called an election. Your friend Tonia must be over the moon."

Ginny heard Della's words like a broadcast from another planet. "Is that what happened?"

Again, Della frowned. "We should get you to a doctor or something. You seem a bit…" She looked hard into Ginny's eyes for a while, perhaps trying to read the mind behind them. In frustration, she said, "I've got to get back inside, Gin. There's this meeting… Look, where are you right now? Your body, I mean. Are you somewhere safe?"

Ginny nodded, although she wasn't sure. Are you safe in a home where people come and go at will, replacing your appliances and laying you out on the bed in pink pyjamas? "I saw Cal," she said, remembering the roses in her kitchen. "We talked. He told me he loves me. I think he might be…"

What? Insane? Running the country? A delusion?

"OK, listen," Della said. "I want you to go back to your unit. Get out of the tank and lie down on the bed." Ginny didn't bother to explain that she was avoiding the tank because it wasn't hers. "I'm going to call your friend Babs – she lives in Brisbane, doesn't she? – and tell her to get round to your place. I'll get a docbot to pay you a call too, and I'll call your dad and tell him you're back. You just rest, and don't go anywhere." She took Ginny by the shoulders. "Promise me you'll stay home." Ginny nodded. "I'll get rid of this damned meeting and then I'll come and see you. OK?"

Ginny forced a smile. "OK. Thank you."

"Go on, now."

Ginny left Della in the lobby of her building, looking worried, and went back to her unit. She got off the bed, took off the pyjamas and took a shower. She dressed in her overalls, dismayed to find that all her clothes had been laundered and pressed and hung neatly in her wardrobe. Then she went to the kitchenette and stared at the food printer. She was starving hungry or she never would have touched the thing. She popped up the interface and flicked through the extensive snacks menu, finally choosing a meat pie. When the printer pinged, she took the pie and sat down on the sofa with it. It tasted good, really good, and she felt better for having eaten. The world felt more solid, less like a dream.

While she made herself a cup of coffee, she rang her father.

"Ginny? Where have you been, darl? I was worried sick."

"I'm fine, Dad. I was just visiting a friend." She bit the bullet. "How are you and Mum?"

"That's why I've been trying to reach you. You wouldn't believe what's been happening here in the past couple of days." She steeled herself for the news. "I got a promotion," he said, announcing it as if he'd won the lottery. "They've made me Regional Manager. I couldn't believe it. You know I was down to part-time working and, what with all the layoffs and all, I was expecting the worst. Then, right out of the blue, we've been awarded the biggest contract in the company's history and it's all hands to the pumps. The GM called me in yesterday and said how much he valued my work and would I do them the honour of helping steer the company through this massive expansion? His exact words. I didn't even think he knew my name, but it turns out I've been 'on the executive team's radar' for some time now." He shook his head in bewilderment. "It's like a miracle."

Ginny tried to smile but couldn't. She managed to say, "Mum must be relieved."

Her father guffawed. "Her? She's to busy with her own miracle to even notice me." He seemed very pleased about it.

The pie she'd just eaten felt heavy in her stomach. "Her own miracle?"

"She's only gone and got herself a new exhibition. Got a call from the Australian Museum of Art this morning. They're putting on a series of events honouring underappreciated modern artists – or somesuch. They practically begged your mother to display her stuff there. Well, you've never seen anything like it. She's strutting around like a queen telling anyone who'll listen that it's about time she got the recognition she deserves." He chuckled. "She'll be impossible to live with now. You'll see."

She let him ramble on about the incredible timing of it, and the incredible luck of it all, just when things were looking so bleak, and how happy they both were. She tried to look pleased for him and to urge further details out of him, but all she could think was that the timing was, indeed, incredible and that she didn't believe it was luck for one moment. By the time he had hung up, anger and anxiety were gnawing at her insides as if she'd eaten a stew of them cooked up by that infernal food printer.

She looked at her message list, still displayed on the wall. Her eyes were drawn to the one from the Australian Chamber Orchestra. It was a day old and marked urgent. Reluctantly, she told it to play. The face of Bernard Recszyk appeared, familiar to her from news items and ACO concert program notes.

"Ms Galton – may I call you Virginia? – I wanted to be the first to call and tell you the good news." Ginny watched the smiling face with grim foreboding. "Our grant from the Rice Consortium has been approved. Honestly, I'd forgotten we'd even applied for it, but it's extremely generous. It allows us to commission works from three of the country's most promising emerging composers. Several names were proposed and evaluated by a most eminent international panel of experts as part of the grant process, it seems, and yours, I'm pleased to say, was top of the list. Congratulations, Virginia! The terms of the grant are quite spectacular. They not only fund your own time for the next two years to produce a substantial orchestral work, but will pay for our rehearsal and production costs to run a series of performances around the country at top venues – already booked and scheduled, by the way! It's really very exciting and an amazing opportunity for you." He drew a breath as if to settle his fluttering heart. "We need to meet, of course. I'm so looking for–"

She cut it off. *Another miracle.* She slumped into the sofa and closed her eyes. Somewhere in the past few days – or even weeks – reality had become unglued. She had her suspicions but she needed to know just when it had happened.

She called Rafe but there was a message saying Rafe Morgan was no longer at that Net address and for further information she should contact the Federal Police Service, Department of Missing Persons. So she called Dover Richards, the man who had shot her.

"Missing Persons." The face in the display was that of a pretty woman in her mid twenties. A construct if ever Ginny had seen one.

"I'm trying to reach a tagger called Dover Richards."

"I'm sorry, Detective Inspector Richards is on sabbatical. Would you like me to redirect your call to another officer?"

Ginny shook her head and hung up. Was Richards there or not? Was he really on sabbatical? There was absolutely no way to know. Her only certainty was that everyone she called about it would give here the same story. For a wild moment she imagined finding out where Richards lived and staking out his home until he showed up. But how would she get his physical address when every directory, every person she might ask, may be deliberately misleading her?

She put her wrists to her temples and pressed hard. *Is this how it feels to be paranoid? Is that what I am? Have I gone crazy?*

Whatever the answer, Richards was a dead end. He had either been removed, or hidden from her. In a sudden burst of anger, she stomped into the kitchen, grabbed up the roses and threw them into the waste chute. Cal was behind this. Cal had been working her like a puppet from the start. She pulled open a drawer so hard the assorted cutlery and cooking implements jumped and crashed. She grabbed the rolling pin and yanked it out. Stupid bloody thing. She'd bought it on impulse ten years ago and had never used it even once. But now she'd thought of a use for it. She grabbed it by one end, took aim at the food printer and swung it back, shouting, "I don't want your fucking roses, you sick creep!"

"Would you prefer chocolate?"

She screamed and dropped the rolling pin, jerking herself round to see who had spoken.

"I didn't mean to scare you," Cal said. "I just didn't want you to break your new toy."

She goggled at him, her heart pounding. "How did you get in here?"

He gave a wistful smile. "I'm not really here at all. It's just a projection in your–"

She didn't want another lecture on his damned technology. "What the hell is all this?" She waved a hand at the world in general. He seemed to understand.

"I wanted to do something for you. To make up for…" The sentence drifted off with a sigh and a helpless gesture.

She narrowed her eyes and tightened her lips. "It worked, didn't it? The vote was in favour of the bill. It passed. And moments later, you flipped the switch and down came your curtain of lies and corruption."

"You can still join me, Ginny."

"And the very first lie was that the vote went the other way. Then the bastard Government calls a double-dissolution election so that they can all step out of the limelight and let a bunch of mugs get elected who have no idea that they're not really running the country at all." She felt tears running down her cheeks and hated herself for crying. "How could you be part of that? How could you help them turn the world to shit like that?"

He took a step forward, as if he meant to comfort her. She

took a step back and looked for the rolling pin.

"No-one will even notice the difference. You'll see. It's always been like that. The people in power define reality. The victor gets to write history, but they also get to write the present, and the future. Democracy has been a sham since…well, always. It's better to be on the inside."

"Better for you and your criminal friends."

He stopped talking and pursed his lips. "I just wanted to give you another chance to consider it."

"And if I say no, do you take away my dad's job, my mother's exhibition? Is that the deal?"

His eyes widened. He looked genuinely shocked. "No, no. Those are just… I just wanted to help your family out. I wanted to please you."

"By giving me a commission I didn't earn?"

She could see from his alarm that he really didn't understand what he'd done.

"People get preference because of their family and connections all the time, Ginny. Almost everybody with power and wealth got a leg up from someone else with power and wealth. It's the way the world works. You could go all your life trying to 'earn' success and, like almost everyone else without the right connections, you'll fail. I just tipped the scales in your favour a little. People hardly ever deserve their successes in this world, Ginny. There isn't a cosmic karma operating that rewards the good people and punishes the bad. Take the commission. Write something beautiful. You don't get opportunities like this except by the luck of being born in the right circles, but anyone can blow it, no matter who they know."

She wasn't really listening to him. Her mind was in the Public Gallery, with Tonia desperately working at inserting

309

the virus and Dover Richards swinging his gun round towards her. "When did it stop being real?" she asked. "For me, I mean. Did I really go to Sydney to see Della? Did Sorenssen really die? And Chu? Was I ever with you at that oversized mansion of yours?"

He looked a little shifty. "All of that was real. All of it."

"But not when I thought I'd woken up in Canberra and we went to the Parliament worldlet."

He shook his head. "I'm sorry. That got...out of hand."

Ginny felt a bitter amusement at her own gullibility. "I turned you down and you put me through that charade in a fit of pique, didn't you?"

He fidgeted and seemed irritated at having to defend himself. "I wanted to show you just how much I could control reality if I wanted to, how easily I could fool you, or anyone. I just let it play out too long. I didn't know you were so determined to be a hero."

I should have known, she told herself. *When Tonia agreed to help, I should have known. When Rafe was so brave. When everything unfolded the way I wanted it to.* Except for the ending. Cal had let his simulated Dover Richards shoot her. *Because Cal was angry? Because he'd seen enough?*

"You should go now," she said.

He nodded. "I'll keep an eye on you."

"What, like you're Superman to my Lois Lane?"

He gave a wan smile. "Something like that."

"Don't bother. I can look after myself."

He regarded her with sad eyes for a long time. Eventually, he said, "I still love you, Gi–"

"Oh for God's sake, just go!"

He blinked out of existence before she'd finished the sentence. She grabbed up the rolling pin from the floor and threw it at where he'd been, screaming in anger and frustration, tears dripping from her chin. It crashed into the wall in the lounge room and left a dent in the plaster. She was trembling all over. She sat down on the kitchen floor with her back to the counter and wept into her hands.

After a while, the doctor that Della had arranged called to set up an appointment. She told it to go screw itself and the AI politely went away. Later, Della called but Ginny had set her phone to 'busy'.

—oOo—

It was a long time before she got up again. From the light, she judged it to be late afternoon. She was tired and flat and felt hollowed out by her crying. She'd spent a lot of time trying to piece together all that had happened, who the various players had acted for, who had known what and when. It seemed to her that there had been times when the Consortium had acted according to its own agenda, not Cal's. For a moment she actually worried whether Cal was in danger. Then she wondered why the hell she should care. If there was ever someone who had played with matches, it was Cal. But perhaps he had found ways to continue to be useful to the various factions behind the curtain. He'd had ten years to plan this, after all.

She went to the window and looked out. It was showing a peaceful ocean view of white sands framed by pandanus trees. She felt an urge to be there and promised herself a vacation at the seaside, up the coast maybe, where it was warm and secluded, but somewhere with great restaurants for the evenings. She imagined meeting a tall, suntanned guy and having carefree sex in a beachfront cabin with the waves pounding and the cicadas singing. She let the fantasy absorb her for a long, long time while the sun went down and the light grew dim.

There was only Della left in the world she could talk to about what had happened – and Cal, of course. She decided right there that she would never tell Della what she knew, that it would be wrong to burden her friend with an understanding of how their world had changed. It scared her how alone she would be with the knowledge she had. It would forever seal her off from everyone she might meet. *My own virtual curtain*, she thought. *With only me inside and everyone else outside.* The thought started her crying again.

Ages later, she ate a pizza from the food printer, thinking, *What the hell, it's just a machine.* She found a bottle of beer in the fridge and drank it with her meal. On impulse, she checked her bank balance and found, as she knew she would, an astonishing amount of money had been deposited there. So her bank manager had not wanted to talk about her overdraft after all. He probably just wanted to tell her what a valued customer she was, and to sell her a financial services package. It felt strange to know that the expensive vacation she had imagined could be real, that she could turn down the ACO commission if she pleased and still spend the rest of her life writing music. Never working again was a perfectly feasible option. What's more, she suspected that if she blew the money in a Gold Coast casino, or gave it all to charity, the next day she would find her account had magically topped itself up again. And it would keep happening until Cal grew bored with her, or became sick of the sight of her screwing tanned strangers at tropical resorts. She laughed at the idea that she had become a kept woman, like a courtesan from pre-liberation times, only she didn't want it and her benefactor got nothing for his troubles. Not the way she had expected her life to go.

The up-side was that she would never need to deal with those little pricks at UnReality ever again. In fact, she probably had more than enough to buy up the company and sack them both, just for the fun of it. She smiled at the idea as she imagined their faces when she broke the news.

She stood up quickly and took two steps across the room in agitation, her smile wiped away in an instant by the realisation that her little fantasy was exactly the same as Cal's and his colleagues', the exercise of power over other people for personal gratification. It was sobering and frightening. Within minutes of discovering all that money at her disposal, she had begun thinking about hurting people with it. Was corruption so easy? So insidious? Was she no better than Cal and the rest?

She grappled with it as the evening wore into night, hating herself, hating Cal, hating all the selfish, grasping people that made the world so bad when it could easily be so good. She woke up at three AM, curled up on the sofa, uncomfortable and cold, surprised that she could have fallen asleep. She stumbled to her bed and climbed in but slept only fitfully after that until the morning came.

With the new day came a new resolve. She ate eggs benedict from the printer, something she'd never tried before. The she called Bernard Recszyk.

"What if you don't like my stuff?" she asked, without preamble.

The ACO Director was fluster for a moment before regaining his professional smoothness. "Better minds than mine have judged your talent, Virginia. I have no doubt you deserved your win."

"But what if I'm crap?"

His compassionate smile was one he must have used on many a great artist who had succumbed to self-doubt. Part of his job must be to keep these sensitive souls on the rails. "Why don't we let the audiences decide that, Virginia? I'm sure you'll be pleasantly surprised."

"If I don't accept the grant, does someone else get a go?"

His face fell. He looked genuinely worried. "You're not considering refusing the grant are you?"

"Just supposing?"

He swallowed. "It's a stipulation that if any of the nominated candidates turn down the grant, the whole of it is voided. This would be a huge boost to your career, Virginia. Massive exposure. The orchestra too. We'd..." He stopped, realising he was saying too much.

Ginny nodded. "I understand. In that case, count me in. When would you like to meet?"

They made the arrangement and hung up.

Ginny went straight to the tank and opened it. It smelled like a new car inside and its surfaces and displays gleamed like Christmas lights. She jumped in, connected her catheters and went to her studio worldlet. There she looked at her low-quality equipment and the low-quality view. Her first order of business was to upgrade everything to the best she could afford – and that probably meant the best there was. Then she'd go and see Della and try to put her mind at rest. She'd tell her about the ACO grant, of course, but nothing else.

The future wouldn't be so bad. She'd stop watching the news feeds, naturally. There wouldn't be much point. If it wasn't mandatory in Australia, she'd stop voting too, but her vote wouldn't matter. Otherwise things would be much the same as ever. She'd take the Rice Consortium commission and she'd do her uttermost to write something that was as good as she was capable of. Cal was right. An opportunity should be grasped with both hands, no matter where it came from. This was hers and she would give it everything she had. Then, whatever came after, good or bad, she would own it, with as much right as anyone ever had to the lucky breaks they got.

And so what if the world was run by crooks and arseholes? Cal was right about that too. It was all just a matter of degree. The more things change, the more they stay the same. She'd have to put that on a T-shirt. If Cal really was watching, he'd probably get a giggle out of it.

About the Author

Graham Storrs is a science fiction writer living in Queensland, Australia. A former research scientist, IT consultant and award-winning software designer, he now lives and writes in a quiet corner of the Australian bush with his wife, Christine, an Airedale terrier called Bertie, and a Tonkinese cat called Minsky.

His writing credits include three children's science books, and a great many magazine articles, academic papers and book chapters. Since turning his attention to writing fiction he has had short stories published in a wide range of magazines and anthologies. *Heaven is a Place on Earth* is his third novel.

The Timesplash Series

Graham's début novel, *Timesplash*, a near-future, time travel thriller, was a Kindle best-seller (in both the science fiction and the techno-thriller categories).

It is now published by Pan Macmillan (Momentum), as are the sequels, *True Path* (shortlisted for an Aurealis Award in 2014), and *Foresight*.

Contact the Author

Graham is always happy to hear from readers, so don't be shy. And if you enjoyed this book, a review on Amazon, Goodreads, or your own blog would be greatly appreciated.

Follow Graham Storrs on his Facebook page: facebook.com/GrahamStorrsAuthor and on Twitter: @graywave

For details of all Graham's novels and short stories, visit grahamstorrs.com